"There isn't anything going on between us," he said.

"You sleep in your room and I sleep in mine. Our conduct is entirely aboveboard."

"Pretty much so, yes."

"I only kissed you once."

"I know." She hadn't intended for her voice to hold so much regret.

The silence grew long between them.

"Do you want me to give them some explanation? I guess I could say you're my sister or a cousin."

"No. I don't want to lie. Especially not to a preacher. I hate dishonesty."

"Then what do you suggest?"

"I don't know." She shook her head and sighed. "Why didn't I ever think about this before now?"

Carefully he said, "We could let them assume you're my wife."

She looked at him and waited for an explanation.

"It's what they already believe. No one would question it."

Elizabeth exploded. "But it's not true!"

Dear Reader,

This month we're giving you plenty of excuses to put your feet up and "get away from it all" with these four, fantasy-filled historical romances.

Let's begin with handsome rancher Brice Graham and his darling baby girl who will undoubtedly capture your affection in *The Rancher's Wife*, an emotional new Western by award-winning author Lynda Trent. Critics have described the author's works as "sensual" and "utterly delightful." In this pretend marriage tale, an abandoned wife moves in with Brice in order to care for his daughter. Yet complications arise when the two wish to marry for real....

Medieval fans, prepare yourselves for a spine-tingling story of forbidden love in Lyn Stone's latest, *Bride of Trouville*, about a young widow, forced to marry, who must hide her son's deafness from the husband she's grown to love. And don't miss *Conor*, by bestselling author Ruth Langan, in which a legendary rogue teams up—permanently—with a beautiful Irish noblewoman to thwart a plot to murder Queen Elizabeth.

If those aren't enough excuses to curl up with a book, then perhaps half-Apache Rio Santee will entice you in Theresa Michaels' new sigh-inducing Western, *The Merry Widows—Sarah*, about two wounded souls who heal each other's hearts.

Whatever your tastes in reading, you'll be sure to find a romantic journey back to the past between the covers of a Harlequin Historical®.

Sincerely,

Tracy Farrell
Senior Editor

Please address questions and book requests to:
Harlequin Reader Service
U.S.: 3010 Walden Ave., P.O. Box 1325, Buffalo, NY 14269
Canadian: P.O. Box 609, Fort Erie, Ont. L2A 5X3

Lynda Trent

THE RANCHER'S WIFE

KS

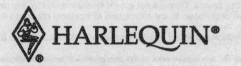

HARLEQUIN®

TORONTO • NEW YORK • LONDON
AMSTERDAM • PARIS • SYDNEY • HAMBURG
STOCKHOLM • ATHENS • TOKYO • MILAN • MADRID
PRAGUE • WARSAW • BUDAPEST • AUCKLAND

ISBN 0-373-29070-5

THE RANCHER'S WIFE

Copyright © 1999 by Dan & Lynda Trent

This edition published by arrangement with Harlequin Books S.A.

Visit us at www.romance.net

Printed in U.S.A.

Books by Lynda Trent

Harlequin Historicals

Heaven's Embrace #59
The Black Hawk #75
Rachel #119
Beloved Wife #154
Thornbeck #232
The Fire Within #314
The Rancher's Wife #470

Harlequin Books

Historical Christmas Stories 1991
"Christmas Yet to Come"

LYNDA TRENT

Lynda Trent has been writing novels for twenty years, using various pen names. Her time travel romances are written under the pseudonym Elizabeth Crane, and her ghost novels as Abigail McDaniels. Romance and mainstream novels, as well as nonfiction, are published as Lynda Trent.

Among other achievements, Lynda Trent has been awarded the prestigious RITA Award by Romance Writers of America for *Opal Fires,* a contemporary mainstream romance novel. She has frequently been a RITA finalist for both contemporary and historical romances. In 1985 she won a bronze Porgy for Best Western Novel in the *West Coast Review of Books*. In 1986, she and her former co-author were named Outstanding Historical Romance Writing Team by *Romantic Times Magazine*. Translations of her fifty-three books are sold worldwide.

To Courtney Jade Trent—a ray of sunshine

Chapter One

Something hurled itself at the side of the sod hut and Elizabeth prayed the storm hadn't torn loose more of the barn. It wasn't a real barn, only a lean-to, not like the ones she had known back home in Hannibal, but it was all the mule had for shelter. Her husband was gone on the horse so the poor mule had only his own body heat to keep him warm in the winter's first snowstorm.

Nothing had gone as Elizabeth had planned when she married Robert Parkins seven years before. She had been seventeen and eager to escape her tyrannical father at any cost. At the time she had thought she loved Robert and that they would live in a pretty home filled with love and children. But she was twenty-four now with neither home nor child. Only Robert, and her disillusionment, and the sod hut they lived in that was, at best, a dubious shelter.

Robert had won the land in a poker game. Forty acres and a gold mine in the new Oklahoma Territory had seemed like a dream come true. Elizabeth should have known better. In the past seven years Robert had been a clerk, a teller in a bank, a merchant's bookkeeper, an apprentice wheelwright and a tinker. He never stuck with anything for long and there had been spells between jobs when he had done nothing and she had supported them by taking in washing and ironing. As fast as she could save money, Robert found it and gambled it away. She had buried the last dream when she first saw the mud hut and the hole in the ground that was supposed to be a gold mine.

The storm winds shifted and her shutters rattled alarmingly. Elizabeth put the straight-backed chair in front of them and sat in it, hoping to keep the shutters closed and the storm out. She had always feared storms and was struggling not to become terrified of this one. Robert had ridden into town for supplies but had been gone for a week on a chore that should have taken two days, three at the most.

As always he had put the journey off until they were almost entirely out of food and Elizabeth was eating as little as possible in order to survive until he returned. The nights were the worst. She lay awake for hours at a time worrying that he might have been killed or that he had simply grown tired of a wife, a sod hut and a worthless gold mine, and had left them all behind.

Robert had believed in the gold mine and had been glad there were no greedy neighbors he would have to fend off once he struck it rich. To Elizabeth, who was accustomed to living in town, the absence of people close by had been frightening. They were all alone on the side of a rocky hill, thirty miles from the nearest town and five miles from another living person.

The gold mine had never yielded a thimbleful of gold, even though Robert had worked it steadily—or at least at a pace that was steady for him. Every day, once she had finished the other chores on the place, Elizabeth helped him chip away at the rock and haul out buckets of worthless rubble. All for nothing. Even Robert finally admitted that.

The land was no good for farming and too small to raise cattle, even the longhorn kind that were said to be able to exist on practically no grass at all.

The only level piece of ground was beneath the hut. The roof was of the lean-to variety and was covered with dirt and grass. While it had provided a measure of coolness that first summer, it was always damp, and downright wet when it rained. As a further inconvenience, bugs nesting in the roof frequently burrowed through and dropped onto whatever or whoever was below. The floor was dirt interspersed with rock, as were the walls. Not one single thing was pretty about it, and the constant dampness was already rotting the treasured quilts and linens Elizabeth had brought with them.

The shutters trembled and shoved against the back of her chair, forcing a wider entrance for the icy wind that seemed determined to rob her of what little heat she had left. Fortunately the gust was of short duration and the weight of the chair closed the gap again. Elizabeth had never been so afraid. At least, she told herself, she didn't have to worry about the hut being blown down since it was built into the hill itself. Assuming, of course, the heavy snow didn't make the roof collapse.

She refused to cry. Ever since she could remember, Elizabeth had hated to cry. It solved nothing and only made her feel vulnerable. Instead, she tried to work up a sustaining anger against Robert. It wasn't hard to do. He had had ample time to ride to the town of Glory, buy provisions, get drunk, gamble away the rest of their money and ride home. A man could easily travel thirty miles on horseback in a day.

So where was he? She tried to blame it on the storm.

It wasn't likely that Robert had started for home and been overtaken by the storm. She had seen it building for an entire day before it actually arrived. Robert was good at self-preservation and would not risk being caught in a blizzard just because she was alone and running out of food.

The direction of the storm's onslaught shifted again and Elizabeth got out of the chair to pace in the small room. There was little furniture to impede her steps. The bed stood against one wall, made bright by her quilts. The table was on the opposite wall, along with the only other chair they owned. A shelf held her meager provisions. In a few short months, the rag rug that once covered most of the wet stone and dirt floor had rotted and had been relegated to the barn for use as rags. She saw no sense in making another.

Her father had been a well-to-do man. Looking back on his house with its clutter of furniture, knickknacks, fringed rugs, pictures on every surface and silently efficient servants, she thought it seemed like a palace. She didn't miss her tyrannical father but she longed for his dry, comfortable house and her mother, who had been dead since shortly before Elizabeth married Robert.

She knew her mother would have insisted that she stay with Robert. The sanctity of marriage had been drilled into her head since infancy. Divorce was an ugly word, and those who were touched by it were no longer entirely decent people. The wives had failed at the one task God had intended for them, according to her parents, and the men were never blamed. It was always said, or at least implied, that the wife had turned despot or slattern and that the husband had been more or less forced to rid himself of her. But surely, if her mother had known what Elizabeth's marriage was like, might she not have encouraged her to leave?

There was no use speculating. Her mother was dead and buried in Hannibal. Elizabeth had no place to go. Her father had never loved her and he would be unwilling to take her in. Besides, she didn't want to go back to the life she had married Robert to get away from. Furthermore, striking out on her own was impossible without money, and Robert had taken all that was left to buy the supplies they would need to get through this winter.

With her lantern in hand, she went to the door and drew the bolt. Cautiously she opened the door a few inches and peered out. The frigid air was thick with wind-driven snowflakes that bit at her face and hands. The snowdrift packed against the door was already two feet deep and more was piling on top of that by the minute. Within a few inches of the door, the dim light from her lantern was swallowed by the blackness of the night and the density of the falling snow.

Elizabeth closed the door again before the rapidly accumulating snow could block it. At this rate, she would be snowed in by morning. How would she get out to the barn to tend to the mule? At least the chickens were long since eaten, so she didn't have to worry about them being buried under snow in their makeshift chicken coop.

What would she do if Robert never came back? The answer was too horrifying to consider.

Knowing she had to get her mind on something else to save her sanity, she fetched the one book she still owned from the tiny table beside the bed. She had read her copy of *The Mysteries of Udolpho* so many times that the pages felt soft and fragile. It was the only thing she had taken from her father's house other than her clothing. This had always been her favorite book and she couldn't bear to leave it behind. Although it was ponderously long, she had memorized pages of it. On nights like this, it was her only friend and companion.

Trying to ignore the howling wind shearing over her low roof, Elizabeth sat at the table, propped up the book in the yellow glow of the lantern and began to read.

Down in the valley Celia Graham glared at her husband and nervously tapped her foot against the floor. "I hate this place!" she said for the fifth time that hour. "It's just like you to drag me away from everyone I love and expect me to live on this godforsaken ranch."

Brice gave her a long look. "At the time you were eager to come here and get away from your mother's interference. And I was under the impression that I was a 'loved one.'"

"That's right! Twist my words about. I don't care anymore. I don't care about anything." Her lower lip protruded petulantly. She hated being stuck here on this ranch, away from her family and the stores she had taken for granted when they were accessible. She particularly cared that she was eight months pregnant; she was tired of being fat and awkward. "No matter what you say, I'm never having another child," she snapped.

He glanced up from the ranch records he was completing. "What does that have to do with it? We would have had children if we stayed in Saxon. I miss Texas, too, but you aren't giving Oklahoma Territory a chance."

"It doesn't deserve one." She looked around the beautifully furnished parlor as if it were a squalid hut.

"This place is ugly. Not at all like Mother's parlor. A man has no idea how to decorate a house."

"You liked it well enough at first. I recall you gloating and saying you couldn't wait for your mother to see it because she would be so jealous."

She hated it when he threw her words back at her. Brice never forgot anything. "That's nonsense. I've never gloated in my life. And to accuse Mother of being jealous!"

Celia hoisted her swollen body out of the chair and glared accusingly at Brice. It was all his fault she had lost her tiny waist—probably forever—and that her hands and feet were swollen and her insides sore from the baby's kicks. She detested children and she couldn't wait to have this ordeal behind her.

She waddled to the carved oak desk and dropped down into the chair. Even crossing the room had been an odious chore. She took out pink stationery and dipped her pen in the inkwell. Dear Mother and Father, she wrote.

For the next half hour she poured out all her hatred of Brice and a lengthy description of all the faults of the ranch. That she wasn't accurate didn't bother her in the least. She was unhappy and that was all that mattered.

The mellow voice of the mantel clock sounded the hour. Celia suspiciously checked the time with the gold watch she wore on a chain about her neck. The mantel clock was one of Brice's purchases and she was waiting to discover it in error.

She ended the letter, put it in an envelope and sealed it. Awkwardly she stood and crossed the room to the door. Her house slippers made no sound on the Oriental rug.

In the central hallway Celia stopped and called out, "Consuela!"

A dark-haired woman several years older than Celia hurried to her.

Celia handed her the envelope. "Have Manuel post this tomorrow."

Consuela glanced at the front door, which rattled beneath the storm's assault. "There is much snow, Señora Graham. He might not be able to get to Glory tomorrow."

Celia gave her a cold stare. "You heard my orders, Consuela. A bit of snow won't hurt your husband."

"Sí, señora."

"I'm ready to go to bed now." She turned and started up the stairs. She didn't tell Brice good-night, nor did he call out to her, though he probably heard the entire exchange. She had left the door to the parlor open so the room's heat would be stolen by the near-freezing hall.

By the time she reached the top of the stairs, Celia was exhausted. She did as little as possible these days; any exercise at all made her heart race and caused a headache to pound in her temples. She passed Brice's bedroom and went into her own room with Consuela close behind.

She waited impatiently for Consuela to take out her warmest nightgown and turn down the bed's cover. Although the brazier had been lit, the room was still uncomfortably cold.

As Consuela undressed her, Celia said, "I hate being so fat and ugly. I hate it!"

"No, no, *señora*. A woman with child is beautiful," Consuela said quickly.

"Your hands are so cold. Can't you hurry? As for me

being beautiful—that's horsefeathers!'' She thought for a moment. "What do your people do to hurry a birth? I'm sure you must have some way."

Consuela's hands paused, then she continued unlacing Celia's dress. "There is no safe way. And you are still a month or more away from your time."

"I don't see how a few weeks could matter to the baby and they matter a great deal to me." She pouted thoughtfully. "There must be some way to hurry this birth along." Celia was still pondering when she went to bed.

By morning the storm had passed, moving quickly south and east up and over the Ouachita Mountains. Through her window on the south side of the hut, Elizabeth could see that a few muddy clouds straggling behind the fierce storm were just making their way up the foothills. To her immense relief, the sky overhead was making an effort to brighten.

Using her dishpan, Elizabeth scooped most of the snow away from her door and began cutting a path toward the barn. Her progress was slow but relentless. She finally made her way to the barn and was able to tug open the doors.

At first the tiny, dark room was cold and still, and a lump formed in her throat with the thought that she was the only living thing that had survived the night. But then a shuffling sound pierced the darkness and hope rose in her. As her eyes adjusted to the dimly lit interior, she saw her mule in the far corner of the barn still on his feet. When she stepped toward him, the mule saw her and began making a raucous noise of welcome.

She hurried to him and patted his furry brown neck. "I'm so glad to see that you're all right. I've been worried about you.'' He snorted and flicked his tail. Beneath her palm she could feel him shivering. "I'm sorry you're so cold. This barn has cracks in the walls I could put my hand through.'' She should have been more insistent that Robert repair the barn before winter came, but how was she to know he would leave and not come back for so long?

"I can't leave you out here to freeze,'' she said firmly. Desperate conditions called for desperate measures. She tipped over the water tub and kicked it until the ice inside fell out.

Carrying the tub with the bag of feed inside and leading the mule, she went back to the hut. The mule balked at going into the house but she tugged on his halter until he reluctantly stepped over the threshold. The hut had been small to start with. With the mule inside it was more crowded that she had thought possible.

"I hope I'm not making a big mistake with this,'' she muttered to herself as she tied him to the back wall. "At least he won't freeze.''

She filled the mule's tub with snow and put it within his reach. He would have water to drink as soon as it melted. The mule made a poor companion and a smelly one, but she was no longer alone or worried that he was freezing to death in the barn. She put another log on the fire and took up the quilt she was making out of her oldest dress and Robert's worn shirts. When Robert came home, he would most likely be angry at her having the mule in the house, but Elizabeth didn't care. She would do whatever she had to do in order to survive.

Another three days went by and Robert still wasn't home. The snow had partially melted and, with the warming trend, the mule had gone back to his former lodgings. Elizabeth's entire store of food consisted of two handfuls of cornmeal, twice that much flour, two strips of dried venison and a handful of beans. Her lamp oil would be gone after another night, maybe two, and she would be left in the dark. She could wait no longer for Robert to return; she had to find food.

She went to the barn and put the bridle on the mule. There was no saddle; the only one they owned was on the horse Robert had ridden to town, but Elizabeth didn't mind that. She had learned to ride bareback soon after their arrival. With one of Robert's sheathed hunting knives tucked into the pocket of her woolen cloak and his rifle in hand, she led the mule to the stump she used as a mounting block. The only problem with riding bareback was that if she got off the mule away from the house, she couldn't always get back on him. But that was just something she would have to deal with.

She swung her leg over his back and as she righted herself astride him and tightened her knees against his ribs, she noticed he was considerably bonier than he had been when she had ridden him last. His feed was almost gone and she had been able to give him only half rations for the last few days. Settling herself as comfortably as possible, Elizabeth nudged him forward. He flicked his ears back and forth in protest but crossed the yard and started down the hill.

Elizabeth had never shot a rifle in her life and wasn't sure how to take aim on game, but she had to try. If she couldn't find food she would have to attempt the ride to town and that would be dangerous, because she wasn't entirely certain of the way. She had only been there once and the Territory had all been so new to her that she hadn't remembered much about it. At the time she had thought she would have no reason to need this information. She tightened her mouth and kicked the mule into a trot.

She continued moving downhill because it stood to reason that game would head for the warmer valley below and away from the windswept hills, some of which were almost as tall as mountains in Elizabeth's opinion. Besides, the going was easier in this direction.

Once she saw a rabbit sit up on its haunches and freeze, its nose twitching, but by the time she put the rifle to her shoulder, it began running away and she knew she had no hope of shooting it with it bobbing and darting about. She also wasn't too sure what the mule would do if she fired the gun while astride his back. Certainly Robert had never taken him when he went hunting.

For that matter, if she shot anything much larger than a rabbit, how would she carry it home? Even if the mule would stand still while she draped a dead animal over its back, how could she lift a deer that high? She wasn't even positive she knew how to dress one. She fought back a wave of panic and let the mule pick his own way through the drifts of melting snow.

Several hours later Elizabeth topped a low hill and found herself looking down at the ranch of her nearest neighbors. A two-story frame house stood in a grove of native cottonwood trees, its sides as white as new snow. Behind it was a proper barn—not like the one that housed her mule—and several pens made of unpainted boards. In the corral closest to the barn were horses and a couple of milk cows. Dotting the slopes on the far side were quite a few white-faced cattle, obviously the property of her rather affluent neighbors. The scene was as pretty as a picture in the books Elizabeth had left behind in Hannibal.

Without thinking, she smoothed her dark hair back into its bun and straightened her dress beneath her wool cloak. From the looks of the place, she felt sure their pantry was well stocked. She hated to have to ask for food, but she had no other choice.

By the time she rode into the yard, two barking dogs came to meet her, their tails wagging. Not far behind them was a tall man with broad shoulders and chestnut-brown hair. He smiled at her. "Afternoon, ma'am. We don't get many visitors out here."

Elizabeth found it difficult to speak. His eyes were a warm brown and his skin tanned by the sun. Despite his size, his voice was gentle and held a hint of what she thought might be a Texas drawl. When she realized she was staring at him and hadn't spoken, a blush rose in her cheeks. Quickly, she looked away for a moment, then said, "Hello. My name is Elizabeth Parkins. We're neighbors."

"We are?" He looked puzzled. "I didn't know anyone had settled around here."

"We live up the hills from here. On the place that used to belong to Mr. Snodgrass."

"Snodgrass?" Understanding lit his face. "Do you mean Old Zeb's gold mine?"

"That's the place," she said with a sigh.

"Come in and warm up. My wife will be pleased to meet you." He grinned up at her. "My name, by the way, is Brice Graham." He held the mule so she could dismount.

She couldn't help but notice that his dark eyes were on her, not staring, not leering, but nevertheless not straying either. Breaking eye contact, she shifted the rifle from one hand to the other, not sure how she was going to gracefully get off the mule without dropping the gun.

Unexpectedly, she found herself wondering why a graceful dismount was suddenly so important. The sound of her neighbor clearing his throat drew her attention, and when she looked back at him, he had extended a hand as if he might be intending to hold her at the waist to help her down. Before she allowed herself another thought, she thrust the rifle into his hand and hurried herself to the ground, almost losing her balance in the process. Feeling a bit awkward and unsettled at the direction her thoughts had been heading, she cast him a quick smile, then busied herself straightening her clothing again.

"Are you alone?"

She looked back at him and this time found his rather intent gaze unsettling in a way she didn't dare examine. Swallowing the lump in her throat, she answered, "Yes. I was trying to shoot some game."

"I see." He tied the mule to the porch rail and motioned for Elizabeth to precede him up the broad front porch steps. "I believe you said 'we' live in Old Zeb's place?"

"I'm married." She almost winced at the admission. "My husband—his name is Robert Parkins—has gone to town for supplies. I'm alone at the present." She hoped she didn't sound too stilted. Robert was forever telling her she tried to put on airs. For some reason it was important that this man know she was married and not available. Or maybe all those thoughts were on her side alone.

As he opened the door for her, he said, "Forgive me for asking, but if your husband has gone to town, why are you having to hunt for food?"

Elizabeth stepped into the wide entrance hall and sighed with pleasure, distracted by the beauty of her neighbor's home. Ahead of her a massive staircase curved gracefully up from the polished oak flooring of the foyer to the second floor and was flanked by wallpaper in a lovely floral design. To her right was a tastefully decorated parlor with garnet-colored upholstered furniture and small marble-topped tables. To her left was a library. A real one, like the ones in Hannibal. She automatically took a step toward it before she remembered herself.

"Ma'am?"

He had asked her a question. Elizabeth drew her dignity about her again. "Robert has been gone for weeks."

"Glory is only a day's ride from here."

"I know. I'm not sure of the exact day he left. We have no calendar." She had been recording the passage of time by making notches in a stick. Robert thought that was foolish, but she had been determined to hold on to whatever civilization she could.

Brice's brow furrowed in concern. "Perhaps something happened to him. I'd be glad to send one of my men to look for him."

"No, no. That won't be necessary." As much as Elizabeth hated being alone, she didn't want anyone to go in search of Robert. Her husband's temper wasn't that even these days and he would resent her fetching him home like an errant child. Just the thought of him left her cold inside. "I imagine he's doing business of some sort." She supposed it could be loosely termed that if Robert was gambling. At least it was business for the saloon.

"Let me send some supplies home with you. That's the least I can do."

"I hate to oblige you." It was true. Having to ask strangers for food and lamp oil was galling to her pride.

"I insist." He smiled down at her and she felt the ice around her heart melt. "Come into the parlor and rest a bit. You must be tired. This gun isn't light." He stood the rifle in a corner of the foyer and showed her into the parlor.

The house had been decorated in a way Elizabeth thought would please any woman. The soft upholstery's color was echoed in the rich draperies flanking the windows. White lace covered the glass panes, yet let sunlight stream through. The walls were light in color for a parlor but Elizabeth liked the idea of sitting among pink roses and twining vines. The parlor was separated from the dining room by portieres of gold damask with a deep fringe. "Your home is beautiful! Your wife has excellent taste. Have you been here long?"

"I was the first settler in these parts. Once I had the ranch established, I brought Celia here as my bride." He saw a woman enter the far end of the hall. "Consuela, will you tell Celia we have company?"

The woman stared curiously at Elizabeth before hurrying away.

Elizabeth moved about the parlor, trying not to behave as if she had never seen luxury before, but letting her senses drink in the rich fabrics, snowy laces and tatting, the clean smell of a room with a real floor.

She heard footsteps approaching the room and turned to smile at the woman who was entering the parlor. As Brice made the introductions, Celia's gaze traveled over Elizabeth as if she wasn't sure she wanted her in the best parlor. If Celia was glad to see a neighbor woman, she showed little sign of it. Elizabeth self-consciously touched her faded gingham dress.

"Do be seated," Celia said coolly. "You'll have to forgive my appearance. I didn't expect company."

"I didn't intend to come calling," Elizabeth said awkwardly. "I was hunting game and found your ranch by accident."

Celia wrinkled her nose. "You hunt?"

Brice said firmly, "I knew you would be glad to meet our neighbors. You see? We aren't as isolated as you would think."

His wife gave him a dismissing glance. "I apologize for the state of my house. Brice had it furnished before I ever laid eyes on it, and you know what peculiar tastes men have."

Elizabeth watched the exchange of veiled animosity and wasn't sure how to reply. She settled for a silent smile. Eager to find a neutral subject, she said, "I see you're expecting a child. Is this your first?"

Celia nodded vehemently. "It's my *only* one. Do you have children?"

"No. We have no children." She still felt guilty for not having borne a child after seven years of marriage. The years ahead would be so lonely without children in them.

"I'll have Consuela gather some provisions for you," Brice said. "You're welcome to stay and visit for as long and as often as you like, Mrs. Parkins."

"Thank you," Elizabeth replied.

When he was gone, Celia leaned forward to say, "It's so nice to have a woman to talk with. I detest this place. It's so lonely!"

Elizabeth nodded. "Yes, it is. This is nothing like I expected."

"Nor I!" Celia looked gratified to hear someone agree with her. "Brice thinks it's wonderful here but I would rather move back home. Wouldn't you?"

"I don't have much to go home to. There's only my

father, and he wouldn't welcome me. You see, Robert and I eloped and he never forgave me."

"He may have changed his mind and be unable to let you know. We get almost no mail in this awful place. Once this baby is delivered and I can travel again, I'll go back home. Brice can follow or not, as he wishes."

"I've often wanted to do just that! It's amazing how alike we are."

"I would say we have little in common. Brice thinks I'm terrible for wanting to leave. He's keeping me here entirely against my wishes." She glanced toward the door.

"Is he cruel to you?" Elizabeth whispered.

Celia rolled her expressive blue eyes. "I couldn't begin to say what my life is like. I never knew a man could be so cruel. Mother was right when she warned me against him." She sighed with dramatic misery. "How I've wished I could change the past and be a carefree girl again."

"It's as bad as that?" Elizabeth was too familiar with Robert's rages and abuse to take such a statement lightly. "Would your father not come after you if he knew you were so unhappy?"

"Of course he would. Father is the dearest of men. But I can't travel like this." She opened her shawl slightly to indicate her pregnancy. "No, I can't escape until the baby is born and I regain my strength." She shuddered. "I tremble to think what Brice will say or do when he knows I'm leaving." She paused dramatically.

"How terrible! To look at him, you'd never guess he's mean tempered."

"I know. That's how he duped me into marrying him. I'm sadder but wiser now."

"When will the baby arrive?"

"Soon, I hope."

"Please send for me when it's time. I live in Mr. Snodgrass's hut." Elizabeth hesitated at the look Celia gave her. She no longer appeared quite as friendly. "But I don't know anything about birthings."

"Consuela will do all that. I suppose I should have someone else with me when the time comes."

"Of course. I'll come as soon as I hear from you." Elizabeth was determined to befriend this woman. She looked at the mantel clock. "I have to be going now. It's later than I thought."

"Must you?" Celia asked petulantly. "We've only begun to talk and I'm so lonely here."

"I might lose my way if I wait until nightfall. I'm not too familiar with the Territory."

"Very well. It wouldn't do for you to lose your way."

They stood and Elizabeth pressed Celia's hand in friendship. She smelled of talcum and rose water. Elizabeth was again aware of her faded and patched dress. It had been so long since she had been able to dress like a lady and indulge in handwork that was pretty rather than utilitarian. It was a shame such a fine lady was trapped in an abusive marriage. "I'll come back as soon as I can." She left Celia behind in the parlor. It was obvious that walking or even standing was uncomfortable for her.

Brice heard Elizabeth in the hall and came to her. He held two gunnysacks tied together. "You have enough supplies here to last several days. I put in some lamp oil as well."

"Thank you." Elizabeth felt awkward around him now that she knew he was cruel to his wife.

"Is something wrong? Did Celia say something to upset you?"

"No, no! I mean, nothing is wrong." He was so handsome, she thought, and his dark eyes looked so kind. One could never tell by looking that he was so terrible.

"It's nice to know the nearest neighbor is less than an hour away," he was saying as he walked her out the door.

"I'm that close? I mean, I've ridden for hours."

"The quickest way home is to head for the rocks shaped like sheep, then turn past them and go toward the mountain with the gap in it. I only saw Old Zeb a few times, but I know the way to his hut." He gazed thoughtfully at her. "I had no idea someone was living there now."

"Robert won the place in a poker game. We've been there several months."

"You've had time to improve it, then." He laughed. "Old Zeb was content if he had rocks to scratch in for gold and a shed over his head. He was always convinced there was gold in that hill somewhere. It didn't matter to him that no one has ever found any around here."

He seemed so friendly, so pleasant. It would be easy for a girl such as Celia to be swept away by him. "The place was a letdown, I'll admit. Robert believed he had found a bird's nest on the ground." She heard the exasperation in her voice and blushed. A wife wasn't supposed to speak ill of her husband, certainly not to a man she had met less than an hour before. "The mine will make a good root cellar," she added brightly. She neglected telling him that she had been unable to get even potatoes to grow in the poor, rocky soil.

"Are you certain that you don't want me to send a man to look for your husband?"

"No, that's not necessary. Robert is the sort to stay gone for as long as it pleases him. Not that I fault him for that," she added quickly. "He will come back any day now. He may even be there now for all I know. I'll pay back the provisions when he arrives."

"No. Please. We grow most of the food ourselves and lamp oil is cheap. I want you to accept these things as a welcoming gift. I'm only sorry it's been delayed."

Elizabeth tried not to show the reluctance she was feeling at having to leave. At least she knew now how to find Celia and the ranch. But how could she visit? Robert wouldn't want her away from home for hours. There was always so much work to do there.

Brice put the bags over the mule's back and balanced them so they would ride well. "You ride bareback," he commented.

"We only have one saddle. I don't mind, except it's difficult to mount." She started to lead the mule to the steps so she could get on him.

Before she knew what he was about to do, she felt Brice's hands on her waist. The next minute she was in the air and sitting astride the mule. He handed her the rifle and stepped away. There was an expression in his eyes that she didn't fully understand. The feeling of his strong hands on her waist, even for so short a time, was indelibly impressed on her memory, and her blood raced faster because of it. No, it wouldn't do for her to come for a visit. "Thank you," she said, noticing her voice sounded breathless. In a steadier voice she added, "You've been more than generous."

"Think nothing of it, ma'am. On the frontier we look after one another."

She told herself she was being foolish. He was only being friendly. How could he be as bad a person as Celia

had said and have such a warm smile? She gave him a
shaky smile and kicked the mule into motion. She could
feel his eyes on her as she rode away and her body
responded in a way she couldn't explain, given all she
knew about him and the fact that she was a married
woman. It took an effort not to look back.

When she reached the hut she lugged the bags off the
mule's back, surprised that they were so heavy. Brice
had lifted them so easily she had thought they weighed
much less. She took the mule to the pen beside the barn
and turned him loose. As she went back to the hut, she
dusted mule hair from her skirt. What an impression she
must have made in that immaculate parlor. She only
hoped she hadn't left mule hair on the garnet cushion of
Celia's chair.

Elizabeth took the bags into the hut and put them on
the table. Opening them was almost as exciting as opening gifts on Christmas morning. Brice hadn't been
stingy. There was a good-sized bag of flour and another
of cornmeal, a string of peach leather and two of apple
leather, a cone of sugar, several strips of venison and
beef jerky and enough lamp oil to last much longer than
he had indicated.

Elizabeth carefully put the provisions away. Even
though she had enough basic supplies to rest easy now,
she wasn't going to be so foolish as to waste any of it.
Especially the lamp oil. The nights were too long and
black when a lamp couldn't be lit. She felt almost tearful
with gratitude.

For a forbidden moment she remembered how pro-
vocative his gaze was when his eyes had met hers and
how his teeth were white and straight when he smiled.
If she didn't know better, she would say he smiled often—but smiles were at odds with a mean nature. She

put her hands on her waist where he had touched her. He was strong yet he had seemed so gentle. She would have to be careful when she visited Celia and not let herself begin to trust Brice. He seemed to be the opposite of all Celia had confided.

She felt guilty for wondering if Celia had been truthful. Surely no woman would say her husband was abusive unless he really was. She had every reason to believe her yet all she could think of was how different he seemed to be from Robert. And how she still seemed to feel the way his hands had touched her when he put her on the mule and how her pulse had raced when their eyes met.

It was only natural, she told herself hastily. Robert had been gone for weeks, and even when he was home, making love with him was no longer pleasurable. Looking back on it, she wasn't sure it ever had been. Not when he was usually finished before she began to warm toward him. She had tried to convince herself that it was always like that between a man and woman. Men were supposed to enjoy sex but ladies were not. She, like most women, had received that message obliquely all her life.

Elizabeth didn't believe it.

She was a lady born and bred, but there had been times she had enjoyed having Robert touch her. Sometimes she had liked it a lot. If he were willing to go slower and wait for her to reach his fever pitch, wouldn't she enjoy lovemaking as much as he did?

Her mind drifted back to Brice. Would it be different with a man like him, strong and gentle?

She resolutely put her mind on the mundane chores of her daily living. Thoughts along that line would only lead her to trouble.

Chapter Two

After telling Elizabeth how miserable she was, Celia was more determined than ever to hurry the birth of the baby and leave Brice. He dearly wanted this child and she smiled to think how it would hurt him to see her leave with it. It was no more than he deserved for bringing her here.

She bullied Consuela until the woman produced a concoction of mandrake, bitter apple, cotton root and squaw vine. It tasted foul and left a bitter residue in her mouth, but within an hour she felt the first contraction.

Consuela put her to bed and sent word to Brice in the pasture that the baby was coming. He arrived sooner than Celia thought possible. Between contractions she berated him for putting her in this condition. As the contractions grew stronger and she began to hemorrhage, her reproaches grew shrill with her panic. She hadn't expected so much pain. She could tell by Consuela's face that something was wrong. The baby should be small and easy to birth since it was a month from full term. Why was she having such pain?

When Brice had first come into the room, Celia saw Consuela hide the empty bottle in the bottom drawer of the wardrobe that blocked the doorway that connected this room with Brice's. If something went wrong and she lost the baby, Celia intended to show the bottle to Brice and blame it all on Consuela.

But why wasn't the baby coming?

Brice ached to see Celia's pain. He had known she didn't want children but he had believed she would change her mind once she had one. Besides, there was no effective means to prevent pregnancy except for abstinence. Celia hadn't wanted him in her bed and that made her pain and misery all his fault. Since she moved to this room, he had allowed himself one lapse in respecting her wishes and this was the result of it.

Brice was a kind man and he hated knowing Celia was suffering because of him. "Do you want me to send a man after Elizabeth Parkins?" he suggested to cheer her.

"No!" Celia snapped. "You know she lives in Old Zeb's mud hut. I don't want white trash around me. Certainly not at a time like this. I want my mother and my aunts!"

"Elizabeth struck me as a good woman. She certainly isn't white trash. And she's a lot nearer than your mother and aunts."

"Go away, Brice! Get out of my sight! I wish you were dead!" She screamed at him so hysterically a bead of spittle ran down her chin. She didn't notice.

Brice left without a word.

Cal, his closest friend, had come in from the bunkhouse and was waiting downstairs in the back parlor. He was called Wandering Cal because of a cast in his right eye. Brice didn't know his last name or where he came from, but they had been friends for years and Cal was his right-hand man on the ranch.

"She doing all right?" Cal asked. He was a man of few words.

"I don't know. It's too damned early for the baby to come. It's too early!" He paced to the hearth, then to the window. "What if I lose them, Cal?"

"Probably won't." Cal sat by the fire and picked up a piece of kindling to whittle. He looked entirely out of place in Celia's back parlor, even if it wasn't as grand as the formal front one. Cal was more suited for the barn.

"I should have sent her back home when I saw she didn't like it here. I kept thinking she would change her mind after a while. I was wrong."

"Wives belong with their husbands." Cal didn't like Celia and never had. He had only come into the house to keep Brice company. Celia never allowed him, or any of the other hired hands, nearer than the back porch.

An agonized scream made Brice cross to the door, hesitate and go back to the window.

"Go to the barn," Cal suggested. "I'll come tell you when it's over."

"No, I have to stay here. If Celia can live through it, I can stand to listen." But the next scream drained the blood from his face.

Cal looked up at the ceiling and paused in his whittling until the sound died away.

Brice started pacing again. He had to keep moving, even if he wasn't going anywhere. Every sound from Celia's bedroom tore at him.

The terrible wailing continued. Hours later Celia's voice had grown hoarse. Brice went up the stairs and back into her room. She no longer looked like herself. Her skin was pasty-gray and her blond hair hung in damp strings about her face. Circles like dark bruises lay under her glassy eyes.

Consuela looked at him in fright. "The baby is not

coming. It still does not show. I think it is turned sideways.''

There was no need for her to explain to Brice what this meant. He had seen enough calvings to know it couldn't be born this way. ''Can you turn it?''

Consuela shook her head. ''Señora Graham will not let me try.''

Brice went closer to the bed. ''We have to turn the baby, Celia.''

''No! I don't want either of you to touch me!''

He sat beside her on the bed and held her arms gently but firmly. ''You don't have a choice in this. You're getting too weak. Consuela, can you do it?''

''*Sí,*'' she said reluctantly. She was clearly afraid of her mistress, but she prepared to turn the baby nonetheless.

Celia screamed as if she were dying, but Brice held her, speaking to her gently in spite of the names she was calling him.

Minutes later, Consuela went to the washbasin and washed her hands. Brice released Celia, who struck him repeatedly until he left the bed. ''Well? Did it turn?''

Silently she shook her head.

''I'll try.'' He went back to Celia and tried to steel himself to her string of curses. A few minutes later he found a tiny foot, then another one. ''I have him!'' he said triumphantly. ''Push, Celia!''

Soon the baby lay screaming on the bed, waving her fists in protest at being born. ''It's a girl, Celia!'' he called out. ''She's so tiny!''

He finished tying off the cord and held her up so Celia could see her. ''Isn't she a beauty?''

''Ugly,'' Celia croaked out. ''She's ugly!''

''No,'' he said with a laugh as he went to sponge her

clean at the washbasin. "She's going to be a rare beauty someday! Celia?" The room was suddenly too quiet.

Consuela stopped cleaning Celia and stared at her face. Then she looked at Brice, her eyes filled with fear and dread.

"Celia?" he repeated. He wrapped the baby in the towel and went to his wife.

Celia's eyes were fixed and growing dull. Her pale lips moved. Brice leaned closer to hear what she was saying.

"I hate you. And I hate your baby." The last word was so broken as to be almost incoherent. A sigh of breath escaped from her lips and she didn't draw another one.

"Celia!" Brice shouted. "Celia!"

Consuela eased away from the bed. "Señora Graham is dead. I see her spirit leaving!" The woman's eyes were dilated with fear.

Brice stared at Celia's body in disbelief. She couldn't be dead! Sometimes women were in labor for days and lived. Celia had only labored for a few hours. She was young!

Nevertheless, she was dead.

The funeral was simple. Cal and some of the other men built a coffin, and Brice, with Consuela's help, laid Celia in it.

Numbly Brice decided to bury her a little distance from the house. He and Cal dug the grave.

Because no one was available to serve as the baby's wet nurse, Consuela made a baby bottle from an empty whiskey bottle and diluted cow's milk to a strength the baby could digest.

Brice went through the necessary motions of laying Celia to rest and caring for the baby, but part of his mind refused to accept the truth. They had no longer loved each other and Celia's last words had been of her hatred for him, but he still felt a deep loss. Was part of it guilt? He had indirectly put her in mortal danger. She had never been robust and the pregnancy had been hard on her. And her heart had given out because it couldn't stand up to the stress of hard labor. Still, she shouldn't be dead. She was young. Brice spent the next few days in a fog.

When he woke up one morning to discover Consuela and her husband had left in the night, the strength of determination began to build in him. He had lost Celia, but he was not going to lose the baby as well!

From that moment on, Brice began to heal.

By now Elizabeth was becoming accustomed to the idea that Robert wasn't coming home. At times this still terrified her because she had the rest of the winter to contend with alone. At others she was almost glad. With him gone there was no one to argue with or tell her she was wrong every time she opened her mouth. No one to chip at rocks while she did all the chores, no one to mess up the hut once she had everything in order.

She was beginning to realize how little Robert had done and was becoming resentful that she had allowed him to get away with it. If he came back, she vowed, it would be different. He would pull his own weight or leave.

Such thoughts sobered her. She had no way of enforcing them and, even if she did, why would she want this hovel to herself? If Robert wasn't coming back, she would be smarter to go back to Hannibal, swallow her pride and return to her father's house, begging his forgiveness. That alone was thought enough to make her know she would never return. There were worse situations than the one she was now in.

In the long days of solitude she taught herself to hunt. At first she missed everything she aimed at and got a bruised shoulder for her efforts. But gradually she started hitting the game more often than she missed and finally became a fairly good shot. The lack of money to buy more ammunition gave her incentive. She wasn't sure what she would do once the bullets were gone. When the ground was clear of snow, she gathered hay and grass for the mule.

Elizabeth was good at making provisions last. She had learned it by necessity over the past seven years. She ate only what she really needed, and when she killed game, she didn't waste any parts that could be boiled, dried or fried. She was even learning to tan hides so she could replace the soles of her shoes when they wore out. Little by little she had come to think of Robert as gone forever, and struggled to fill the void he left.

Loneliness was the worst part. There were times when she thought she would go mad if she didn't hear a human voice. During these times she sang or talked aloud to the mule or quoted the poems she had learned in school or did verbal math problems. Anything to hear something other than wind and silence.

Frequently she considered going back to the ranch to visit Celia, but the weather was so unpredictable she was afraid to go so far from home. Also, she knew Celia and Brice would insist on giving her more provisions, and she was too proud to accept charity when she had no means of repaying it, even though her meal and flour were almost gone.

There was the constant worry of how to replace the things she couldn't make for herself, such as the lamp oil, the bullets, cotton cloth for a dress when her two remaining ones became threadbare. She had no money at all and no way to make any. A few times she even went into the mine and chipped halfheartedly at the barren rocks in hopes of finding the gold she knew wasn't there.

Another snowstorm came and she was again stranded with the mule in her hut. The mule didn't seem to like the arrangement any better than she did, but she wouldn't leave him in the barn where he might freeze. The second day of the storm, she realized how fortuitous her decision had been when the weight of the wet snow caved in one end of the barn's roof. Had the mule been inside, he would almost certainly have been injured or killed. Elizabeth tried not to think about the ponderous load of snow over her own head or to wonder how much more weight the roof could bear without collapsing.

When the snow finally started to melt, a portion of the roof crumbled into her hut and landed on her table as she ate. She would have been hard-pressed to say which upset her more, the hole in the roof or the loss of food she could ill afford to replace.

Something had to be done. Elizabeth was becoming more and more aware that she couldn't stay here indefinitely. But where could she go? If she went to Glory she might be able to earn her living by washing clothes and ironing, but, until she had money, she would have no roof over her head. Without a house, where would she wash and iron? She could try to sell her land and the sod hut, but who would be fool enough to buy them?

She considered going to Brice's ranch and asking for a job as housekeeper. By now Celia's baby would have been born and Elizabeth had always liked children. Perhaps she could be the baby's nanny and later its tutor. She was well educated and there was no school in the valley. Such a job would be a joy.

But with such an arrangement would come the problem of living under the same roof with a man who was already in her dreams too often and whose temper was reportedly as bad as Robert's.

Elizabeth hated herself for her dreams about Brice. In them he was far more than a friend. Brice could never be her lover. Not ever. She was married to Robert and was stuck with him, like it or not. And Brice was married to Celia. All marital obstacles removed, Elizabeth vowed to avoid another abusive man.

Faced with no recourse but to relocate to Glory, Elizabeth began thinking in terms of how to find the town. All she remembered about that leg of their journey was her anticipation of finally reaching their new home and that it had been all uphill. She would start off in the direction Robert had taken the day he left and hope that she'd recognize enough of the landmarks to avoid getting completely lost. The mule wouldn't travel as fast as the horse, but she would get there eventually. There had been no trouble with Indians that she knew of, and being a laundress wasn't the worst fate in the world. At least she'd be alive.

As she was planning for her departure, she heard a horse ride into the yard. For a moment she was frozen. Could it be Robert? She ran to the door and threw it open.

Instead of Robert, Brice was dismounting from a prancing bay. He grinned at her and her heart skipped. "I hope I'm not barging in," he said as he tied the animal to a bush.

"No. Not at all. Come in." She was heartily glad she had moved the mule back to the pen and had cleaned the hut as well as possible. All the same, she was embarrassed at him seeing where she lived.

Brice ducked in order to get through the doorway into

the hut, his hat in his hand. His eyes glanced about and his face was carefully expressionless. He took the chair she indicated and laid his hat on the table. "Is your husband around?"

"No, he never came back." Her illicit dreams hadn't done Brice justice. He was far more handsome than she remembered and his voice was deeper and seemed to resonate somewhere within her. She abruptly looked away.

Brice leaned forward as if he hadn't heard her correctly. "He didn't? You're still alone?"

She refused to meet his eyes. "I don't believe he's going to come back. Not after being away this long. I'm planning to move to Glory." Almost defensively she added, "I can't make it here on my own."

He glanced up at the sky that showed through the roof over her head. "I don't see how you've made it this long."

Tears rose in her eyes and she blinked them back impatiently. "I manage quite well. Better than you might expect. I finally learned to shoot, and I found a spot down the stream that is level enough to plant a garden, which I'd planned to do come spring. I'm only going to Glory because I can't figure out how to buy bullets or calico or lamp oil. Other than that, I could make it here just fine."

"I wasn't finding fault. I was complimenting you."

Elizabeth drew in a steadying breath. "I'm sorry for the way the place looks, but there's not much you can do with a sod hut." She still felt as if she should defend herself and her life-style.

Brice was quiet for a moment. "I want you to come back to the ranch with me."

Her eyes met his. "Why?" If he was offering her charity she didn't think she could stand it.

He looked away. "A lot has happened since you've been gone. Celia had the baby." He paused for a long time. "The baby—a girl—is well. Celia didn't make it."

Elizabeth reflexively took a step forward. "No! Celia died?"

He nodded. "It was a terrible thing. There was nothing we could do. When the baby came, I thought she would be out of danger. But she died before she ever touched the baby."

"How terrible!" Elizabeth felt stunned. It had never occurred to her that Celia would die. "She was going to send for me when she started labor. Why did no one come?"

Brice gave her a measured look. Quietly he said, "She changed her mind. She told me not to send for you."

Elizabeth stared at him. She didn't believe a word of it. Her stomach turned at the idea of Celia crying out for the company of a woman and Brice refusing to send for her. He really must be a monster as Celia had said.

"Why are you looking at me like that?" he asked.

"No reason." She averted her eyes.

"Consuela left. She didn't give me any warning. One morning she and her husband, along with all their belongings, were gone. She never liked it here. I guess I can't really blame her. But that leaves me without anyone to look after Mary Kate. I hate to ask you, but I need the help. In addition to room and board, I'll pay you a salary."

He was offering her the best possible of alternatives. He might be abusive, but she would have to take her chances. For now, she still had her pride. Elizabeth lifted her chin. "I will care for your child. I have an education. As she grows older, I'll be able to teach her to read and write and do arithmetic."

"It sounds like a perfect solution." His soft voice

warmed her like a summer's breeze in spite of her dislike of him. "I came here thinking I'd have to argue your husband into letting you come, at least until I could find someone to take Consuela's place."

"But I'm not coming because I have no other option. It's important that you understand that." Celia was gone, but she could at least keep the baby safe. That might be necessary for its survival.

He smiled. "I understand. You'll still have this place and the land it stands on. I can send a wagon up for your belongings."

"That won't be necessary. I can tie it all in a quilt and put it on the back of the mule. Most of this can stay right where it stands." She would have no need for a rain-stained table and two chairs that didn't sit evenly, or a bed whose mattress hadn't been really dry since summer. Her few personal belongings wouldn't even fill a quilt.

"I'll go catch the mule for you," he offered.

She looked around the room for the last time. The colorful quilt she'd covered the bed with seemed to be struggling in vain to make the place bright and cheerful. The other was draped over the table to hide the stained wood. She folded the smaller one and put it in the center of the larger one, then plucked her other dress and night-gown from the peg that had been hammered into the rock of the back wall and laid them atop the folded quilt.

There was no need to take Robert's clothes. She had no use for them, and he might come back at some time.

She put her precious copy of *The Mysteries of Udolpho* in the center of the quilt and tied the opposite corners to make a pack. Again she looked around the room. She had lived here for months, yet all she had to take with her was a bundle that she could carry in one arm. With a sigh she went out to meet Brice and the mule.

He tied the bundle behind his saddle, then, as he had done before, he encircled her waist with his massive hands and lifted her onto the mule's back. His touch sent her senses reeling even more this time than before. She reminded herself what sort of person he was. Why did she always find herself drawn to the wrong sort?

Trying to keep her composure from slipping away entirely, Elizabeth said, "Although I'm coming to live in your house, Mr. Graham, it's to be understood that I'm only taking care of the baby and doing the housekeeping. You and I… That is, I'm only taking Consuela's place as nursemaid and housekeeper. Is that understood?"

"It's all I've asked of you," he said quietly.

Elizabeth felt a blush rising. "I know. I just wanted it to be understood from the very beginning."

"Of course. Your bedroom door has a lock on it, but you won't need it. I'm a man of honor. I have no intention of taking advantage of you."

"Good," she said as she tapped her heels against the mule's sides. She hoped she wasn't putting herself in danger by agreeing to live in his house. She was fairly certain no other adult lived there. But by his own admission, he had no interest in her, and that would make her job easier. She should be glad of it. This way they each knew what the other expected.

All the same, she wished she hadn't brought it up.

"Why the name Mary Kate?" she asked as they rode down the hill.

"It's my mother's name."

"It was a good name." But wouldn't most men have named her after the wife they had just lost? This seemed to be further proof of his coldness toward Celia.

When they topped a rise and Brice's ranch came into

view, she couldn't conceal her quick intake of breath. The ranch was even more beautiful than she remembered.

Brice noticed her reaction and smiled. "I know. It affects me the same way." His manner was matter-of-fact, not in the least boastful. "I love the West. This part of the state reminds me of my boyhood home in Texas. The winters here are tougher, though."

She glanced at him as they rode down the incline. "I would imagine so, Texas being all desert and tumbleweed."

He chuckled. "No offense intended, but I'd bet even money that you've never been there. It's actually quite beautiful, even the part out west that's like a desert. The eastern side where I was raised is rolling hills and piney woods."

"If you love it so much, why did you leave?"

"My brother inherited our ranch when my father died. My stepmother and I never did see eye to eye on anything, and Papa always believed everything she said against me. There were hard feelings between my brother and me, so it seemed like a good idea for me to pack up and leave. Papa did, however, leave me money, and I bought this place from one of the sooners who rushed in here to homestead when the government opened the Territory for settlement. He had only been here a short while and had done nothing with the land."

"I would think the money would have been the better inheritance."

He grinned again. "Not if you're a Texan."

"I gather you met Celia in Texas?"

He nodded. "We married after I built this ranch. Her parents weren't at all happy about me taking her so far away. They blame her death on me."

Elizabeth studied his face for any expression of guilt. There was none.

"Celia was never robust. She was sick off and on all her life. Maybe if we'd stayed right there with her family she would have died anyway. I don't know."

"I'm sorry about your loss," she said sincerely. "Losing her in childbirth must have been very difficult."

Again he was silent. "It's a funny thing about the frontier. It seems to bring out things in people that, in settled places, they never discover."

He didn't elaborate, and she didn't think she should press him to explain.

They rode to the barn and left the animals with one of Brice's hired hands, who looked at her with curiosity but didn't ask any questions. Brice carried her bundle as if it weighed nothing at all.

The back of the house had a porch almost as long and wide as the front. A broom and a mop in a bucket stood beside the chimney. A gray cat lay on the step in the sunlight. The back door was covered with wooden gingerbread that matched the front entrance. Brice had spared no expense on this house. Elizabeth was again struck at the disparity between this house and her hut.

The kitchen was large and built inside the house, unlike many of the older homes in Hannibal, which had their kitchens in a separate building. The hearth was deep, high enough to walk into, and of a width that would accommodate the roasting of a whole steer. Hanging on the walls and from a rack suspended from the rafters were utensils of every size and description. Elizabeth was glad she hadn't bothered to pack the single iron skillet and iron pot she owned. Everything she could possibly need was here.

"We had a cook for the first couple of years but she

became homesick and went back to Texas. Consuela was her cousin, and I'm surprised that she stayed as long as she did. When the cook left, everything fell onto Consuela's shoulders.''

"Where is the baby? Surely you didn't leave her alone here while you went after me?''

"Of course not. Wandering Cal is with her.''

"Wandering Cal?'' she asked doubtfully.

"He's my foreman. He's called that because his right eye has a way of wandering off to one side. Cal has been with me since a year or two after I came here. Mary Kate is safe with him.''

"I think I should go get her.''

Brice led her into the wide hall that served as a foyer and across to a back parlor. "We're back. Mrs. Parkins, this is Cal. Cal, has Mary Kate given you any trouble?''

The man stood and gingerly handed the baby to Elizabeth. "Pleased to meet you, ma'am. Nope, her and me's been playing.'' His deep, gravelly voice sounded at odds with his words. He was as tall as Brice, several years older and far more grizzled. He looked more like a bandit than a nursemaid. Elizabeth automatically held the baby closer.

Mary Kate regarded her solemnly with large blue eyes. Then she spotted her father and gurgled happily and waved her plump arms and legs.

Brice grinned, and when he touched her arm with his forefinger, Mary Kate grabbed it and tried to put it in her mouth.

Elizabeth found herself smiling and felt love growing in her heart. No one could see this baby and not fall in love with her. "She's beautiful! And her eyes are as blue as Celia's.'' She looked up at Brice's dark ones.

"One baby looks pretty much like another, if you ask me,'' Cal said in a rumbling voice.

Mary Kate cooed to him as if she saw right through his facade of disinterest. To her relief, Elizabeth saw a faint smile lift his lips. He immediately removed it.

"I'm going back to work if you don't need me no more." He looked at Brice as if he was going whether he was needed or not.

"Go ahead. I'll be out as soon as I get Mrs. Parkins settled in."

Cal nodded as he grabbed his hat and left without a word to Elizabeth.

"He's talkative today," Brice commented when they were alone. "I've spent days on the trail with him and not heard him say a word. Mary Kate is a good influence, I guess."

"What do you know about him? He looks as if he chews bullets as a pastime."

Brice laughed. "Cal is a mystery. He has no past, no family, no ties to any place or thing. He owns only his clothes, a horse and tack. He was a drifter, and for some reason decided to settle here."

"You don't know anything about his past? How do you know he isn't wanted somewhere by the law?" She couldn't get over the foreman's rough appearance, in spite of the gentleness he had shown with the baby.

"That's not unusual on the frontier. A lot of people make no mention of their pasts and no questions are asked. If they've made some mistakes back home, they've come west for a new start, and that's what they're due."

"But what if—" she began.

"He won't answer any questions, so you may as well not ask him. All I know is he's reliable and smarter than he seems. He's pulled me through some tough times. No, don't worry about Cal. He won't do you any harm. More than likely he'll ignore you altogether. That's how he treated Celia. She never liked him but she got used to him.''

''It's really none of my business.'' She hugged the baby. ''What do you feed her?''

He took her back outside to the springhouse that straddled a small brook not far from the rear of the house. Elizabeth wrapped the baby beneath her wool cape as she followed him. ''The cows give milk but it's too rich for her. Consuela and I experimented until we hit upon a combination of milk and water that doesn't upset Mary Kate's stomach. That's it in the crock there.''

Elizabeth nodded.

''Her bottles are lined along that wall.'' Brice indicated a shelf of empty whiskey bottles that had been fitted with rubber nipples. ''Consuela found it easier to fill them out here than to carry the crock to the house, fill one and bring it back to the springhouse.''

''This time of year I can't see much need to keep them here. The back porch should be cool enough in the shade.''

Brice nodded. ''I think so, too.'' He gave her a searching look. ''I'm glad you've come. I can't manage all of it on my own. Not and keep the ranch running.'' His voice was soft and sincere.

Elizabeth drew her cape closer around the baby. ''I'll have no trouble doing these things. We'll get along just fine.'' Mary Kate lifted her head and studied Elizabeth closely, her tiny brows furrowed in infant thoughtfulness. Elizabeth found herself smiling.

Brice was watching her. ''You have a pretty smile.''

At once it disappeared. Elizabeth wasn't used to compliments. She stepped out of the springhouse and started across the gentle slope to the house.

''Did I upset you? I didn't mean to.''

''I'm not upset.''

"You look upset."

"Well, I'm not." She refused to look at him, even when he held the back door open for her.

"Come upstairs. I'll show you to your room and Mary Kate's." He picked up her bundle from where he had left it in the kitchen and led her through the house and up the stairs.

Elizabeth was glad to follow him. This way she could look at him without being seen. His compliment had left her feeling uncomfortable. He was newly widowed. He had no business complimenting a woman. He was still in deep mourning, even if he wasn't wearing black. And for that matter, why wasn't he? In Elizabeth's opinion, no recently bereaved man should be able to smile, let alone to smile in a way that made her world rock. She had been alone too much. That had to be it.

Brice indicated the first door in the upstairs hall. "This is my room. If you ever need me in the middle of the night, all you have to do is call out."

"Why would I need you in the middle of the night?" she asked suspiciously.

"In case the baby gets sick."

"Of course." She felt her cheeks warming and hoped he didn't notice.

"Your room is here." He opened the door to the bedroom that adjoined his own. "In the summer you can leave the veranda door open and the room will be cooler. There's always a breeze here in the summer. We share the veranda, but you can trust me to respect your privacy. As you'll notice the door between the rooms has been blocked shut by Celia's armoire."

She nodded, not trusting herself to speak.

He looked around at the room as if he were deep in thought. "This was Celia's room. During her pregnancy she was ill quite often and preferred to sleep alone. But even before that she had taken this room for her own. It was the way she wanted it.''

Elizabeth gazed around the room. That explained why the wallpaper was sprigged with roses and violets and why the curtains were lace. Not one item in the room was masculine.

"This is rather delicate, but I don't know of any other way to say it," he began awkwardly. "Celia's clothes are still here. I didn't know what to do with them, and they didn't fit Consuela. If you'd like them, you're welcome to them. I think you're about the same size. Otherwise, I guess I'll have to burn them."

"It would be a waste to burn clothing!" Elizabeth exclaimed. All the years of her marriage, she had seldom owned more than two extra dresses. The thought of burning a garment was unacceptable. Cloth was too difficult to acquire. Dresses weren't simple to make. "I can make them over if they don't fit. But won't they be unpleasant reminders to you? I don't want to offend you."

"No, I would rather someone get some use out of them. She had some she never even wore." He stepped back into the hall. "You can have anything in the room." He went across the hall to a room painted in a shade of pale rose. "This is Mary Kate's nursery."

There was no need for him to have pointed that out. It was obvious that someone had spent hours making baby blankets, gowns and bonnets. Crib-sized quilts lay folded at the end of the baby's bed. It didn't escape Elizabeth that pink was the predominant color. If Mary Kate had been a boy, several baby things Celia had made would have been too feminine for his use.

As if Brice were following her thoughts, he said, "Celia's mother sent all these things. As you can see, she was determined that the baby would be a girl. I don't think she has much use for males. Celia came from a house full of sisters and two maiden aunts, in addition to her parents. The absence of women out here was very disturbing to her.''

"I see."

"I had hoped she would become friends with you."

"I hoped so, too."

"You can change anything you like in the nursery or your room. All I ask is that you leave mine alone."

"I'll only go in there to clean."

Their eyes met, and Elizabeth was aware of the intimacy of their surroundings. She stood there holding his child and speaking of his bedroom in the most ordinary of tones. She had to look away. She wasn't entirely sure she could trust him not to take advantage of her.

"Do I make you nervous?" he asked.

"No," she said a bit too quickly. "Why would you wonder such a thing?"

"Maybe it's because you make me nervous as hell." He turned and left the room without further explanation.

She stared after him.

Chapter Three

Brice tugged at the leather strap he was threading into the buggy harness. The air in the barn was still and colder than the air outside but he didn't mind. He could use some cooling off.

Elizabeth had been at the house only half a day, and just knowing she was there was driving him to distraction.

"Damn!" he muttered as he yanked on the strap. It twisted and lodged firmly behind the concho. He frowned at it.

"Want me to do that?" Cal asked from the nearby stall. He was grooming a mare that was due to foal soon. Cal was much better with animals than with humans.

"No, I can do it."

Cal turned back to the horse. The rhythmic sound of his brushing picked up again. After a while, he left the stall and passed Brice on the way to the tack room. Brice could hear the man's unspoken comment. They had worked together so many hours that words were seldom necessary.

"That bright bay can draw the buggy," Brice responded. "She's a smart trotter and she'll look good in harness."

"Yep."

"It'll be good for Mary Kate to get out in the fresh air. Children need sunshine, too."

Cal only glanced at him and tossed the horse brush into the box by the tack door. He reached through the doorway and got a lead rope.

"I'm doing it for Mary Kate, not Elizabeth."

Cal took a long time looping the lead neatly in his left hand. "I thought her name was Mrs. Parkins."

"That's what I said. Mrs. Parkins."

One of Cal's rare grins spread across his wrinkled, weathered face as he sauntered back to the stall.

Brice tugged the strap through the concho and this time it threaded straight. "You talk too much, Cal. I've noticed that about you before." He grinned at the man.

Cal only grunted. He snapped the lead onto the pregnant mare's halter and led her out of the barn to the feedlot to graze on hay he'd spread there earlier.

Brice picked up the ranch end of the strap and started working it through the other side of the harness. He heard footsteps behind him and said without turning, "She's pretty. Did you notice that, Cal?"

"Who is?" Elizabeth asked as she looked around. "Are you talking to me?"

Brice jerked his head around. "I thought you were Cal." Politely he got to his feet and nodded a greeting.

"He's turning a horse out into the feedlot."

"I was saying the bay mare I bought to pull this buggy is pretty," Brice improvised. He noticed Elizabeth was small, several inches shorter than Celia had been. In the dim light of the barn her hair was as black as a crow's wing. Unlike what he had remembered, her eyes weren't dark also, but gray. A silvery color like storm clouds. "The harness strap was in bad shape and I thought I'd better repair it before the buggy is needed."

"You really have a buggy?" she asked.

"It's right over there."

She went in the direction he nodded and found the buggy in the area behind the stalls. "It's beautiful! And the lamp is brass!"

He smiled. It was good to do something for someone who noticed an effort had been made. "It didn't look that good when I bought it. There's been some elbow grease put on it, I have to admit." He had polished the lamp to a brilliant shine rather than return to the house and Celia's constant complaining.

"I haven't ridden in a buggy in so long!" Her voice was filled with wonder. "I hadn't thought I ever would again."

"Where's the baby?"

"Asleep. She took a whole bottle of milk and fell asleep while I rocked her. I came out to thank you again for bringing me here. I already love her. You're a very lucky man."

Until today he would have argued that there was no truth in her last statement, but things had already changed. "She's a good baby. I don't think she'll give you much trouble."

Elizabeth came back to him and touched the harness. "Do you take the buggy out often?"

"It hasn't been used since I brought it home. I thought Celia might like to use it but by then she wasn't well. I got it for her."

"How thoughtful of you." She looked at him in surprise.

"Once the weather is warmer, you and Mary Kate might like to take it for outings."

"Thank you. That would be nice." She went to the stall and looked at the horse inside. "I've always loved horses. We had one almost this color back in Hannibal."

"You and your husband, you mean?" It would do him good to remember she was married.

"No, my father."

"Do you like it out here?" he asked.

"No, I don't. Life is too hard here." She was thinking of the privations in the sod hut and Robert's abandonment. "I intend to go back to Missouri eventually." She touched the horse's velvety nose.

He hadn't expected this answer. Elizabeth was so independent he had thought she would love the freedom of the frontier. "If I hear of a train returning east, I'll let you know," he said stiffly.

"Thank you. I won't be able to afford it for quite a while. And then there's Robert—wherever he is."

"You shouldn't worry too much about your husband. There are a lot of things that can hold a man up out here. It could be his horse went lame and can't travel." It was the only excuse Brice could think of. Even that didn't hold water. If he were Robert and had a wife, especially one like Elizabeth, waiting for him out in the hills, he would buy another horse or walk home before he would leave her stranded for so long.

"Robert can take care of himself. He always does." She glanced up at him as if afraid she had given too much away. "I should be getting back to the house. I don't want Mary Kate to wake up and be alone."

He watched her go to the barn door. At the entrance she turned.

"Would you like a ham for supper?"

"That would be great."

"How many do I cook for?"

"Just me. The men eat in the bunkhouse." He was looking forward to not eating with them. Ezra Smart might be all right at trail cooking, but a man could tire of beans and beef after a while. Brice had liked Consuela's cooking well enough but she put red peppers in everything, and after a while that grew tedious as well.

"I'll have it ready just after sundown." She gave him a smile and stepped out of sight.

Brice stood staring after her. She even knew to time meals to the hours a man could work! Celia had insisted on dinner at six o'clock year-round because that was the time her parents had always eaten. She hadn't even tried to understand that some days he had to work for as long as there was daylight. Ham. His mouth watered just thinking about it.

"You look like somebody whopped you in the head with a poleax," Cal commented as he strolled back into the barn. He went to the gray gelding's stall and opened the gate.

"She just came out to say the baby is sleeping," Brice said defensively.

"Is she going to keep you posted every time that girl nods off?" Cal hooked the lead to the gray's halter and led him to the tack room.

"Of course not." Brice went back to working on the harness. "She's cooking ham for supper."

Cal grunted. It was a customary sign of his approval.

"You want me to ask her to set an extra plate? You know you're welcome at my table anytime."

This time the man's grunt had an edge of humor.

"Celia isn't there now and her opinions don't matter anymore. You're my foreman and my friend. If you want to eat in the house with us, it's fine with me.'' He was thinking that might be safest. If Cal was there he wouldn't be alone with Elizabeth. "I'll tell her to set you a place.''

"Nope. Rather have beans.''

Brice shook his head. "You're an odd one, Cal. How you can eat Ezra's food every night is a mystery to me.''

"He ain't fussy.''

Brice knew Cal would never forget or forgive Celia for driving him out of the house, even if she was dead and buried now. It was still her dining room as far as Cal was concerned and he had vowed not to set foot in it again. Celia had been too picky about most things. A man couldn't work around cattle and horses all day and not smell like them from time to time. Or at least a man like Cal couldn't. He was barely house-trained at all. Just the same, Celia could have been more tactful.

He remembered every word Elizabeth had said and how she had looked when she said it. The brief visit had told him a lot about her. She was conscientious or she wouldn't have cared if Mary Kate woke up alone, and she appreciated a good buggy when she saw one. And she wasn't that fond of her husband.

Brice found himself dwelling on that information. He couldn't blame her for feeling the way she did about her husband. The man was a bastard for leaving her in a situation like that. But she was still married, whether she liked the man or not. Brice had to remember that. He also had to remember she was no happier in the Territory than Celia had been.

He was lonely. He knew that all too well. Even before Celia had died, he had been lonely. That wasn't hard to do in the house with a woman like Celia. What he had taken for shyness when he was courting her had turned out to be mere shallowness. Her delicate health that had stirred him to such protectiveness had been an irritation when she used it as a weapon to keep him at a distance. He was wiser now and more wary, but he was also damned lonely for a woman's company.

He worked the strap into place and buckled it. Finished at last! For a while there he had thought the harness would win the struggle.

"I'm taking Partner out for a ride," Cal said as he tossed a blanket and saddle over the animal's back. Partner flicked his ears back in protest and lifted a back hoof as if considering a kick to Cal's leg. Cal slapped him on the flank and Partner put his hoof back on the ground.

"I'll see you in a day or so." Brice grinned at Cal. It was a standing joke between them. Cal broke horses by saddling them and riding out onto the range. He came home when the horse learned to obey bridle signals and not before. It was the easiest and quickest way to successfully train one.

"I'll be back before dark," Cal assured him as he tugged on the saddle cinch.

"I wouldn't put money on it. The day is pretty well gone."

Cal responded with another guttural sound. This time the utterance seemed to mean he disagreed. He led the horse outside before mounting.

As soon as he was in the saddle, Partner flattened his ears and tried to get his head down to buck. Pulling up on the reins, Cal held the horse's head firmly up. Partner lunged forward, and by the time they topped the hill, he was running full out.

Brice laughed softly to himself. The horse couldn't throw Cal, and one way or another, Partner would know something about reining before he saw the barn again.

Cal was kind to animals—but he was more stubborn than they were.

Mary Kate was an easy baby to tend. Elizabeth laid two kitchen chairs on their sides in one corner of the kitchen to form a pen of sorts and put the baby there with an assortment of wooden spoons to play with until supper was prepared. Elizabeth had to remind herself over and over not to become too attached to the baby or the house because she had no intention of staying. If Robert returned, he would certainly insist that she go back to the sod hut. If he didn't, she would go back home to her father and hope he would forgive her for leaving with Robert.

She also couldn't get too attached to Brice. That was a different matter altogether and a far more difficult one. She clearly remembered that Celia had said he was cruel to her, no matter what his attitude toward Elizabeth might be. After living with her father and Robert, Elizabeth found cruelty easy to believe of any man. Elizabeth always seemed to be drawn to the men who were bad for her. Even if she were free, she would do well to avoid an entanglement with Brice. And having Mary Kate just a few feet away was a constant reminder that Brice had only been a widower for a short while.

When supper was ready and staying warm in the brick warming oven, she made a puree of potatoes mixed with juice from the ham for the baby. Elizabeth had older cousins with infants and she had known how to care for babies for years. Her father had often sent her to stay with cousins for months at a time to help care for their children. Without her mother's milk, it was important for Mary Kate to eat food as soon as possible.

She held Mary Kate in her lap and slowly fed her

spoonfuls of food. The baby grabbed at the spoon and gulped as if she hadn't eaten in a week. Elizabeth laughed. "You're a greedy little one, aren't you? That's good. You go for everything you want in life and don't let anyone hold you back."

Mary Kate gurgled happily and potatoes rolled down her dimpled chin.

When she had eaten all she wanted, Elizabeth changed her into a clean gown and diaper and rocked her as she fed her a bottle of milk. Mary Kate gazed up at her as she drank the milk, occasionally giving her a toothless grin that dribbled milk onto her cheek. Elizabeth felt a tug of pure love that touched something deep inside her.

The baby soon fell asleep and Elizabeth put her in her bed. As she pulled the quilt over the baby, she touched the soft golden down on Mary Kate's head. Nothing was softer than a baby, she decided. Mary Kate sighed and snuggled into the familiar warmth of her quilt. Elizabeth put a stuffed bear in the bed so that Mary Kate wouldn't be lonely when she woke up, then went downstairs.

By the time she had the table set, she heard Brice washing up at the pump on the porch. When he came inside, his hair was damp from the water. He stopped when he saw her bending over the spider on the hearth to stir the beans. She looked back at him and smiled. "Ready to eat?"

"I'll run up and change my shirt." He backed toward the inside door. "I won't be but a minute."

"There's no rush." She started ladling the beans into a serving bowl. She hadn't cooked much because she wasn't used to having many choices in what she ate. Even during the better times, she and Robert rarely could afford more than a meat and one other dish. Ham, beans, potatoes and corn bread were like a feast to her. She had even baked some of the dried apples into a pie. Would he think she was wasteful? She wanted to keep this job. It was her ticket back to civilization.

When she heard Brice coming down the stairs, she lit the other two lamps that made the dining room bright enough for the meal. To save lamp oil she had set the table in the dimmest light possible. She brought in the steaming bowls and put them nearest the head of the table where she assumed he would eat. Although she wasn't sure she was supposed to join him, she had put her plate to one side.

"Is this all right?" she asked when he came into the room. "I can eat in the kitchen if you'd rather."

He gave her a long look. "No, I want you to eat with me. You aren't a servant, Eliz—Mrs. Parkins. I never meant that you should feel you are one."

She felt the blush rising again. "I just didn't know. In my father's house only the family eat at the dining room table. I didn't want you to think I was overstepping my boundaries."

He held her chair and she slid into it hastily. Robert had never once done that for her. He sat at the end of the table and said, "This looks wonderful!"

Elizabeth smiled but didn't meet his eyes. "I also made an apple pie. I know it's extravagant, but I felt...I wasn't sure if you like desserts."

"You can make whatever you please. I'm not picky. Just hungry."

She passed him the corn bread. "Mary Kate has been an angel. I made her a place to play in the kitchen and she was no trouble at all. She's upstairs asleep," she added.

"Do you have brothers or sisters?" he asked.

"No, I was an only child. I have many cousins,

though. That's where I learned how to care for babies. I had hoped to have a large family, but apparently that won't be.''

"You're young. They may still come." He watched her for a moment but gave no clue as to what he was thinking. "Beans?"

"Thank you." She put some on her plate and left the bowl where he could reach it for seconds. She was trying so hard to do everything perfectly that she was barely allowing herself to breathe. "You said you have a brother. Are there others?"

"No. Just the two of us. We're half brothers, really. James used to remind me of that often. We never got along all that well. Otherwise we could have worked the ranch together and I would have stayed in Texas."

"Do you regret the move?"

"Not anymore. I can be my own person here and not have to answer to anyone."

She looked at him in amazement. "That's almost exactly what I told myself not long ago!" She caught herself. "Of course it's different for a man."

"You're welcome to stay here for as long as you like."

Elizabeth pushed the beans around on her plate. "We'll have to see what happens. We don't always get to do exactly what we want to do. Especially not if Robert shows up. I have obligations. Things are expected of me." Her voice trailed off and she glanced at him. He was watching her in that oddly exciting way. Hastily she straightened and handed him the potatoes.

"I already have some." He seemed amused at her eagerness to change the subject.

"So you do." She put down the potatoes. "Is that the baby crying?"

"No. I don't hear a thing."

"I left her door open so I would know if she wakes up. I don't want her to cry and me not hear her."

"You're kind. I knew you would be."

"I don't hold with letting babies cry. Suppose it's a weakness of mine—perhaps not having had one of my own. All they need is food or a hug or..." She bit off the rest of her sentence. Diapers weren't a fit subject for the dinner table.

"Consuela thought crying would make her lungs strong."

"I won't let her cry. Not unless I can't find how to make her happy. I never saw a child spoiled by being loved and treated with kindness, so if you don't agree with that, it's best that we clear the air now."

"Why are you so determined to argue with me?"

She looked at him in surprise. "Is that what you think? I never meant to leave that impression. I'm not bad-tempered. Not at all. I..." She flushed with embarrassment. He was the one who was bad-tempered, and now the word lay between them.

"Hold on. I didn't mean it that way. You go off on tangents faster than any woman I've ever known."

"I talk too much. Robert is always telling me so. I'll try to be more careful." She sighed as she broke off a bit of corn bread from the wedge on her plate.

"I like hearing conversation. Cal never makes a sound unless it's necessary. It's damned lonesome when no one is talking." He caught himself. "I'm sorry. I should be watching my language. It's been a long time since I had a conversation with a woman."

"I don't mind," she said honestly. What did it mean he hadn't had a conversation with a woman in a long time? Celia hadn't been gone so very long. Surely they talked before she died. Still, months of silence when you were used to having a wife about could seem like a longer time. "Sometimes Robert and his poker friends would turn the air blue. It doesn't embarrass me."

"He allowed his friends to talk like that in front of you? Why would he do that? Why not go to a saloon where no one cared how anyone else was talking?"

"He was of the opinion that the house was his and that I should adjust to it. My father would have agreed with him in principle, even though he hated Robert and would have cut out his own tongue before admitting that they saw eye to eye on anything."

"It sounds as if your life hasn't exactly been a bed of roses, even before moving to Zeb's sod hut."

"My parents had a nice house in Hannibal. My father built it for my mother as a wedding gift."

"That's the first time you've mentioned her."

"She died."

"I'm sorry. You must miss her."

"She never made much of a wave as she passed through life," Elizabeth said thoughtfully. "Some people don't, you know. They can live out their entire lives without others taking particular notice of them. She wanted me to be more like that. She said I would be happier if I could learn to be accepting of whatever came to me. But I can't. I just can't sit back and never express an opinion of my own."

"Neither can I. Celia certainly wasn't like that. She wanted life to conform itself to her whims. She wasn't always easy to live with."

Elizabeth frowned at him and pushed the bread plate in his direction.

"What did I say to upset you?" Brice asked.

"How can you ask that? Celia is barely in her grave

and you're discussing her faults? I found her quite likable. We had a lot in common.''

"Did you?'' he asked in a cool tone.

"Mr. Graham, I feel we must be honest with each other if we are to live under the same roof. I'm married and I came here only for the job and for the sake of the baby. You and I don't have to like each other. Although I only saw Celia once, I considered her to be my friend and I'm loyal to her memory. No other relationship between us is possible.''

"You're assuming a great deal. It takes more than one visit to make a friendship. And, I assure you, Mary Kate's well-being is my top priority.''

"Celia was the first woman I had seen in months. I must insist you treat her memory with respect, at least in my presence.''

"I knew her better than you did and you have no right to call me to task.''

"I see.'' Elizabeth stood and picked up her plate. "I think the less contact we have, the better it will be.''

"I think you're right.''

She swept past him and finished her meal alone in the kitchen. It wasn't the way she had intended the first meal to turn out, but she felt it was better to get everything out in the open from the beginning. Otherwise she might make a fool of herself.

That night Brice awoke to hear Mary Kate fretting in her bed. Automatically he swung his feet out from under the cover. He had pulled on his pants and was halfway to the door before he was really awake. With a yawn he went out into the hall and down to the nursery door.

At the doorway he stopped.

Elizabeth was already there. The baby was in her arms

and she had started to sing to her softly. She opened the window to get the bottle she had left there to stay cool. Her hair was loose and flowed down her back in thick waves to below her waist. Her gown was white and loose but the lamplight showed him tantalizing glimpses of her silhouette beneath the concealing fabric. She looked younger and more vulnerable than she had during the day.

She turned to take the baby to the rocker, and Brice stepped back into the dark hallway before she could see him. He was wearing no shirt or shoes and he didn't want to alarm or embarrass her. When he heard the sound of the rocker moving in pace to her song, he looked back around.

Elizabeth was rocking and feeding the bottle to Mary Kate while she sang softly and smiled down at her. They made such a scene of domestic tranquillity that Brice felt emotion tighten his throat. As Elizabeth's hair swayed with the rocker and undulated about her, he wondered if it could possibly be as soft as it looked. Certainly it was longer and thicker than he had guessed. Mary Kate reached up a pudgy arm and gathered a fistful of it and held on. Elizabeth smiled at her.

Quietly Brice backed away from the room and retreated down the hall without making a sound. Once in his room, he closed the door and sat on the side of the bed. Maybe it had been a mistake to ask her to come here.

At the time it had seemed only logical. He needed a woman to take care of the baby and the house; she needed a decent place to live. But it wasn't working out so simply. She had made it plain at dinner that she didn't like him and would prefer not to be around him. The unfairness of it hurt him, because he had offered her

room and board as well as a salary. Why did she dislike
him so? At least, he consoled himself, there was no
chance of him forming an attachment with another
woman who disliked his ranch. When she left, there
would be no regrets.

Although her song was too soft for him to hear from
his bed, Brice listened to it in his heart. It was a tune
any mother might sing to a child, but Elizabeth's voice
was beautiful, and the loving way she had looked down
at the baby had touched him deeply. He would never be
able to ignore her presence in the house the way he had
done Consuela's. He would have to be very careful with
his feelings toward Elizabeth.

Brice got to his feet, strode to the veranda door and
stepped out into the night. The air was much too cold
for comfort but he welcomed it.

He stayed there trying not to think those thoughts that
had driven him out into the cold until he heard the quiet
sound of Elizabeth's bedroom door closing and the rustle
of her bedclothes. The walls were too thin at times. Listening to Celia move about in that room and knowing
he would never be welcome there had been galling but
not so tempting as to hear Elizabeth settling into the
same feather bed. Drawing a deep breath, Brice went
back into his room and closed the door against the night
air.

He gazed for a long moment at the door that connected his room to hers. Celia had blocked that passage
with a heavy armoire. Unless Elizabeth had looked
closely, she probably hadn't noticed the door was there
at all. Celia's gesture had been purely antagonistic; she
had known he would never force himself on her. And
once she was with child, she had made it clear that he
would never be welcome in her bed again. The baby had

fulfilled her duty as she saw it. To prove she meant it, she moved permanently into the other bedroom. He had spent a lot of sleepless nights after that.

He was only fooling himself to think he could live with Elizabeth in the same house without her presence having an impact on him. Something deep in his soul had come to life the first time their eyes met. It was a measure of his desperation over Mary Kate's welfare that he had thought they could live tranquilly under the same roof. There was only one decent thing to do. Tomorrow he would send Cal in to Glory to look for Robert. He should have done so right away.

He took off his pants and tossed them over the arm of the chair beside his bed. The sheets felt uncomfortably cold when he slid between them. Brice hated to sleep alone, and he had never been able to sleep in a nightshirt. That was one of the first matters he and Celia had argued about—if you could call it an argument when her side consisted of crying and pouting and making him guess what was wrong for days before unloading her grievances on him at the top of her lungs.

Elizabeth would never be that indirect. She had proved that at dinner. Elizabeth would tell him straight out and in no uncertain terms what he had done that displeased her. He found himself smiling in the dark. Such honesty would be refreshing. As much as he hated to argue, he wouldn't mind so much if he could be certain what the subjects were from the beginning.

But she didn't like him for reasons he didn't understand, and her primary goal was to leave the Oklahoma Territory and return to her people in Missouri. It was for the best that her stay at the ranch was temporary, given the way she disliked him and how he didn't dislike her at all. Yes, he had to find Robert for Elizabeth and another woman for Mary Kate. And he needed to do it soon, before emotions exploded between them.

Chapter Four

By the time Elizabeth had been at the ranch for two months, she found herself actually enjoying living there. Brice had sent Cal into Glory to look for Robert, but he had been unable to find him. A few people remembered seeing him months before yet no one had any idea where he might have gone. Elizabeth had taken the news with an outward show of calm but Robert's disappearance only cemented her inner conclusion that he had deserted her and never intended to return at all.

Mary Kate now knew Elizabeth well and considered her to be her own personal possession. Her small face would light up as soon as Elizabeth came into the room and she'd hold up her hands with an angelic smile on her face to signal that she wanted to be picked up and carried. Elizabeth loved the baby as much as she would have if Mary Kate had been her own child.

Brice was a larger part of Elizabeth's life than she would have preferred. Because she considered it part of her job, she planned her day around those times when he would appear for meals, and centered the menus around his likes and dislikes. He still had shown no sign of cruelty, but Elizabeth was certain he was capable of it. As were all the men she had known well. She had to remind herself constantly that Celia had had no reason to lie about it and that she mustn't read more into his kindnesses than might be true.

After supper Brice liked to sit in the library and go over the ranch's accounts or read. Elizabeth had been drawn to that room since her first glimpse of it. When Brice was gone during the day, she often went into the library and stroked the leather spines of the books and read the titles. To do more seemed like an invasion of his privacy. But eventually her desire to read overcame her reticence.

After putting Mary Kate down for the night, she went to the library door and paused. Brice sat at his mahogany desk, the lamp making a puddle of yellow light on the polished surface. He was bent over several papers, adding numbers and making notations beside the columns. He must have sensed her presence because he looked up. "Yes?"

Her mouth went dry. What if he refused to let her read his books? Her father had always discouraged her from reading. "I was wondering..." She hesitated, not sure how to go on.

He put down his pen. "Yes?" he repeated.

She went to the nearest shelves and touched the books lightly. "Have you read all these?"

"Yes, I have. I like to read."

"So do I. I was wondering if, well, if I might borrow a book from time to time. I would be careful with it and be certain to bring it back when I'm finished." She looked at him beseechingly.

"You like to read?"

The hint of amazement in his tone rankled her. "I told you I can read. My mother taught me even before I started school." She was trying not to sound defensive but was doing poorly. "Forget I asked." She turned to leave the room.

"Wait." He leaned back in his leather chair. "I never said I wouldn't let you read my books. I'd be glad to share them with you."

Elizabeth turned back to him, embarrassed and feeling more defensive than ever. "Are you making fun of me? You may have found me living in a sod hut, but I do have an education. If I'm here that long, I'm quite capable of tutoring Mary Kate."

"Please accept my apology if I have offended you in some way," he said with genuine sincerity. "I know you're educated—I can tell by your speech. And you have a copy of *The Mysteries of Udolpho* that looks as if it's been read almost to pieces."

Still on her guard, she drew a calming breath and said, "It's my favorite. Have you read it?"

"Several times. Even in Texas we know about Mrs. Radcliffe. As a matter of fact, I have another of her books." He rose and went to the shelf nearest the front window. Here it is." He pulled out the book and gave it to her. Their fingers accidentally touched and both backed away hastily.

"The *Romance of the Forest*," she read. Just knowing it was by Mrs. Radcliffe made her mouth water. She caressed the book as if it were alive. "I'll be very careful with it."

"If you'd like, you may sit in here with me. I'm almost through with the accounts and planned to read myself."

Elizabeth found herself smiling. "I'd like that." She went to one of the wing chairs and sat down. Her eyes went to the book again. It was almost too good to be true that he would let her read his books. She had occasionally considered taking one without his knowledge, but her reverence for books had been too great. It would be tantamount to going through the personal things in his room for her to secretly take one away.

"I'm surprised you felt you had to ask permission," he said.

She discovered he was still watching her. "I don't take another person's things without asking. I'd never do that. Not even simply to borrow it."

He put down his pen as if the prospect of talking to her was more intriguing than his work. "You told me once that your father had a library in your house. You must have enjoyed it."

She looked down. "Father discouraged me from reading. I read every book he owned, but I never let him know about it. I know I just told you I never borrowed without permission, but this was different. He wasn't a reader and owned the books only because it was the thing to do. *Udolpho* really belongs to him. If he knew I had taken it, he would be furious."

"I want Mary Kate to enjoy reading. The world is available through books. There have been times when I relied on escaping in these books and have had adventures by the barrelful without ever leaving this room."

"Did Celia enjoy reading?"

"No. She never read a single book in her life as far as I know. She knew how to read and write but didn't like to do either."

Elizabeth thought about that. As much as Elizabeth wanted to like her, Celia hadn't struck her as a woman who would enjoy reading. "Some don't, I suppose, and there's nothing wrong with that. Father didn't, for instance. Mother read and I guess my love for books comes from her. We spent many hours reading to each other while the other sewed. It was how we spent most of our evenings. Of course, my father was never aware of it. He was hardly ever home in the evenings."

"I hope you'll do the same for Mary Kate, assuming you're still here."

Brice got up from the desk and came to sit in the chair opposite hers. A low fire burned in the hearth, casting flashes of red and gold upon his face and down his side. The lamp beside her didn't quite illuminate him. "I think you must begin to think in terms of Robert being gone indefinitely. He should have come back long ago and, as you know, Cal couldn't find anyone in Glory that knew of his whereabouts."

"I know. In a way, I didn't expect him to come back. Not after the first couple of weeks." She rested her head against the chair's back and watched the flicker of colors against the medallions on the ceiling. "I wonder from time to time if he's dead. Robert wouldn't be beyond simply riding away and never coming back, but it's hard to believe he would leave me—or anyone—with no provisions and not tell me that he wouldn't be returning. That seems almost inhuman."

"I've thought that, too."

"I could have starved to death if you hadn't been here. Even if I had set out for town on the mule as I'd planned, I doubt I could have found it. I was foolish not to pay closer attention to which direction we took and to landmarks along the way. Or for letting Robert put off going after supplies until we were out of virtually everything. There are many things I would do differently if I had it to do over again."

"If you had done differently, you might never have come here to the ranch. And to Mary Kate," he added.

"For that reason I wouldn't wish matters changed."

"Nor would I. Though I would like to take Robert out behind the woodshed, so to speak, and teach him how to treat a lady."

"I think that was the main problem between us," she said thoughtfully. "He couldn't get past the idea that I have an education and that I think beyond the basics of getting through a day. I don't think Robert ever wondered why the sky is blue or the grass green or how fruit trees know how to bud in the spring. Much less as to what the stars really are and whether man will ever discover a way to fly."

"To fly?" he asked with amusement.

"I read a story about a man who wanted to fly so badly that he glued feathers on his arms and taught himself. But he flew too near the sun, the glue melted, the feathers fell off and he fell out of the sky." She smiled at him. "Ever since, I've wondered what it would be like to sail around in the air with the birds. I realize it will never be a possibility, but you have to admit, the idea is intriguing."

"It is at that."

"Sometimes at night, I look up at the stars and it's as if I can see them dancing. What could they really be? Why are they there?"

"I've heard they are suns like ours, but so far away as to seem to be pinpricks of light."

"Doesn't that make you burn with curiosity?" she asked. "It does me. Thousands of suns, all hanging there in space. What else is out there?" She laughed. "You'll think me foolish. I won't put odd ideas into Mary Kate's head, I promise. But I do wonder."

"So do I.'

"Mysteries have always fascinated me. That was one

reason I didn't mind when Robert decided to come west. The frontier was a giant mystery to me. I couldn't imagine land that no one had ever lived on and miles of prairie without a single person on it. Now I can imagine it all too well.'' She smiled wryly. ''I thought we would never get here or find Mr. Snodgrass's place.''

''I'll bet after you found it, you were even more amazed,'' Brice said with amusement.

''That's putting it mildly.'' She wrapped her arms around her body. ''I knew it wouldn't be a grand place like this, but I had hoped for a floor, at least, and a ceiling that didn't rain bugs onto my dinner table.''

''I had the lumber for this house hauled in by wagon,'' he said as if deep in thought. ''After it was built, I had the furniture brought here the same way. It wasn't easy, but I was determined. A few pieces are from my family, the others I bought.''

''Celia was a lucky bride.''

''She didn't think so. The house didn't suit her. She wanted one like her parents', and she hated not having neighbors. I guess she never believed how big the frontier is. The furniture pleased her, but she always felt it was too masculine, that I should have let her choose it. That's why she sent off for floral wallpaper for most of the rooms. She didn't realize how impractical it would have been for her to be here before the furniture arrived. I slept on the floor in an empty house for weeks. She would have hated that.''

''I think any woman would want some say in furnishing her house. I shudder to think what Robert would have chosen. He saw that sod hut as only a minor inconvenience.''

''Celia wasn't cut out for frontier life. I should have known that. But we see what we want to see, I guess.''

"I did the same with Robert. I saw him as daring and reckless and not at all like Father. We had such grand plans. But those aren't traits that make for a steady marriage. He's too fond of gambling and has an eye for the women." She sighed. "He wasn't dashing at all, only wild."

"Elizabeth," Brice said, "I'm glad you're here. To look after Mary Kate."

"So am I." She looked up at him.

His face was in dark shadows but she could see light from the fire faintly reflected in his eyes and on his cheek. His hair fell across his forehead like a raven's wing. He leaned closer to her, and drew her to her feet to stand in front of him. She knew he was about to kiss her. She knew she should push him away. Instead she closed her eyes and tilted her lips up to his.

The kiss was gentle, filled with wonder. His lips were warm and firm on hers, yet soft. A warmth rushed through her and seemed to burst into flame. She felt the fabric of his coat beneath her palms but had no memory of embracing him. She held him close, not willing ever to let the kiss end. Eagerly she opened her mouth to his.

Brice ran his hands along her back under the light weight of her indoor shawl. It felt incredibly intimate. Everywhere he touched caught fire with passion. Elizabeth hadn't known she was capable of such an immediate response. Desire thundered in her veins and the floor seemed to rock beneath her feet. She held him closer out of reflex, not thought. She heard a soft murmur and realized it had come from her.

When he finally lifted his head from her, he didn't release her. Instead they stood silently embracing. She could hear the quick pace of his heart beneath her cheek. The kiss had affected him as much as it had touched her.

Even now the floor didn't seem completely steady beneath her feet. His cheek resting on the top of her head was so right, so natural.

At last he raised his head and gazed down into her eyes. She thought if he apologized she would die. Instead, he touched her cheek and ran his fingers along her skin as if he were memorizing it forever. "Elizabeth," he whispered, saying her name as if it were an endearment.

She put her fingers on his lips to stop him. "Don't say it. I already know we shouldn't have."

"Why did you think I was going to say that?" He kissed her forehead and let his lips linger before pulling away. "I don't regret this. Do you?"

She knew what her answer should be. Her mother had been quite specific. Any unwarranted caresses from the opposite sex should be firmly rebuffed in such a way that would discourage them being repeated in the future. This was especially true of a married woman. She took a deep breath to steel herself. "Yes. We... You must never take advantage like this again."

"Take advantage," he said with a frown. "It seemed to me that you enjoyed that a great deal."

"I'm a married woman, Mr. Graham."

With her head held high and clutching the book, she hurried from the room and ran up the stairs.

When she was safely in her room, she leaned against the door and tried to calm her racing heart. Only part of her shortness of breath was due to the speed at which she had taken the stairs. For the most part, she was still breathless over his kiss and the unexpected passion it had ignited. If she had stayed in the library another minute, she might have gone back into his arms.

Elizabeth closed her eyes. What had she done? It was

one thing for a man to give in to carnal thoughts and another entirely for a woman to do the same. She had kissed him like a wanton and had enjoyed it thoroughly. Even now in her self-recrimination she wanted him.

She went to her bedside and removed her clothes. His book lay on her pillow like a memory of him. She reached in her dresser drawer and took out a soft gown of fine cotton. Like her dress, it had belonged to Celia. She almost never wore her own dresses. They were faded and nearly worn out from having been washed so many times and Celia's were almost all new and of pretty colors.

She yanked the gown over her head and buttoned the front all the way up to her neck. Then she stood in front of her mirror and stared at herself decked out in a dead woman's nightgown and hungering for that same woman's husband. Slowly her aching for Brice was replaced by a keen embarrassment and self-loathing. Celia had been her friend—or she would have been, had she lived! She had warned Elizabeth about Brice! She pulled down the covers and climbed onto the feather mattress. She would do whatever was necessary to keep herself away from him. The last thing she wanted was for Brice to think she was easy prey.

The pillow lumped under her head. She had almost started to dread leaving the ranch. Life here was so peaceful and so easy compared to her former life, and she loved Mary Kate. If only Brice didn't ignite such longings in her. After that kiss he would know she wasn't as cold toward him as she pretended. She had to be far more careful in the future. Somehow she could learn to do this. Surely she could.

Through the wall she heard the muffled sounds of

Brice moving about in his bedroom. The wall had never seemed so thin.

She looked at the armoire that almost hid the door that connected the rooms. That it had been placed in that position had told her more than anything else that Celia hadn't exaggerated her dislike and fear of him. No woman who loved and desired her husband would symbolically place a huge armoire in front of the door that connected her bedroom with his. The armoire did its job so well she had lived in the room several weeks before she had noticed the door.

She heard the creak of the ropes that supported his mattress and knew he was in bed. In her mind she could see him lying there just as she was. His thoughts must be just as confused. What had happened in the library had gone against everything she had resolved when she agreed to move to the ranch.

How naive she had been to think she could live in his house and not grow too fond of him, or want him as a man.

Elizabeth turned to her side and curled into a ball of misery. Why on earth had she kissed him? Worse, why had she enjoyed it so thoroughly? She was disgusted with herself.

She made herself look around the room. Celia's bed, Celia's curtains at the windows, Celia's furniture standing against the walls. Celia's house. Celia's husband— the man with the cruel streak. It was still possibly true. Robert hadn't treated her badly before they were married. Brice might change, too.

After several long minutes she quelled the longing and picked up the book. Elizabeth had always prided herself on her common sense. She couldn't have him and that was that. She had had a momentary lapse in common sense but that was over now. A moment's indiscretion needn't ruin her future as long as it never happened again.

She picked up the book and opened it to the first page. Mrs. Radcliffe loved words and she used an uncommon amount of them to describe anything. Elizabeth welcomed the need to concentrate on the book and not on the man in the next room.

Her efforts, however, weren't entirely successful.

Elizabeth saw the buggy approaching as she was hanging out clothes. Visitors were so rare, she stopped her chore and ran to find Brice. He was as amazed as she had been.

They stood on the porch and waited for their guests to drive close enough to be recognized. Elizabeth felt him tense and looked up at him.

"It's Celia's parents! I was afraid they might do this!"

"Are they here for a visit," she asked doubtfully. Nothing about the older couple looked congenial.

The couple drove into the yard. They had seen Elizabeth standing beside Brice, and their faces were grim. The man climbed out of the buggy and assisted his wife. Still neither smiled. Elizabeth could see a strong resemblance between the woman and Celia. Her eyes were as blue as Mary Kate's.

"I didn't expect a visit from you. Welcome to my ranch." Brice didn't sound as if he was welcoming them at all.

"We aren't here for a visit," the man answered angrily. "You know why we're here."

"We've come to get our granddaughter," the woman said.

"I see you're as friendly toward me as ever." Brice motioned toward the door. "Come in and warm yourselves by the fire."

"We don't plan to be here that long. Where is she?" the woman demanded.

Brice gave her a maddening smile. "May I present our guests?" he said to Elizabeth. "This is Lorna and Hillyard Lannigan, Celia's parents. Mr. and Mrs. Lannigan, this is Elizabeth Graham. My wife."

Elizabeth stared up at him in amazement.

The couple looked up as if they were going into shock. "Wife!" they exclaimed at once, and glared in unison at Elizabeth.

"How can you be married? Celia has only been gone five months!" Lorna was so angry her words were like daggers.

"That's a long time in the Territory. Elizabeth was a widow on the land next to mine. Mary Kate needed a mother, Elizabeth needed a husband. It was that simple."

Lorna and Hillyard stared from Brice to Elizabeth.

"After all," Brice added, "you said in your letter that Mary Kate couldn't be properly brought up by a single man. I took your advice."

"What do you have to say for yourself?" Hillyard fired at Elizabeth.

"I...it was sudden. But it answered all our needs," she stammered. She could have pushed Brice off the porch for springing this on her.

"You scarlet hussy!" Lorna spit out. "You and Brice must have been carrying on before my Celia died!"

Brice stepped forward warningly, but Elizabeth could fight her own battles. "I was Celia's friend," she said with frigid dignity. "You have no right to accuse me of such a thing! Brice and I had scarcely exchanged words prior to her death. You are in Brice's house—our house—and you may not stay if you're going to be rude to either of us.''

Brice gave her a surprised smile, as if he were gratified that she could take care of herself.

"We're still taking our granddaughter with us when we leave,'' Hillyard growled.

"No,'' Elizabeth said firmly, "you are not. I regret you've come so far for nothing, but you must know the child belongs with her father. With us.''

"I told you that in my letter,'' Brice said. "You're welcome to visit her but Mary Kate stays here.''

"Show her to me,'' Lorna commanded. "Where is she?''

"She's taking a nap upstairs.'' Elizabeth turned to go up the stairs. "I'll show her to you.''

She was glad she had closed the bedroom doors to cut down on drafts. There would be no way of explaining why they had separate rooms. She was also glad she still wore the narrow gold wedding band Robert had given her. At the nursery she opened the door and led them to the crib.

"Look at her!'' Lorna cried out so loudly the baby awoke. "Look, Hillyard, isn't she the very image of our Celia?''

"They could be twins,'' he rumbled in agreement. "Her hair is like pure gold.''

Lorna picked up the child. "She has my eyes,'' she announced.

Elizabeth saw Mary Kate's lower lip start to tremble and she took her from Lorna. "She's not used to company, and she didn't finish her nap.''

Lorna paid her no attention. She was surveying the

room. "My little quilts are here, the dresses I sent. Everything seems to be here."

"You made her some beautiful things," Elizabeth said to put the woman in a better mood. "You must have sewn for months."

"Nothing is too good for our grandchild. That's why we can't allow her to stay in this wilderness."

"She's safe here," Brice said from the doorway. "Mary Kate stays here and that's final."

"Brice," Elizabeth said quickly before another argument could escalate. "I'll put the Lannigans in the guest room and have their horse taken to the barn and fed."

"I'll do that." He looked reluctant to leave Elizabeth alone with them. "I'll be right back."

"You've come a long way," Elizabeth said. "Would you like to freshen up?"

Lorna frowned at her. "I cannot believe that my Celia is barely in her grave and her husband has already replaced her. You called yourself Celia's friend. No friend would do what you have done."

"Things are different out here," Elizabeth said. "Some matters move slower and others faster. When the housekeeper, Consuela, left, there was no other woman here to take care of Mary Kate. Brice loves her, but he has to run the ranch. I was living alone under difficult circumstances. It only made sense for me to come here and solve everyone's problem."

"Celia wrote us often about Brice's cruelty toward her," Hillyard said. "It would curl your hair, the things he put her through."

"I can only say he has shown me nothing but kindness. With Mary Kate he's gentle and loving as a father should be. You need have no worries about her safety."

"The child's place is with us. We can give her advantages that are impossible here. There's no school, no neighbors. When she's a young lady, who can court her out here?''

"I don't know," Elizabeth admitted. "But I have an education. I'll teach her everything she could learn in school.''

"You," Hillyard said as he drew himself up, "are a woman. Schoolteachers are men. At least the ones of any merit are.''

Elizabeth controlled her temper. "I'll leave you with Mary Kate while I see that your room is ready.''

She was putting fresh sheets on the bed when Brice brought in their bag. "How could you tell them we are married!" she whispered under her breath.

"It was all I could think of at the time.''

"How will you explain our having separate rooms? What will you say to them when I go back east?''

"I don't know," he admitted. "I didn't expect them to show up on my doorstep.''

"You've certainly put us in a fine pickle," she muttered as she snapped the sheet in the air over the bed. "Married indeed!''

Dinner that night was full of strained silences. Elizabeth finally tired of trying to engage her angry guests in conversation and let the silence reign. Seeing the Lannigans' treatment of Brice explained why he wouldn't have wanted to live near them. Having met them, Elizabeth was hard-pressed to remember Celia as the angel she had become in Elizabeth's memory. Perhaps, she thought, Celia had had more faults than she had credited her with at the time.

No one wanted to sit in the parlor and visit after the meal. Elizabeth did the dishes alone because Lorna didn't offer to help. Hillyard sat alone on the front porch and smoked. She wasn't sure what transpired between Brice and Lorna in the parlor, but Brice was angry as they all went upstairs to their bedrooms.

Elizabeth would have walked past Brice to her own room, but he deftly steered her into his. "I'll check on the baby."

The Lannigans breezed past without so much as a good-night and shut the door more loudly than was necessary.

Elizabeth stood in Brice's room, uncertain what to do. She had no intention of sharing it with him, but she didn't want the Lannigans to find her living in a different room. Since they were supposed to be newlyweds, it would look odd.

Brice soon returned, carrying the sleeping baby.

"What are you doing with Mary Kate?" she whispered.

"Making sure they don't leave with her in the middle of the night. That wouldn't be beneath them." He put the baby in his large bed and covered her. "Mrs. Lannigan told me that Celia wrote that she was leaving me as soon as the baby was born. Since Celia intended for them to help her raise the baby, she insists that Celia meant for them to have her."

"She was going to leave you?"

"We weren't happy together, but I had no idea she would go that far. Celia would have done just about anything to hurt me, so it's probably true."

"She was really like that?" Elizabeth was having to shift her opinion of Celia and she didn't like that. "That's very difficult to believe."

Brice shook his head. "You're basing all you know about her on one brief visit. Anyone can be pleasant company. I'm sure she showed you just what she wanted you to see."

Elizabeth frowned. "That doesn't change the position you've put me in. I'm not spending the night in here."

"I don't expect you to. The Lannigans would hear the hall doors opening and closing, so you'll have to use the veranda door."

"Oh." She felt foolish for not having thought of that. "I suppose that would work."

Brice went to the veranda and opened the door. "Good night, Elizabeth," he said with a smile.

"Good night," she said coolly to cover the effect he had upon her.

The Lannigans left the next morning. While Brice didn't actually tell them to leave, he came close to it. Elizabeth expected Lorna to shower the baby with tears and kisses on parting, but she scarcely gave her a hug. All her emotions were centered on her hatred of Brice and, by association, Elizabeth.

"You're making a tragic mistake in refusing our daughter's last wishes," Lorna told him. "Mary Kate will be little more than a barbarian if she continues to live here."

"I assume Celia was so busy complaining about me, she didn't mention the proposed town?"

"What town?" Hillyard asked.

"She was so lonely here, I wrote back east and offered land and a house to each wagon if the settlers consisted of a teacher, a preacher and a man to run a general store. Four families have agreed to come. Mary Kate won't grow up a barbarian."

"It's a likely lie," Lorna fumed. "Celia would have written to us about that."

"Not if she was determined to portray me in the worst possible light."

Elizabeth was having to struggle not to show her own surprise at this revelation. A town was going to be built here? It was too good to be true.

"Have a safe journey home," Brice said to the Lannigans in an unconvincing tone.

They left as angrily as they had arrived, driving in the direction of Glory. From there they would travel east to the railroad spur that ran south to Texas.

"A town?" Elizabeth asked as soon as they were out of earshot. "Here? You never told me about that."

"I only recently heard my offer had been accepted."

"You could have told me!"

"I wasn't in a hurry to lose you." He turned and went inside, leaving her to wonder what he meant by that.

A town, she thought with amazement. The arrival of townspeople would mean a wagon train and a way for her to go back east. Would she have enough money by then? She had a great deal to think about.

Chapter Five

Almost overnight spring came to the Oklahoma prairie just north of the Ouachita Mountains, spreading swaths of wildflowers of every color across the hills and along the greening valley. Elizabeth, relieved to be rid of winter, took Mary Kate outside whenever she had a spare moment and let her play on a pallet beneath the trees.

Since the night Brice kissed her, they had avoided being alone whenever possible. Elizabeth didn't let herself look too deeply into his eyes or let their hands accidentally touch during the course of daily living in the same house.

She was sitting on a quilt spread on the grass with Mary Kate when Brice came up from the barn. He stood for a moment watching them. Mary Kate braced her pudgy legs and concentrated on heaving herself up and crowed with delight when she succeeded with only a little help from Elizabeth.

"She'll be running everywhere before long," he said as he came to them and squatted down by the quilt.

Mary Kate gurgled and dropped to all fours to scoot toward him.

"I've never known a baby to be so determined to

walk," Elizabeth told him with a smile. "All my cousins were barely crawling at seven months. That could be their mother's fault, though. It's a firmly held belief in my family that standing too early makes a baby have bowlegs."

"It's not true, is it?" he asked with concern.

"No, of course not. I've known a score of women who let their babies stand up whenever they were able and not a single one of them has bowlegs. All babies' legs look a little curved. Once she starts walking they'll straighten out."

"I was very fortunate to find you."

Elizabeth glanced at him suspiciously before averting her eyes. He did the same.

"I meant I was fortunate to find you for Mary Kate."

"I understood you to mean that."

"I came over to tell you that I'm going into town. Is there anything you need other than the usual things?"

"You're going into town?" Elizabeth asked. Robert had said almost the same words to her before he left. "Today?"

"If I start out now I'll be there before dark. Cal is following with the wagon."

She turned away so he wouldn't see the concern in her eyes. "I need flour and meal. And sugar, of course. Coffee. Could you get some thread? Mary Kate is outgrowing everything she owns and I've used up all the flour sacks. I'm going to cut up that pink flowered dress and make her some clothes."

"I can get cloth. The feed store has some in the back room and I hear there's a new general store now. What color do you want?"

Elizabeth thought for a minute. "Blue would go with her eyes."

"Blue it is, then."

As he got to his feet she said hesitantly, "You will be back, won't you?"

He looked down at her for a long moment. "Yes. I'll be back tomorrow."

She looked away, embarrassed at her words. "I was just wondering."

"I'm not Robert. I have no intention of deserting anyone." He gave her another enigmatic look and went toward the house.

Elizabeth watched him until he was inside. Logic told her he wouldn't leave a prosperous ranch and his baby daughter. But she had thought Robert wouldn't walk away from everything he owned, either.

The baby sensed her change of mood and crawled into her lap. Elizabeth hugged her close. She was being silly to worry. Brice would be back.

When he came back outside a few minutes later, he had a poncho rolled up under his arm in case of rain. He also had a revolver strapped to his leg. She had never seen him carry one before and she couldn't stop staring at it.

"I'll be back before dark tomorrow," he said to her. "You'll be perfectly safe here. Lucky Jones is going to keep an eye on things until I get back. If you need anything, go to any of my men and they'll take care of it."

"I'm not afraid," she lied.

"All the same, I wanted you to know Lucky is in charge."

Elizabeth nodded. She had liked Lucky from the first day she met him. He was about Cal's age but looked as if he laughed frequently. Like Cal, Lucky had no history and she doubted that Jones was really his last name, but she felt safe with him.

"I'll be back before dark tomorrow," he repeated. He bent and kissed Mary Kate on the top of her sun-warmed head. She was examining a blade of grass and didn't look up. "Goodbye, Elizabeth." He looked at Elizabeth as if he was about to speak, but turned and walked away toward the barn.

Not long after that she heard horse hooves and watched him ride his bay gelding away from the ranch. Minutes later, Cal drove the wagon out and down the valley toward town. Because the wagon was slower, Brice had ridden ahead to make arrangements at the livery stable and find a room.

She didn't think for a moment they would return by the next evening. With a sigh she picked up Mary Kate, bundled up the quilt with her free arm and went inside.

The house was too quiet. Even though Brice was seldom inside during the day, she knew he was around somewhere and the house seemed to reflect that. In his absence the rooms were too large and silent.

She fed Mary Kate a bottle of milk and put her in the pen she had devised from chairs. Mary Kate picked up a gingham doll and chewed on it thoughtfully.

There was no reason to cook if Brice wasn't going to be there. She and Mary Kate could make a meal from the leftovers from the night before. That left Elizabeth with a lot of spare time.

She cleaned the house while the baby didn't need her attention but she couldn't keep her mind on her work. Brice would reach Glory and get some of his business finished before Cal got into town. She wondered if he would visit with the loose women that were certain to be in any town that had a saloon. Did he have one he was partial to? He was single and had a man's natural desires. Maybe that was the reason he had been in a hurry to get there.

She hated to think of Brice laughing and drinking with a saloon girl and doing who-knew-what with her upstairs. She told herself it was no business of hers what he did. She had no claims on Brice and she was only going to make herself miserable with such thoughts. All the same, she remembered having to fish Robert out of several bars during their marriage for one reason or another, and she had no false impressions about what went on there.

Elizabeth picked up Mary Kate and went in search of Lucky. She found him in the barn where he was doctoring one of the expensive Hereford bulls Brice had bought to improve his herd. "He looks as if he has a mean temper," she observed.

"Yes, ma'am, but he's going to fetch us some fine calves." Lucky tickled Mary Kate's tummy with one forefinger. "Is there something I can do to help you ladies?"

"I have a piece of furniture I'd like to have moved. You'll need help."

Lucky went to the feedlot door and whistled. In a couple of minutes a young man barely out of his teens trotted into sight. "Avery? Miss Elizabeth has something she wants us to move for her."

Elizabeth was surprised to find this was how the men referred to her. It made sense, she supposed. No one stood on ceremony out here.

Avery followed them through the barn and caught up with them by the time they reached the house.

"It's in my bedroom." She led them upstairs and when she was in her room, she pointed to the armoire. "Would you move it over to that wall, please?"

"Sure thing," Lucky said. He got on one side of the massive piece of furniture and Avery on the other. "Lift easy, boy. This thing weighs a ton." They both strained and the armoire rose.

Elizabeth stayed out of their way and was relieved when the armoire was safely in place on the far wall.

Lucky straightened and rubbed his back. "I do believe that thing is getting heavier with the years. It was hard enough to bring it upstairs and harder still to move it to cover the door. I sure hope it stays where it is for a while."

Elizabeth smiled. "It will. I'm not one to move furniture around often."

"That's real good to know, ma'am."

Avery just grinned and looked at the floor. He was shy to a fault.

"I have some cookies in the kitchen if you'd like some as we pass through," she offered.

"I'd like that," Avery said, speaking for the first time. "I don't reckon I've seen a cookie since I left Ma's house."

She took them downstairs and into the kitchen. She made sure both had ample cookies to fortify themselves on the trip back to their work.

Avery grinned as he bit into his and said, "Thanks, Miss Elizabeth."

"We're much obliged," Lucky seconded. "I do believe these are the best cookies I've ever tasted."

"Thank you for helping me."

As they left, she and the baby went back upstairs. The room was in much better proportion with the armoire back where it should be. It towered eight feet with a carved pediment of plumes curving around a sphere. She had never seen a prettier one.

The door she had uncovered was dusty, and Elizabeth put Mary Kate on the floor while she cleaned it. Like the other doors in the house, it was made of pine that had been stained to resemble oak. Beneath the crystal doorknob was an ornate brass plate that covered the hole for the knob and the keyhole for the lock. Elizabeth turned the knob and heard a soft click as it opened.

Brice's room beckoned her. She stepped through and looked back at her own room. The door would probably never be opened again, but while he was gone, she could see the house as it had been meant to be seen. With the door open, the bay recess on Brice's front wall was properly balanced by the sweeping windows in her room. With it closed, Brice's room had odd proportions.

"There now, Mary Kate. Doesn't that look better?" she asked. The baby glanced up from her explorations of the fringe on Elizabeth's bedspread.

Elizabeth closed the door again and heard the latch click into place. He might never notice she had moved the armoire and besides, she liked it better where it now stood. Again she wondered at Celia having wanted to block him out of her room. It hadn't been a necessary measure, of course, because he had access to it from the hall as well as from the veranda. No, this move could only have been meant to hurt Brice.

Shaking her head, Elizabeth took Mary Kate downstairs to make her dinner.

Late that night she tossed and turned in her bed, listening to the house creak and settle about her. A wind was blowing through the cottonwoods and causing the shutters to tap lightly against the house. Elizabeth wasn't afraid, but she was far from sleep. This was the sort of night that seemed more lonely than others. In the far distance she heard the faint rumble of thunder. Rain was on the way.

She got up and went in to look at Mary Kate. The baby was sound asleep, her fingers curled like the petals of a flower. Elizabeth pulled the cover over her and gave her a gentle good-night kiss. She was a good baby and almost always slept through the night.

She went back to her room and opened the door that connected it to Brice's room. His room was as thoroughly masculine as he was himself.

She didn't understand him. Everything about Brice seemed gentle, yet Celia had been afraid of him. Or at least she had implied as much. Not once had Brice unleashed the cruel temper that Celia had attributed to him. To Elizabeth, this made no sense. To Mary Kate he was more loving than any father Elizabeth had ever seen. He adored the child, and Mary Kate loved him.

And there was the memory of their kiss. Elizabeth never forgot how it had felt and it had been repeated far too often in her dreams. There had been passion in the kiss, but no demand. She hadn't feared that he would take her by force, though she had been afraid she would offer herself to him. It had been far too long since a man had kissed her in that way. And Brice was very good at it.

That was all it had been, she told herself as she moved about his room. She had only come in here because the approaching storm made her nervous and this room was heavily imprinted with Brice's personality.

She had to save every penny of her money so she could get away from Brice and the temptation to fall in love with another man of Robert's caliber. Brice had shown her nothing but kindness she admitted, but people were generally good to company. He'd said it himself about Celia.

She pulled out the stool and sat on his bed. Why did she feel so safe with him? Even his belongings calmed her. She lay back on the soft bed and let his pillow cradle her head.

For a long time she lay there, not knowing when or if she would ever be able to do this again. At last the need to sleep crept over her and she went back to her own bed.

Brice awoke before dawn as he always did. Cal was stirring on the other side of the bed and coming awake. Without speaking, Brice swung his feet over the side of the bed and stood up. Because of sharing a bed, he had slept in his long johns. He pulled on his pants, then his socks and boots.

Cal yawned and scratched his head. He had made good time and had arrived in town before the sun was completely down. Unlike Brice, he had spent some time at the saloon before turning in. Cal wasn't a drinking man but he did love a game of poker. He would be going home several dollars richer.

"Are you going to clean out some more pockets while I'm stocking up?" Brice asked as he buttoned his shirt.

"Might."

"I should be ready to leave by midmorning."

"Won't take me that long." Cal gave him one of his rare grins.

Brice chuckled. "I'll come to the saloon to get you."

He went downstairs and into the dining room. Every time he came to Glory, he stayed at this boardinghouse. The only other place that rented rooms was over the saloon, and he didn't like the sound of men laughing and arguing over the discordant notes of the piano or the softer and more disquieting sounds from the girls' adjoining rooms.

The woman who ran the boardinghouse smiled when she saw him and set a plate for him with several other men who had slept over. Brice soon ate, paid for their room and Cal's meal and left.

From the edge of town where the boardinghouse was located to the center of town was only a short walk. Although Glory was growing, it was still small and had the feel of the frontier about it. The streets were dirt and the few boardwalks were narrow and not very long. Most of the store owners considered it unnecessary to build walkways when there were so few ladies about.

Brice went to the feed store and ordered medicines and feed for the livestock he kept at the barn. The herds on the range had plenty of new grass to sustain them, but the horses needed oats for daily work and the sick bull had to be fed. The owner knew Brice well and promised to have his purchases loaded in the wagon by the time he was ready to leave.

The new general store was next to the barbershop. Its walls still had the look of fresh pine and smelled faintly of the sawmill. Brice went in and looked around. As Cal had told him, there was everything he was likely to need. He shook hands with the man behind the counter and gave him the list of staples Elizabeth had prepared.

"I'll start gathering this up. Feel free to look around for anything you might have forgotten to put on the list. I've got a new load of flour in and I'll try to pick out sacks with a matching pattern for you. Just make yourself at home."

Brice ambled across the store to the women's notions along the far wall. He felt out of place here but he was

determined to get what he had come after. A woman
with a tape measure around her neck came to wait on
him. "I need blue cloth for a girl's dress."

"How old is the girl?"

"She's a baby. About this big." He held his hands
apart to measure Mary Kate's size.

"We have some lovely gingham here. This is popular
with the women for their little ones." She showed him
a bolt of blue cloth sprinkled with tiny flowers.

Brice grinned. He felt like a bull in the kitchen in this
department. "That'll do just fine."

The salesclerk didn't bother to ask him how much he
wanted. She knew to the inch how much cloth would be
needed for a small girl's dress.

"I'd like to get some more cloth," he said on inspi-
ration. "For a woman. She has dark hair and her eyes
are gray."

"How large a woman is she?"

Brice held his hand at about shoulder level. "She
stands this tall and is about this big around." He made
a circle with his hands.

The woman nodded. "Most of the women like pink."

He shook his head. Pink wasn't right for Elizabeth.
"How about the stuff over there?"

She went to a bolt of deep rose cloth that was the
color of one of the wildflowers that dotted the valley.
"This would make up a pretty dress. I have some ma-
chine-made lace that would turn it out nicely indeed."

"Just pick out whatever she'll need."

The woman measured out the rose cloth along with
yards of frothy cream lace and satin cording. "I don't
know how many buttons she'll need so I'll just put in
what women usually buy on an average. It depends on
the pattern, you know."

Brice nodded, though he didn't know. "And thread. She said especially to get thread."

"What color?" The woman put spools of the shade to match both fabrics and waited for his answer.

"She didn't say. Pink, maybe?"

She pursed her lips as if she would rather walk through nails barefoot than wait on a man at the fabric counter. "Why don't I give you some of the blue and rose, and maybe some black and white as well? That should go with most things. Does she need extra buttons?"

"She didn't say she did."

"Ribbons?"

He smiled. "Yes, she needs some ribbons." He picked out a handful of colorful ribbons and carried his purchases to the man at the main counter.

"Looks like you've taken up sewing, Brice. Getting lonely out there, are you?" the man joked.

"Not as lonely as it used to be, Ed. Doing a lot of business, are you? You've got plenty of room in this new building."

"Yeah, we were cramped for space in the back room at the house. We had several new families move in just before winter set in. They have lots of children and that means lots of yard goods. I like to see big families." Ed laughed as he added up the purchases. "How's that baby doing?"

"She's growing like a weed. She's going to be walking before long."

"Already? Seems like just yesterday she was born." Ed remembered the baby's birth had taken Brice's wife. "I miss seeing Miss Celia. I reckon it's real hard for you without her."

Brice hesitated. "I have someone to watch after Mary Kate and keep the house."

"That's good." Ed turned the paper he'd been writing on so Brice could see it. From upside down, he pointed with his pencil. "This here's the yard goods and notions, here's the flour, meal, sugar, beans and all."

Brice reached in his pocket and brought out a fistful of money. As he counted it out, Ed wrapped the cloth in brown paper and tied it with string from the ball inside a metal cage on the counter. "Is your wagon out front?"

"Not yet. Cal is bringing it around."

"I'll watch for him. Much obliged." He held out his hand to shake Brice's.

Brice shook hands and left. He felt good for having bought Elizabeth cloth for a new dress. Women loved new clothes. He had sometimes wondered if she minded wearing what Celia had once owned but had decided she must not. He wouldn't have objected to wearing Robert's if the circumstances had been reversed. Clothes were clothes. The dresses looked very different on Elizabeth than they had on Celia. He wouldn't have recognized them if he hadn't known where they came from. Elizabeth had curves in places Celia had only flat planes.

Cal was already pulling onto the street. By his promptness Brice thought he must not have found anyone willing to part with more money over a game of poker. Cal had a reputation as a man who didn't often lose, and it was becoming harder for him to find men to play with.

Brice looked in the flatbed behind the seat at the carefully stacked feed bags and vials of ingredients to mix for the medicines his animals would need over the next few months. "Pull down to the general store, Cal. Ed is watching for you. I'll go get my horse."

As they were riding out of town, Brice saw Oscar Pellam, the undertaker, sweeping the boardwalk in front of his establishment. Brice reined in. "Go on ahead, Cal. I'll catch up with you."

Cal acknowledged with a nod.

Brice rode over to Pellam and dismounted.

"Good day, Mr. Graham. A lovely day after the night's rain, isn't it?" He made even cordial greetings sound dolorous.

"A fine day," Brice responded. "Could I ask you a question?"

Pellam stopped sweeping and folded his long hands on the broom handle. "Of course. There's not more tragedy out at your ranch, is there? Such a shame about Mrs. Graham. You have my deepest sympathy."

"Thank you. I was wondering if you had reason to do business with a man named Robert Parkins."

"Parkins," the undertaker repeated as he pondered. "Was he a dark-haired man of about thirty years? On the slim side?"

"I never saw him. He went missing from Old Zeb's place back before Christmas and never came back. Left a wife out there."

"Come in for a spell." Pellam led the way into his funeral parlor.

Brice glanced around and was glad to see none of the coffins was inhabited. He had never been comfortable in places of this sort.

Pellam took him to the inner office and thumbed through a stack of papers. "Here it is. A couple of drifters found a man frozen to death on the plain and brought him here. I had never seen him before so I assumed him to be a drifter, too." He opened a drawer and took out a pistol and gun belt, a man's folding coin purse and an envelope. From the envelope he took some hair. "I always do this. It comforts the ladies to have a bit of the deceased's hair to make a mourning brooch or whatever." He dropped it back in the envelope. "Do you think this could have been Robert Parkins?"

"It probably was. I can take the things to Mrs. Parkins and she will know. If it's not him, I'll bring them back to you on my next trip into town."

"Fair enough. I gave the man a decent burial in the cemetery. If it's him, you might tell the widow that I'll be glad to put his name on the grave. If she wants to purchase a headstone, she'll find my prices reasonable."

"I'll tell her. Much obliged." Brice went back out to his horse, tucked the few belongings into his saddlebag and mounted. Freezing alone on the prairie wasn't a good way to die, but there were worse ways. And it would explain why Parkins never returned. He wondered how Elizabeth would take the news.

They reached the ranch just as the sun was going down. The sky was awash with a vivid red with streaks of gold and purple. A full moon was edging over the eastern horizon as the sun disappeared behind the western one. As the wagon clattered into the yard, Elizabeth stepped out onto the porch. When she saw Brice, she began running down the steps, then caught herself and slowed to a sedate pace as she went out to meet him.

"I told you I'd be home today."

She clasped her hands in front of her as if to restrain herself. "I'm glad to see you. Mary Kate will be, too. She's been cranky all day."

"She's probably teething again." He looked down at her and wondered again how to show her the items Pellam had given him. He didn't want to be a source of pain for her. It had to be done. He untied the saddlebags and rested them over his shoulder before reaching in the wagon for the package of material. "I brought you something."

"The cloth for Mary Kate?" Elizabeth asked hopefully.

"I hope I bought the right amount. Let's go inside where we can see better."

When they were in the back parlor Elizabeth pulled the string from the package he gave her and folded the paper back. "Look at all the cloth! Why, this will make a dozen dresses for Mary Kate!"

"The blue is for her. The reddish colored one is for you."

"For me?" Elizabeth looked at him in surprise. "But I don't need a new dress."

"All women need new dresses. I told the woman to put in whatever she thought you'd need."

Elizabeth held up the handful of ribbons. Her eyes met his questioningly.

"Those are for you. Mary Kate doesn't have enough hair as yet to need ribbons." To his surprise, her eyes filled with tears. "What did I do wrong?" he asked cautiously.

"Nothing. You did everything right." She brushed at her eyes and held the ribbons close to her along with the rose fabric.

"If nothing is wrong, why are you crying?"

"I'm not!"

"Yes, you are." He went to her and lifted her chin so she had to look into his eyes.

"It's just that you're so...kind." She pulled away from him. "I don't think I've ever known a man as kind as you are. It's like Christmas morning!"

Brice hadn't fully understood until now how bleak Elizabeth's life had been. What he had brought her would have been no more than a passing amusement to Celia or his mother or most of the other women he had known. Once again he found himself wondering why she had been treated so shabbily. She certainly didn't deserve it.

"There's something else as well," he said reluctantly. "What did Robert look like?"

She looked at him questioningly. "He's not as tall as you and his hair is darker. He's thin. His eyes are green."

The description was close to the one Pellam had given him. He started unbuckling his saddlebag.

"Did you see him?" she asked impatiently. "Is he in Glory?"

Brice took out the pistol and gun belt and the coin purse. Elizabeth made no sound, but she picked up the purse and stared at it. Brice handed her the envelope. When she looked inside her eyes filled with tears. "What happened to him?"

"He froze to death between here and Glory. Since the purse is empty, he must have been on his way home, or the drifters that found him kept the money."

Elizabeth slowly sat down and stared at the purse and clippings of hair.

"Mr. Pellam gave him a proper burial, but he didn't know what name to put on the grave. It's in the Glory cemetery. He will put up a wooden cross or you can buy a headstone."

"Robert is dead," she said slowly.

"I'm sorry to break it to you like this, but I wasn't sure it was him. I'm sorry, Elizabeth." Neither of them noticed how easily he used her given name. "The next time I'm in town, I'll have Mr. Pellam carve a stone and put it in place.''

She nodded silently.

From upstairs he heard a fretful cry.

Elizabeth lifted her head and started for the door. ''She's not feeling well,'' she said in that same numbed tone. He followed her into the entrance hall and up the stairs. ''I think she was running a bit of a fever this afternoon and she hardly ate supper.''

She paused at the door to her own room to put down Robert's belongings and the fabric. Brice looked past her and saw the armoire standing against the wall where it had been originally. He looked at the uncovered door and back at the armoire.

Elizabeth moved past him to the nursery. Mary Kate was sitting up and weaving from side to side as she whimpered. ''What's wrong, honey? Look who's come home.'' She picked up the baby and Mary Kate clung to her, still crying weakly. Her eyes met Brice's. ''She's burning up with fever!''

He touched the baby and was surprised how hot her skin was. ''What's wrong with her?''

''I don't know. Will you light her lamp?''

Brice tried not to let his concern show. Babies got sick all the time. Maybe they all ran a high fever when they did.

Mary Kate flinched away from the light as if it hurt her eyes. Her cheeks were feverishly red and her eyes were glassy. She seemed hardly able to hold up her head and was still making that miserable sound. Perhaps most telling of all, she hadn't reached for Brice as soon as she saw him.

Elizabeth cuddled her and murmured soothing words to her. To Brice she said, ''I have to break her fever.

Will you bring me a basin of water and a cloth?'' As he went to get the things she had asked for, he saw Elizabeth start to undress the baby. At least her concern for the baby had shaken her out of her shock over Robert's death, he thought.

By the time he returned, Elizabeth was inspecting Mary Kate for a rash that might foretell measles or chicken pox. He felt a dread growing inside him. ''What do you think is wrong?''

Elizabeth pursed her lips. ''I don't know. She doesn't have a rash yet, but I wonder if it could be measles.''

''Where would she get it? Is there sickness at the bunkhouse?''

''Not that I know of.'' Elizabeth put the baby on her lap and dipped the cloth in the water. When she touched Mary Kate, the baby cried louder and tried to pull away. ''I know, darling. I know it feels cold, but I have to cool you off. It's going to be all right.''

Brice watched her as if from a long distance away. Babies died from high fevers. Mary Kate was much too hot to be merely teething. He could tell by looking at her that she was sick.

Elizabeth glanced up at him. ''Go help Cal unload the wagon. I can manage here.''

He was reluctant to leave but there was nothing more he could do to help Elizabeth. He hated to hear Mary Kate cry like that. ''I'll be back as soon as I can.''

Elizabeth nodded. Crooning to the baby, she wet the cloth again.

When Brice returned Mary Kate was calmer but she was still alarmingly hot to the touch. ''Lucky says young Avery is down sick,'' he told her. ''He collapsed this afternoon. Looks like it may be scarlet fever. Cal is tending to him in the bunkhouse.''

Elizabeth shuddered. "Have you had it?"

"Yes. How about you?"

"I think so. I guess I'll know soon enough. Avery was in the house along with Lucky to move that armoire for me. Maybe she caught it then."

"I've heard it runs like that from one person to another. Did he pick her up?"

"I don't think he even looked in her direction."

"Well, however it happened, it looks as if she's got it." He smoothed his daughter's damp hair and she looked pitifully up at him. "Come here, sweetheart. Let me hold you for a minute."

Mary Kate laid her hot cheek on his chest and he could feel the temperature as if it were a branding iron. "Do you know any other ways to break a fever?"

Elizabeth shook her head in silence. Her eyes were large and haunted. Brice knew she was frightened.

"She's going to be just fine," Elizabeth said firmly. "I'm not going to let anything happen to her."

Brice nodded. He knew neither of them would get any sleep that night.

Chapter Six

Elizabeth looked up from rocking the baby. Her face was pale and tired but she refused to go to bed. Brice had worked with her all night trying to bring down Mary Kate's temperature. With the pearly light of dawn, the baby seemed to be a bit cooler.

"Is it down, do you think?" Elizabeth asked anxiously. "I think she's asleep."

Brice touched Mary Kate's head. "I can't tell. Maybe a little." He didn't want to give Elizabeth too much hope.

"Look at her little face. She's as red as can be except for around her mouth. It's scarlet fever, all right. I had hoped Lucky was wrong about Avery." She sounded exhausted.

"Go get some sleep. I'll watch Mary Kate."

"I don't want to leave her."

"She may become sicker, and you'll need to be able to think clearly. It won't help her if you collapse from exhaustion."

Elizabeth nodded and laid the sleeping baby in her bed. "Watch her closely. If she gets worse, wake me."

"I will." He sat in the rocker and gazed at his daughter. She seemed so tiny in the bed. He could hear the breath rasping in her throat. Mary Kate lifted her hand in her sleep and scratched at the rash on her face. Brice gently moved her hand away.

Scarlet fever was a disease to be feared. No one knew just how it passed from one person to another, but he had once heard of an entire ranch that had contracted the disease. People died from scarlet fever. As far as he knew there was no cure. It ran its course and what happened, happened. Brice was willing to have the fever himself twice over if it would spare his child.

Ever since Mary Kate's birth, she had been like a miracle to him. She was so tiny, yet she had survived the difficult birth and until now had thrived. He prayed silently that she would grow healthy again and not become sickly like her mother. Celia had used her frailty as a weapon, and it had been an effective one. She had become sick easily and healed slowly. Would Mary Kate be like that?

He closed his eyes and rubbed them. He was near exhaustion himself. Riding in the saddle all day was grueling work and he had stayed up all night along with Elizabeth.

Would Elizabeth catch scarlet fever? A person who survived having it once never caught it again, but she wasn't certain that she had had it. He could barely remember his own bout with it. He had been small and knew he was immune primarily because his mother had told him so. Mary Kate would have to be told when she was older that she had had the disease. He prayed there would be an occasion to tell her.

The hour passed slowly. Mary Kate awoke and he tried to give her a bottle, but she turned her head away fretfully. Her throat looked red and sore and she didn't want to swallow. Next to her pale gold hair, her face was a fiery scarlet.

Elizabeth didn't sleep as long as he had hoped she would, but she was more rested than before she lay down. She had changed into a clean dress and her hair was brushed into a neat bun. "Go get some rest. I can take care of her." She took the baby from him and picked up the bottle.

Brice shook his head. "I'm fine. Maybe I should go out to the bunkhouse and check on Avery."

"If you must, but when you come back to the house, I want you to rest." Her eyes met his. "Her fever is down now but I may need help when it comes back up."

"You think it will?"

She nodded. "Fever is like that. It's nearly always lower in the morning than the afternoon. Go look in on Avery, then get some sleep."

Brice made his way out to the bunkhouse, feeling as if he were asleep on his feet. He was looking forward to a brief respite in bed.

The bunkhouse was behind the barn and had a detached kitchen beside it. It was the first building Brice had built and he had lived in it until the house was finished. It was a long, low building with only a couple of windows. Usually, no one was inside during the day, so sunlight wasn't needed, and the lack of windows made it easier to heat in the winter.

He went through the door without knocking and waited for his eyes to grow accustomed to the dim interior light. Avery was on his bunk, lying perfectly still. Brice lit one of the lanterns beside the door and pulled up one of the ladder-back straight chairs so he could sit beside Avery. He could see from the rise and fall of the young man's chest that he was breathing, and he was relieved. "How are you doing?" he asked.

Avery slowly opened his eyes. "I feel like hell," he whispered. "My throat's on fire." Like Mary Kate's, his face was bright red except for the telltale whiteness around his mouth. "Am I going to die?"

"No." Brice made himself sound more positive than he felt. "I've seen worse cases than this and they lived."

Avery nodded. Brice could see that talking hurt his throat. He got Avery a tin cup of water from the pump outside. "Drink this. You can't let a fever run its course without drinking water. You'll only get sicker."

"I can't keep anything down."

"Just sip it." Brice was glad Mary Kate, unlike Avery, was retaining the little liquid she was able to swallow. A high fever would burn a person past recovery, he had heard.

Avery took the smallest sip, then closed his eyes as if he had expended what little energy he had.

"Can I get you anything?"

The young man rocked his head from side to side without opening his eyes.

"I'm going back to the house now but I'll be out to check on you after a while."

Avery nodded.

Brice was reluctant to go. Avery was barely more than a boy, and he was as sick as Mary Kate, maybe sicker. Cal and the other men had too much work to do for anyone to stay with him all the time. His rash had spread from his face to his chest and hands. Clearly he had been sick for a longer time. Brice hated feeling so helpless, but there was nothing more he could do to render aid.

He left the bunkhouse and, as he passed the barn, he

saw Lucky riding in from the pasture. "I just looked in on Avery. The boy's really sick."

"Yeah, I know. Does he look like he's going to pull through?"

"I don't know. Mary Kate has it, too."

"No!" Lucky looked at him with compassion. "How sick is she?"

"Not quite as bad as Avery, I don't think, but his rash has already spread. She may be that bad by tomorrow. Elizabeth is with her now. We sat up with her all night."

"I'll keep an eye on Avery. I had scarlet fever when I was sixteen. Avery's young too, but he's tough. I don't expect we'll lose him."

"I sure hope you're right." Brice waved as he turned to go back to the house.

The stairs seemed to be a mile long. By the time he reached the second floor, he was so tired his hands were shaking. All the same, he went to the nursery first. "How is she?"

"She took a little milk and it's staying down. I'm going to put some water in a bottle and give her that. How's Avery?"

"He's pretty sick. Lucky is going to stay near the bunkhouse and keep an eye on him."

"Go get some rest. You look as if you could collapse."

Brice didn't argue. He went to his room and had stripped off his clothes before he reached the bed. Just getting out of the clothes he had put on the morning before made him feel better. As he was about to pull back his covers, he noticed an impression on his bed. The feather mattress showed where someone had lain there.

He was puzzled for a minute. Why would anyone

want to lie on his bed? Then he glanced at the door that connected his room to Elizabeth's. Only one person could have done it. He was smiling as he got into bed. There was only one reason that he could think of for her to have done that. She had missed him. The thought triggered a warm glow around his heart. She cared for him.

He was asleep almost before the thought finished forming.

By the next day Mary Kate was bright red from head to toe but her temperature had dropped. Her tongue had the appearance of a ripe strawberry. Even though her fever was better, Elizabeth wasn't convinced that the disease was leaving the dangerous stage. Mary Kate was less fretful but she looked terrible.

Avery was recovering more slowly but he was feeling better. No one else on the ranch came down with scarlet fever and Elizabeth was beginning to relax. That night Mary Kate fell into a peaceful sleep for the first time since the fever had started and Elizabeth sighed with relief. "I think she's out of danger."

Brice gazed down at the baby. "I think you're right."

"We'll still have to watch her closely. As I recall, the worst complications can happen for about three weeks." She touched the baby's face gently so as not to waken her. "She's strong though. She'll be all right."

"You think so? That she's strong?"

"Look how quickly she started improving. She's doing better than Avery." The bunkhouse was a male domain but Elizabeth had gone out from time to time to check on Avery and take him food that was more palatable than anything Ezra Smart could cook. "He's still so weak he can barely get out of bed, and this afternoon

Mary Kate made a halfhearted attempt to play. No, she's going to pull out of this without any lasting problems.''

"I hope you're right.''

They left the nursery and went downstairs to the front porch. A spring-scented breeze was tossing the long grasses on the hills and wildflowers nodded in agreement. Evening was throwing long blue shadows across the rolling hills and the sun was setting in the trough cut by the valley. Streaks of crimson and topaz crossed the clouds.

"I'm sorry about Robert,'' Brice said. "With all that's been going on you haven't had time to mourn properly.''

"I think I've known for a long time that he must be dead. I mourned him then and I don't have any mourning left.'' She glanced at him. "Don't think I'm hardhearted. My marriage wasn't a happy one. Robert could be mean when he drank and he drank a great deal of the time.''

"I'm sorry for that, too.''

Elizabeth studied him. "You aren't at all the way I expected you to be.''

"What did you expect?''

"It doesn't matter.''

"I got a letter today. A man rode out from town to bring it.''

"A letter?'' Mail was so uncommon Elizabeth was excited even though she knew the letter had to be from someone she didn't know.

"It's from the man who headed up the train that brought most of the settlers to Glory. The train bringing our settlers has formed and will be heading west soon. As slow as the mail is, they could arrive in a few weeks.''

Elizabeth pressed her fingers to her lips. "It's almost

too good to be true! But what about your land? Won't they try to take over the grazing land?''

"None of them are ranchers. I made that clear in my advertisement. The town will be near the edge of my land but anyone wanting to run cattle will have to settle past this place and down toward that low range of hills. That will put them within a reasonable distance from the new town, but not encroaching on my land.''

"Neighbors! That means children for Mary Kate to play with.''

"And friends for you as well.'' He sat on the railing and gazed down the valley as if he could already see the houses going up. "The site I have in mind is down the valley there on Puma Creek. The creek never runs dry in that spot and will supply enough water until wells can be dug. There are cottonwoods and pines and some scrub oaks, so the place is already pretty. The flat land will make building easier. We'll be able to see the town from here, but they won't be on our doorstep.''

"What if more families want to come here? What if they want to make it a real town and not just a settlement?''

"I've set aside land enough for that. See that clump of cottonwoods flanked by the crooked pine?''

Elizabeth shaded her eyes and managed to pick out the trees he indicated. "It will be there? That close?''

"That's the place. What do you think? Is it too close?''

"No, I'd say that's just right. When she gets older, Mary Kate can ride there safely, or even walk that far.'' She tried to picture the grove with houses in its midst but couldn't imagine it. "I wish I knew when they will arrive.''

"It depends on how hard a winter they had east of

here and whether the spring rains bring flooding. They aren't coming from that far. The wagon train leaves from western Missouri. It's pretty much flat land between here and there, I understand.''

"Neighbors!" she whispered almost to herself.

"I know it's lonely out here for a woman. It's not so bad for me because I'm working with the cowhands all day, but you must miss having a woman to pass the time of day with.''

"I do miss that." Elizabeth smiled. "I had a neighbor in Hannibal that I was fond of. We both cried when Robert decided to come west. I think about her from time to time and wonder what she may be doing.''

"There's been talk in town about the railroad putting a spur through to Glory. Once it's set up, you could write her." He was watching her closely.

Elizabeth looked at him in amazement. "I never thought of that. I could, couldn't I?''

"Civilization is coming to the Territory. It's not just open prairie anymore." He was watching her instead of the sunset. "You haven't mentioned going back east with the wagon master. Do you still intend to go?''

Elizabeth turned away. "Of course." She wasn't strong enough to resist him when he looked at her that way.

"Why did you turn your back to me?''

"I thought I heard Mary Kate," she lied. "I guess I was mistaken.''

Brice put his hands on her shoulders. "I don't think we can ignore forever what's happening between us.''

"I have no idea what you mean." The touch of his hands seemed to burn her skin even through the layers of fabric. "I've always intended to leave. I told you that from the very beginning.''

He turned her around to face him. "How long are we going to pretend that we don't want each other?"

She opened her mouth, but no words came out. For the first time in her life, Elizabeth was speechless.

He, too, was silent for a long moment. "I guess I was mistaken." He abruptly went into the house, leaving her alone on the porch.

Elizabeth started to call after him but stopped herself in time. She still wasn't certain that he was saying he wanted her in marriage or in any other way. His words had been so full of possible meanings that she was confused. Could he have meant "want" in terms of their business arrangement? He hadn't tried to kiss her since that night in the library. He hadn't even tried to hold her hand. He couldn't possibly know how often and how erotically she dreamed about him.

She felt anger at herself flare. Both of them were newly bereaved. He couldn't court her. Most of the time he barely acted as if he liked her. She avoided him as often as possible with the intent of not caring too much for him. So what did his words mean?

She leaned her face against one of the columns that supported the upstairs veranda. Life had become so complicated since she met Brice.

Three days later Mary Kate's rash had faded away and she seemed to be her old self again. Unlike Avery, who was peeling even on his tongue and feeling thoroughly miserable, she had almost no peeling skin at all. Elizabeth kept her comfortable with clover-scented lotions and frequent baths in baking soda. She didn't hold with the adage that people, especially babies, became sick if they were bathed regularly. Elizabeth herself bathed almost every day of her life and had never suffered any ill-effect. For that matter, Brice also bathed frequently.

Sometimes this caused a problem. One evening, Elizabeth had to go out to the barn to find eggs for a recipe and happened to come around the corner just as Brice was standing there naked and rinsing the soap from his body by pouring a bucket of water over his head. She stopped dead in her tracks, her mouth dropped open and she felt a blush rushing to her cheeks. He was magnificently muscled and there wasn't an ounce of spare flesh on him anywhere. Then she realized she was staring and that Cal was watching her stare. She gathered up her skirts and ran back to the house.

"What are you laughing about?" Brice asked Cal, his eyes still closed against the onslaught of water.

"Nothing." The amusement was clear in his voice.

Brice wiped the water from his eyes. "It wouldn't hurt you to bathe once in a while yourself. The last time you rode upwind of me I thought we were coming up on a buffalo herd." It wasn't true, but they had bickered over bathing for as long as Cal had been on the place.

Cal only grinned.

Brice glanced around the barn. They were alone. Even the sick bull had been let out into the feedlot. "I hope you're not going strange on me, Cal."

Cal tossed him a linen towel. He was still grinning.

Puzzled at what the joke could be, Brice frowned slightly as he dried off. Although the day was warm, his wet skin felt cold and he was glad to pull his clothes back on. "Will you look at the bull before you quit for the day? I'm thinking he could go to pasture in a day or two." He fastened his shirt and stuffed the tail into his open pants. "I'm heading for the house."

Cal actually chuckled. "Tell Miss Elizabeth hello for me."

This was more social exchange than Brice had ever known Cal to utter. "Tell Elizabeth hello? All right." He was more puzzled than ever.

He went up the slope to the house, running his fingers through his hair to dry it. A good breeze was blowing. In the summer that was good news but during the winter it hadn't been welcome. Soon the days would be hot and a breeze of any kind would be good.

He went into the kitchen and grinned at Mary Kate in her play corner. "Hey, honey." She gurgled at him and clapped her hands. The movement caused her to lose her balance and she sat down hard.

Brice looked at Elizabeth. She hadn't turned since he came into the kitchen. "Evening, Elizabeth. Cal says to tell you hello."

Her reaction was startling. She whirled on him, cheeks blazing. "You can tell Cal to keep his hellos to himself! And so can you!" She gave him a glare and ran from the room, her face a mask of embarrassment.

Brice stared after her until the stair wall cut her from his view. "What the hell was that all about?" he asked himself, more in amazement than anything else. He went to Mary Kate and picked her up. "Are you going to grow up to think like a woman, honey? No, not you. Not your daddy's darling."

Mary Kate patted his face and cooed in agreement.

Elizabeth stopped running when she was in her room. It was just like Cal to tell Brice she had seen him in the altogether. Men joked together about things like that. She was so embarrassed she was short of breath.

Not that she had minded seeing him—that was the problem. She had been struck dumb and would have probably stayed rooted to the spot if she hadn't seen Cal there as well. Brice had a beautiful body. Elizabeth had rarely seen even Robert with his shirt off. It simply wasn't done. Robert hadn't been built anything like Brice. Not at all.

In her mind, she could still see the expanse of bare skin over the cords of muscles. His buttocks were firm and rounded. Fortunately his back had been turned toward her so she knew he hadn't seen her. But Cal had apparently filled him in on all he missed. Why had she stood there staring at him? It wasn't at all like her.

More important, how could she face him over the dinner table having seen him in no clothes at all and knowing that he knew? She dropped down onto her chair and leaned back to rest her head on the rattan webbing. Until a few minutes ago, she hadn't realized he bathed in the barn. She assumed he made do with the washbasin in his room. She resolved never to go around that corner again without making enough noise to signal her presence to whomever might be in there.

But that didn't tell her how to look him in the eye at the dinner table. If she hadn't stood there and stared, she could pass it off as what it had been—an accident. But to just stand there!

She could wring Cal's neck.

She waited as long as she could before going back downstairs. Brice was stirring the beans on the fire spider. He had already put plates on the table along with the bread she had baked that morning. When she came in, he looked up and watched her to see what she was going to do next.

Elizabeth averted her eyes. "How was your day?" she asked in clipped tones.

"Same as always. How was yours?"

"I don't want to talk about it."

"Do you want to tell me what you're so mad about?"

"No!" She spooned up the beans into a serving bowl and gave it to him to carry to the table while she carved the roast from the side oven.

"Is it something I've done?" he asked when he came back to her. "Damn it, Elizabeth, I haven't seen you all day. What has you in such an uproar?"

She paused. "What did Cal tell you?"

He stopped and thought. "Nothing. He said to tell you hello. That's all. For him it's a lot, but you know how Cal is."

"He didn't tell you—" She caught herself in time. "He didn't say anything else?"

"No. Was he supposed to? Cal isn't the best one to send messages by. What should he have told me?"

Elizabeth rubbed her forehead. "Nothing. Forget it."

Brice stared at her but finally shrugged. "If you say so."

"Just wash up—" She bit her lip. "Sit down and eat before it gets cold."

She was so thankful that Brice didn't know about her embarrassment she was willing to forgive Cal for his grin of amusement on her behalf.

"Elizabeth, I still don't understand."

"It doesn't matter." Now that she knew her secret was safe, a smile lifted her lips. "I'm going to try Mary Kate at the table tonight. She's too young to eat with us, but she handles her spoon pretty well now and it will be simpler."

"Suits me just fine." He still looked puzzled but was clearly willing to let the matter drop if she was no longer angry.

Elizabeth smiled to discourage him asking any more

questions and got a towel to tie around Mary Kate. She put the baby beside her and ladled a spoonful of beans onto her small plate. Brice had certainly looked good in the barn. She was going to think about that more than once, she already knew.

Chapter Seven

As the earliest of the wildflowers faded and hardier ones took their place, a thread of wagons came up the valley from Glory.

"Brice! Brice!" Elizabeth cried out as she ran to the catch pen where he and several of the men were dehorning a cow with a crooked horn. "The settlers are here! I can see the wagons!" She held to the fence, her breath coming rapidly.

Brice looked up from his work and grinned. "I'll be through here in a minute. I have to get this horn off while we have her down." Cal and Avery were wrestling the cow on the ground while Lucky, mounted on his cow pony, kept the rope tight on her hooves. One horn was growing toward her face and was threatening her eye. "She was too hard to catch to let her go now."

"I'll be on the porch!" Elizabeth gathered her skirts and ran back toward the house. On the porch she hurried around to the front of the house and watched the progress of the wagons. One, two, three…four wagons! Her heart beat faster, not because of the running but from excitement. They were going to have neighbors!

In her eagerness the wagons seemed to take forever

to reach the house. By the time they were there, Brice had washed up from doctoring the cow and was beside her. Elizabeth had gone after Mary Kate so someday when Mary Kate was old enough to understand, Brice could tell her about the time they all had watched the settlers arrive.

The wagons stopped a respectful distance from the house so the hooves and wheels wouldn't rut the yard. Elizabeth, with Mary Kate in her arms, hurried to Brice's side to welcome them. Everyone on the wagons was climbing down and straightening their clothes to make the best impression. Elizabeth was glad to see a number of children and several young couples, as well as a few older ones.

The wagon master shook hands with Brice and tipped his hat to Elizabeth. She smiled back.

One of the younger women came to Elizabeth and said. "My name is Maida Harrison. This is my husband, Edmund." Her voice was shy despite her obvious eagerness to make friends. She appeared to be about nineteen and her husband not much older, which made her about five years younger than Elizabeth.

"Please call me Elizabeth." She shifted Mary Kate to her other hip and gave Maida's hand a squeeze. In her excitement she forgot to give her last name.

"What a beautiful baby!" Maida reached out and touched Mary Kate's hand. The baby responded with a smile.

"This is Mary Kate. I can't tell you how excited I am at having children for her to play with as she grows older."

"Well—" Maida threw a shy smile at Edmund "—we don't have children yet, but we were only married a few days before the wagon train left. They will come in time.''

"Of course they will.'' Elizabeth looked at the other settlers. Everyone was talking and laughing at once. "This is like a dream come true!''

"It is for us, too. It was so kind of Mr. Graham to offer land and houses. We couldn't have afforded to come otherwise. It took most of our money to outfit for the wagon train and buy provisions. Do you know where the land is he put aside?''

Elizabeth pointed in the direction from which they had come. "You passed close to it on your way to the house. Do you see the cottonwood trees down there? The ones with the pine off to one side? That's the place. Most of Brice's land lies to the east and south of the house. The town will be near the border of the property.''

"There are trees!'' Maida smiled up at her husband.

Edmund grinned. "Maida sets a great store in having trees about. She worried when we were crossing the plains.''

"So did I when I came here,'' Elizabeth said. "I was so afraid we would end up somewhere with nothing but sky and dirt.''

Another couple stepped forward and introduced themselves as Ella and Abner Barker. The woman looked vaguely familiar but Elizabeth was positive they had never met. She tried without success to think whom the woman reminded her of.

Her conversation was cut off by Brice saying, "I'm going to show these people where the town will be. Do you want to ride along? It won't take any time for Lucky to hitch up the buggy.''

"You're welcome to ride down with us if you don't want to wait,'' Maida offered.

"I'd love to."

Brice called out to Lucky to hitch up the buggy and meet them at the town site. Elizabeth waited for Maida to climb into their wagon, handed the baby up, then climbed up after her. Edmund got on and slapped the reins on the backs of the team of horses. The wagon started moving with a jolt that reminded Elizabeth of her own journey west.

The town site was as pretty as any could be. Puma Creek was broad and lazy, the trees tall for that part of the country.

"Brice told me once he almost put the house here but at the last minute decided on the rise instead."

"It's beautiful!" Maida tucked her hand into Edmund's. "Where will the houses be built?"

"I guess that's up to each of you to decide."

"I like it right here," Edmund said. "If that's all right with you, Maida."

She nodded enthusiastically. "Can the porch face the creek? It would be so nice to sit on it and watch the water pass by."

"Sounds good to me." He grinned at her and winked. It was clear they were in love and that marriage was still a novelty to them.

Elizabeth smiled. "That puts you on the side of town closest to our house. You'll be my nearest neighbor."

The others were milling about, choosing home sites and laughing with friends. A tall, thin man in his late thirties called for silence. The people slowly stopped talking and gave him their attention.

"Who is he?" Elizabeth whispered to Maida.

"That's Brother Amos Sanders. His wife is the woman standing behind him. Her name is Dorcas. He's the preacher."

"Let's all pray and give thanks for safe delivery to our new home," Brother Amos said in ringing tones. He looked like a man who would rather discuss brimstone than blessings but he did command attention.

They all bowed their heads and Elizabeth jiggled Mary Kate to keep her quiet. Brother Amos's prayer droned on and on. Elizabeth tried not to be impatient. Religion was an important part of civilization and she couldn't afford to be choosy when this was the first preacher she had seen since leaving Missouri.

At last he said, "Amen," and it was echoed by several of the others. He pointed at a place somewhat removed from the trees. "The Lord has shown me this site for the church. How soon can we start building?"

Brice said, "I've sent word to the nearest lumber mill and I expect the lumber to start arriving any day now. I suggest you build the houses first. There's lumber enough for everyone."

"No, brother, the church—God's house—will be built first," Brother Amos said firmly.

Brice shrugged. "That's up to all of you. I won't be able to give you much help. Springtime is a busy time of the year for me. In fact, I may be able to hire some of you men to help me on the ranch. We need a woman to help Elizabeth about the house, too."

One of the older teenagers stepped forward. "I'm real good at housework. I reckon Mama can spare me." She looked at her parents. "Can't you?" They nodded.

Brice smiled at how easily this had been accomplished. "What's your name?"

"I'm Molly McGivens." She smiled at Elizabeth and came to stand closer to her.

"I'm Elizabeth—"

Brother Amos cut her off before she could say her last

name. "I'm pleased at your generosity," he said as he strode over to her. "You and your husband have earned a star in your crowns for this."

Elizabeth spoke up quickly. "No, no, you misunderstand. Brice isn't my—"

"Now, now. False modesty is a failing." He stepped aside. "I'd like to present my wife, Dorcas. This is Mrs. Graham."

"I'm not—"

"I'm pleased to meet you," Dorcas said. Her voice was flat and her face looked as if she never smiled. She was thin to the point of gauntness but looked far from frail.

"But you don't understand—" Elizabeth tried again.

As before, Brother Amos cut her off. "God has told me to have the church face due east. The cemetery—God forbid we'll need it soon—will lie directly to the side of the church. The parsonage will be beyond that."

"That seems like a good plan." Elizabeth knew she should insist on setting her marital record straight, but Brother Amos was rather intimidating. His bony face and glittering black eyes seemed too fiery for confidences. He was the only one of the settlers she wasn't taking to easily.

"My husband is so happy to have this mission," Dorcas said. "So am I. We hope to win souls to glory and bear witness to our faith. Thank you for giving us this opportunity."

"You're welcome," Elizabeth said uncertainly. She was honest to a fault and knew they had the wrong impression but she couldn't bring herself to correct it. What would that fierce-eyed preacher and his no-nonsense wife think if they knew she was living alone in a house with a man who wasn't her husband? They would certainly ostracize them and might even pack up and move farther west. *Later,* she told herself. She would explain to them later, after they were settled in.

That night after Mary Kate was in bed, Elizabeth went into the library to talk to Brice. "I believe we have a bit of a problem."

He looked up in surprise. "What sort of problem?"

"The settlers seem to believe I'm your wife." She sat in the chair opposite him. "I didn't understand they had that misconception at first, but when I met the preacher, he introduced me to his wife as Elizabeth Graham. I tried to correct him, but he wouldn't listen."

He nodded thoughtfully. "I noticed that about him. What about the others?"

"I don't know. As I said, it never occurred to me that they misunderstood, but if Brother Amos did, they must have, too." She faltered. "I found I had no way of explaining why I'm living here alone with you." Her eyes met his.

"This is something I hadn't considered. There isn't anything going on between us," he said. "You sleep in your room and I sleep in mine. Our conduct is entirely aboveboard."

"Pretty much so, yes."

"I only kissed you once."

"I know." She hadn't intended for her voice to hold so much regret.

The silence grew long between them.

"Do you want me to give them some explanation? I guess I could say you're my sister or a cousin."

"No. I don't want to lie. Especially not to a preacher. I hate dishonesty."

"Then what do you suggest?"

"I don't know." She shook her head and sighed. "Why didn't I ever think about this before now?"

Carefully he said, "We could let them assume you're my wife."

She looked at him and waited for an explanation.

"It's what they already believe. No one would question it."

"But it's not true!"

"Elizabeth, I spent some time talking to Brother Amos and he's as close to a religious zealot as I ever hope to meet. If we tell them the truth, he will insist they pack up again and leave. I'm sure of it. The man almost delivered a sermon to me just because I commented on a young couple I saw holding hands. It seems they aren't married and he's been watching them to be sure no improprieties are happening."

"I didn't expect the preacher to be so strict. The pastor at my church back home was kindly and never raised his voice. He was nothing like this Brother Amos."

"And there are the others to consider, too. I don't know where they would stand, but I imagine most of them would have second thoughts about settling here if they were to learn that we aren't married." He looked thoughtfully at the windows that were filled with night but would someday overlook the town. "I don't like to lie either, but I don't see a way around it. Besides," he said reluctantly, "you'll be leaving soon."

"I'm not sure this is the best time for that. I haven't saved enough money to outfit a wagon or pay the wagon master to get me back home."

"I could give you the money if you want to go."

"Certainly not!" She frowned at him. "I'm not one to take charity. No, I'll stay where I am until I can pay for myself. Besides, Mary Kate needs me." She paused doubtfully. "But if you want me to go, I will." She waited for his reply.

"No."

"It would make things easier for you," she argued perversely. "Then you could tell them I was your sister or whatever you like. There will be someone to watch over Mary Kate now. Molly seems kind and Mary Kate likes her."

"Molly isn't you." He sounded angry and she glanced at him.

For a moment she didn't think he was going to elaborate. Then he came to her and took her hand to draw her to her feet. "At first I was only intrigued by you. You came riding in from nowhere on that mule and hanging on to a rifle taller than you are. I was afraid you'd shoot yourself getting off his back." He smiled at the memory.

"Then I saw you smile for the first time and I couldn't stop looking at you. When you smile there are stars in your eyes and there's music in your laughter. I've never known anyone like you."

Elizabeth held her breath.

"I respect you more than any woman I've ever known. I don't know what may become of us. I'm probably wrong to ask you to stay." He hesitated. "Mary Kate loves you. She would miss you so keenly."

She had thought he was going to reveal his own feelings for her, not those of his daughter. Maybe he didn't feel anything for her at all. Certainly if he had permanent hopes for her, this was the time to express them. They could slip away, be married, and no one would ever be the wiser.

The wagon train was composed of married couples, but some of the daughters were of marriageable age.

Women were no longer such a rare commodity on the ranch. Maybe he was thinking that and wanting to keep his life unencumbered until he met his new neighbors.

Elizabeth wanted to ask him point-blank if he cared for her, but what would she do if he replied that he didn't? Not knowing was preferable. She turned to go. "I should go upstairs. It's been a long day."

He nodded. Misery pooled in his eyes but he didn't elaborate on its cause. "I know. You must be tired."

"I shouldn't have.... I'm going now." She had gone to the door before he stopped her.

She left the room and went quickly upstairs before she could change her mind.

Brice sat down in his chair but he didn't pick up his book. What had happened? One minute he had been telling her he didn't want to lose her, the next she had walked out of the room. Did she care for him or not? If she had, wouldn't she have stayed? What had she been trying to tell him when she said she wouldn't leave yet? He was thoroughly confused.

He sat there for several minutes, then went out onto the porch. Down below he could see the campfires. The wagons with lighted lanterns inside glowed like giant pumpkins. Now and then he could see a man or woman walk past the lights and disappear into the darkness. What would their arrival mean to Elizabeth and himself?

Until she had told him about Brother Amos's misconception, it had never occurred to him that their relationship would require an explanation. Elizabeth was so much a part of his life that he hadn't thought what it would look like to an outsider. That nothing sexual had happened between them really didn't matter. They were living alone under the same roof so she was as compromised as she would have been if they were lovers. *Lov-*

ers. Brice wondered what it would be like to be Elizabeth's lover.

What did she want from him? He just couldn't figure her out.

Among the wagons below, the light was extinguished in the one belonging to the young Harrison couple. His imagination told him what they would be doing in the privacy of the wagon.

He went back into the house and blew out the lamp before he went upstairs. He had to know where he stood with Elizabeth. When he reached her room, he knocked on her door.

"What is it?" she asked in a startled voice. Moments later she opened the door, holding her wrapper close about her neck. "Is Mary Kate sick?"

"No, I want to talk to you." He brushed past her into the bedroom and closed the door so the sound of their voices wouldn't awaken the baby.

She stayed at the door, still holding the wrapper close about her.

"How exactly do you feel about me? Spell it out. I can't tell what you're thinking and why you seem to be telling me one thing and then walking away from me." His voice was clipped and angry because of his frustration. "Talk to me, Elizabeth. I'm not leaving until you do."

Anger flared in her eyes and she advanced on him. "You have no right to come barging into my bedroom and demand that I do such a thing! My mule would have more manners than that!"

He noticed she wasn't wearing shoes and that she barely came up to his shoulder in her bare feet. Her face was pale with emotion. If he hadn't known that she had no reason to be crying, he would have sworn that she had been. "I need to know," he said.

"I told you I'm staying for Mary Kate's sake. That's what you want, isn't it? If it's not, I'll leave with the wagon master."

"I don't want you to leave. I've already told you that."

"Then we have nothing further to discuss." She opened the door and frowned at him until he left.

Elizabeth shut the door behind him and leaned against it. Hot tears rose in her eyes. She hated pretending she was immune to Brice. She was probably making a big mistake in not leaving. It could be a long time before she had another opportunity. She wasn't staying only for Mary Kate's sake, though that was a part of it. She loved the baby as dearly as if she were her own. But she was also falling in love with Brice.

Fighting against it was to no avail. He had become part of her world. She couldn't leave without knowing if he would someday love her. She no longer disliked the Territory since being here also meant being near Brice. At times she even liked the harsh beauty of the hills and the soothing loveliness of Puma Creek and the green valley. Someday—assuming he came to love her—Elizabeth would tell him she no longer despised his world. She had to stay where she was until she knew if that day would come.

Chapter Eight

"The buildings are coming along beautifully," Maida said as she helped Elizabeth wash up the dinner dishes. "It's almost like we planted house seeds and are watching them grow." She laughed. "Edmund says I have outlandish thoughts."

"I agree with you. It really is like watching a town sprout and grow."

"I try to stay out of the men's way, but I love walking into our house through what will be the front door and pretending I can see the rooms just as they'll be. It looks awfully small now, but Edmund says houses always look like that before the walls are up. After that wagon, anything will be like a palace."

"I know. I remember my trip out. I thought we would never get here. I grew to thoroughly dislike that wagon." She smiled at the remembrance.

Maida dried the plate and put it with the others. "Is Texas anything like this? Edmund says it's all desert and cactus."

"I've never seen Texas," Elizabeth said without thinking.

"You haven't? I thought you and Brice came from there."

Elizabeth said carefully, "Brice did. I'm from Missouri."

"Just like us! How did you ever meet?"

"It's a long story. Brice has told me that Texas, the part he's from at any rate, has tall trees and rolling hills. He gets homesick for it from time to time."

"I miss my family, but I can't say I miss Missouri. Where did you live?"

"Hannibal. My father is all the family I have left, aside from cousins, and we were never close." She had to be careful not to mention Robert or the circumstances that led to her being at the ranch.

"Your baby is so adorable." Maida looked over at Mary Kate playing with toys in a corner.

"Thank you." It still bothered Elizabeth when people referred to her as Mary Kate's mother or Brice's wife, but she was finding it surprisingly easy to pretend it was true. For a woman who abhorred lies, it wasn't that difficult for her to live one.

"She's beautiful. Her features look like Brice, don't they? I just hope we have a baby that pretty."

"I'm sure you will."

"How is the McGivens girl working out?" Maida asked in a lower tone so she couldn't be overheard.

"Molly is wonderful. Mary Kate loves her and she keeps the house beautifully. I know from experience how hard it is to keep everything clean. Every speck of dust stirred by a cow fifty acres away seemed to land in my parlor."

"I can hardly wait to have a parlor of my own." Maida watched as Elizabeth carried the pan of dishwater to the back door and tossed its contents out onto the yard for the benefit of the grass. Water was too scarce to waste, even if the well was a good one.

Elizabeth came back in, wiped the pan dry and hung it on the wall before doing the same thing to the pan of rinse water.

"I guess the church will be ready for services by Sunday." Maida hung her cup towel over the rack to dry. Her brow furrowed as if something was bothering her. "What do you think about Brother Amos?"

"I'm sure he's a good man. We were lucky to find a preacher willing to come here."

"Of course he is," Maida said quickly. "I'm not one to criticize a man of the cloth."

Elizabeth smiled and said in a whisper, "But personally, I think he's rather full of himself."

Maida laughed and playfully scolded, "Shame on you, Elizabeth! To talk that way!" She lowered her voice, too. "I agree. He walks around just waiting for somebody to do something wrong. I'd hate to be married to him."

"I've thought the same thing. Why do you suppose Dorcas married him in the first place?"

"Heaven knows. She's a plain woman. Maybe he's the only one that asked."

"That wouldn't be reason enough for me." Elizabeth picked up Mary Kate and said, "It's time for her nap."

"Could I watch you put her to sleep? I want to learn everything so when we have one, I won't make mistakes."

Elizabeth laughed. "I don't know that I'm much of an authority, but you're welcome to watch."

They went upstairs and Elizabeth changed Mary Kate into a dry diaper and put the wet one to soak in a covered crock of vinegar water. Later that day she would wash them and hang them out to dry overnight. Earlier, she had filled one of Mary Kate's bottles at the springhouse and had stored it in her room in a smaller crock of cool water. She took it out and dried it off.

"You're giving her a bottle? I assumed she would be fed the ordinary way."

"It didn't work out that way." Elizabeth evaded. She sat in the rocker and put the nipple to Mary Kate's mouth. "She's learning to drink from a cup and won't be on a bottle at all before long."

"So soon?"

"It'll be easier that way, all things considered." She rocked rhythmically. Mary Kate stared up at her, her eyes already becoming sleepy.

By the time the bottle was empty, the baby was almost asleep. Elizabeth laid her gently in her bed, and they slipped quietly from the room.

As they passed Elizabeth's bedroom, she said, "Let me pick up my sewing. I'm hemming a dress, and I can do that while we talk." From one of the lower drawers of the armoire, she got the rose-colored material Brice had given her after his last trip to town. She had carefully unstitched one of her other dresses and was using the pieces for a pattern.

"What a pretty color," Maida said.

"Brice brought me the material as a gift. I've never had one this color. You don't think it's too fancy?"

"Of course not. Why, there were women in my hometown whose dresses seemed to be made entirely of braids and cording and so forth. No, it's not at all too fancy."

Elizabeth was glad to hear it. She had been out of touch with fashion for several years before coming to Oklahoma. Only the plainest of dresses had been appropriate for the hut.

Maida went to the French doors that were open to the veranda. "What a nice breeze. And the view! I believe I can actually see a mountain in the distance."

"You can see it on clear days. I love to sit out there in the evening." She picked up the small basket she used to store her sewing things.

Maida looked at the other set of open doors. "Whose room is this? Do you keep a spare room for guests?"

Elizabeth hesitated. "That's Brice's room."

She looked back at her in surprise. "You don't sleep in the same room?"

"I can hear Mary Kate better from this room." She went to the hall door. "Would you like to sit on the porch? It's nice and cool out there and we'll be out of Molly's way while she cleans the parlor."

Maida wasn't ready to let the matter drop. "Couldn't you hear her as well from this other room? It's only a few feet farther away. Or couldn't Brice move into the room with you?" She followed Elizabeth out into the hall and looked curiously at the closed door that hid Brice's room. "I know it's none of my business, but I should think it would put a strain on a marriage not to share a bedroom."

"It's not as if he's all that far away," Elizabeth said with careful calmness. "Only a door separates the rooms."

"All the same," Maida said as she shook her head. "Edmund and I have decided never to sleep apart if we can help it."

Elizabeth didn't answer, hoping her silence would hint to Maida that she didn't want to discuss it. She opened the basket and took out her scissors. Her needle was stuck in the dress's fabric. To change the subject she said, "We should have a quilting party. I have a top almost pieced."

"That would be nice. I haven't been to a quilting party in the longest time and I do love to quilt. There's not much for us to do but stay out of the way while the cabins are being built. Yes, I think this would be a perfect time for a quilting party."

"It's settled then," Elizabeth said. "Perhaps two days from now? That will give the other women time to organize their chores around it."

"I can hardly wait. I'll tell everyone and save you the trip to the cabins."

Elizabeth was looking forward to it herself. She hadn't realized how much she had missed the companionship of women.

"Edmund, I'm really worried about it," Maida said as she stirred the pot of stew over the open fire. "They aren't sleeping together."

"Honey, everybody has their own ways of doing things. Maybe they just don't want more babies or maybe Brice snores."

"She didn't say he did. And who wouldn't want more babies?"

"Not everyone is as fond of big families as you are," he reminded her. "Besides, it's none of our business."

"But I'm her friend. If we don't do something to help, their marriage may go bad." She gazed at him earnestly. "Don't you agree? We've always said we wouldn't ever have separate rooms."

"I don't know what you think I can do about it."

"You could talk to Brice."

Edmund stared at her. "What? I can't say anything to

him about it! How could I explain knowing what their sleeping arrangements are?''

"You could tell him Elizabeth and I happened to be talking about bedrooms. Tell him anything. The important thing is that he has to think about this arrangement. Nothing is more important than keeping a marriage together.''

"I'm not talking to him about this. Men don't discuss such things.''

"I don't see why not!''

"I'd be embarrassed and so would he. I'm amazed that you talked to Elizabeth about it, for that matter. You should mind your own business, honey. Not everyone knows you mean well when you do things like this.''

"But you know I do. I'm not trying to pry. Please Edmund?''

He had never been able to refuse her anything. "All right,'' he said grudgingly. "I'll try to find a reason to bring it up. But it won't be easy and if I come home with a black eye, you'll know you're the one to blame.''

She smiled at him. "Brice wouldn't hit you. He's a gentleman. He will probably thank you for helping him sort it out.''

"I don't think so.'' Edmund frowned at the flames and wondered how he was going to bring up a subject like that.

"Is everything all right with Elizabeth?'' Edmund asked Brice as they lifted the rafters into place. The other men were busy on their own houses and Brice had come down to lend a hand.

"She's fine. Take your end a bit to the left. That's good.'' Brice put two nails in his mouth and hammered a third one to hold the rafter in place.

"Maida was worried."

Brice glanced at him. "Worried about Elizabeth?"

Edmund sighed and said, "Oh, hell. I'm no good at this. Just forget I said anything."

"All right," Brice said amiably. "This is a good load of lumber. There's scarcely a crooked board in the lot. I wasn't too sure what I'd get, sending off for it like I did. That's the same sawmill that supplied lumber for my house. I guess they recognized me as a customer."

"It's good wood, real true and all." Edmund looked over at the wagon where Maida was hanging out the wash she'd just done on a line stretched from the wagon to a tree. She would ask him questions for certain, and Edmund hated to disappoint her. "So there's nothing going wrong at your house?"

"Not a thing," Brice said as if he couldn't imagine what Edmund could be talking about. "Is everything all right at yours?"

"Just fine. We can't hardly wait to get into the house. I always took a roof for granted." He laughed. "I won't ever do that again. I wasn't cut out for the gypsy life."

"Neither was I." Brice checked the alignment of the rafters. "They look straight to me."

"Me, too."

"Let's get the rest of the walls up inside. We can work on the roof tomorrow."

Edmund was whistling as he resumed nailing. He had given it his best effort and could report to Maida that nothing was wrong between Brice and Elizabeth.

Brice came in to find Elizabeth wrestling the quilting frame out of the attic. "Here, let me do that. What are you trying to do? Fall down the stairs?" He reached past her and took the boards out of her hands.

"I was going to ask you to help me hang it. I had hoped to have it downstairs and clean before you came in."

"I don't mind doing things like this for you. For that matter, there is always a man or two around the barn or feed pen who can lift heavy things for you if I'm not around."

"I meant to ask Molly to help but she went home before I remembered." She dusted her hands on her skirt, then rubbed at the smudge on her nose.

"Why was the quilting frame put up there in the first place? It won't be in the way."

"Celia didn't like to quilt. Her mother sent it to her the first year we were married and she had me take it up that same day."

"It's a lovely frame. I thought she would enjoy needlework. I do." Elizabeth hadn't meant to bring a memory of Celia into this. She seemed to lurk around every corner.

"She wasn't much on doing work of any sort. I guess she thought our quilts would last forever or that her mother would send more when they wore out."

Elizabeth was beginning to think Celia was more spoiled than any adult she had ever encountered so she kept her opinion to herself.

Brice brought in a ladder from the barn and together he and Elizabeth threaded the rope through the set of pulleys and into the ring hooks embedded in the ceiling. When they were done, Brice pegged the frame together and suspended it from the ropes.

Elizabeth pulled it up and lowered it again. "Perfect! I always wanted a quilting frame." She could hardly wait to fasten her pieced top to the frame and get started.

"Your party is tomorrow, isn't it?" he said.

"Yes. I'm really looking forward to it. There's no better way to get to know women than over a common work like quilting or shucking corn."

"Edmund asked me some odd questions today."

She glanced up at him. "What sort of questions?"

"He wanted to know if you were all right and if anything was wrong up here."

Elizabeth sighed. "That Maida! She must have told him."

"Told him what?"

"She went to the nursery with me and when I stopped off in my room to get that dress I'm finishing, she noticed we don't sleep together."

Brice uttered a noncommittal grunt.

"I tried to make excuses but I could tell she was concerned. She thinks a marriage can't survive unless the husband and wife sleep together."

"I agree with her. At least it wouldn't be the sort of marriage that I want." He thought for a minute. "If it would ease her mind, tell her there's something wrong with one or the other of us. Blame it on health."

"That would only make her worry more. I can't tell her that."

"Then let her worry."

Elizabeth looked at him across the frame that separated them. "I hate lying. I should have told the truth about us from the beginning."

"We did what we had to do," he reminded her.

Elizabeth went to the pulley and raised the frame out of the way. "Everything has gotten very complicated, hasn't it?"

"I'm sorry. I'm only trying to protect you."

She crossed the room but at the door she paused. "I appreciate that, Brice, but now how will we ever explain not being married?'' Then she turned and left him behind to think about what she had said.

Elizabeth went to her room and took out the envelope of Robert's hair and the other items Brice had returned to her. She stared down at them, thinking all marriages might not be bad just because she had been unhappy with Robert. The few items she removed from the envelope brought back memories. She took out the hair clippings. They were soft in her fingers and she looked at them more closely. With a frown, she went out on the veranda and held them in the sunlight. The hair glowed with a touch of red. Robert's hair had no red in it at all.

Elizabeth went back to the other things. They were his. She remembered seeing them every day. But the hair from the dead man wasn't the right color. Dread curled in her stomach and she stuffed the lock back into the envelope.

Chapter Nine

"I love quilting parties," Ella Barker said as she and her teenage daughter, Darcy, sat in the dining room chairs Elizabeth had moved into the back parlor around the quilting frame. "My goodness, but you have a lovely house." Ella's eyes were taking in every detail.

"Thank you." Elizabeth was so eager to get to know the other women she had been up since before dawn getting things ready. Molly had instructions to watch the baby, and she was pretty well assured of an afternoon of uninterrupted social exchange. "How is your house coming along, Ella?"

"Real well. My Abner is roofing today. Once we have a roof, we'll move in and finish the rest while we live in it." Ella was the matronly sort and took everything in stride. "What are a few inconveniences as long as you have a house about you? He's looking forward to building the schoolhouse next. He's a good teacher, Abner is."

"Brice and I are so glad you came here."

Maida, who had been helping Elizabeth in the kitchen, came in with a platter of cookies called tea cakes they had made that morning. The recipe was one Elizabeth had learned from her mother, and the sugary cookies were light and buttery.

"Cookies! My goodness, I haven't seen cookies since we left home." Ella took one and bit into it with relish. "These are wonderful. I can't wait to get an oven of my own. This is one thing you just can't make over an open fire."

"Brice says the bricks for the chimneys and ovens are drying nicely. That's the same man Brice hired to make our bricks here."

A knock at the front door signaled more guests. Elizabeth hurried to answer it. Two more women and a teenage girl were waiting on the porch. She opened the door wide. "Come in, come in. I have the quilting frame set up in the back parlor."

Harriet McGivens led the others into the house, extolling its beauty. Dorcas Sanders brought up the rear in total silence. At first Elizabeth thought the woman was too shy to speak, but when their eyes met, Elizabeth was taken aback by what appeared to be resentment that the others had complimented her about her house. Until now Elizabeth hadn't really thought Brice's house would seem ostentatious to the preacher's wife. Apparently she was wrong.

The woman's countenance was as somber as her clothing. Dorcas's dress was black; indeed that was the only color Elizabeth had ever seen her wear. Although the day was warm, her bodice was buttoned to the neck and her cuffs were close about her wrists. Elizabeth couldn't help but feel sorry for the discomfort the woman was enduring, but thought it best not to mention it, since she wasn't sure whether it was Dorcas's choice to dress this way or her husband's edict.

"Molly didn't exaggerate," Harriet said as she looked

about, peering up the staircase and catching glimpses of the dining room and library. "She said your house was beautiful, and it sure is."

"I can't take credit for it," Elizabeth said. "Brice built it and bought the furniture himself."

"He certainly has good taste for a man." Harriet let out a booming laugh. "I can just imagine what Tavish would choose. One thing's for sure, he'd have tartan plaid everywhere." To Elizabeth, she explained, "He's come straight from Scotland, and it's true what they say about Scots."

Elizabeth wasn't sure what "they" said, but was hesitant to ask. She led them into the back parlor, and they greeted Maida and Ella as if they hadn't seen them in weeks, though they were all camped only a few yards from one another.

Ella's daughter, Darcy, sat close to her mother. Elizabeth decided the girl was overly shy and gave her a reassuring smile as they took their places around the quilting frame. The girl smiled back but didn't speak. Elizabeth had seen her talking to young Charley McGivens on several occasions, and it was Maida's opinion that they might be the first couple to be married in the new town.

The other girl was Charley's sister Dorothy, and she was as vocal as their mother. "I love this pattern! Could I borrow it?"

"Of course," Elizabeth said. "I'll trace it for you. It's called Bear Tracks."

Harriet nodded as she touched it. "I have a similar one called Tulip Basket. You just use different colors. It sure did make up nice, didn't it?"

"It sure did, Mama," Dorothy said. "I'd like to make me one in blue and yellow." To Elizabeth she added,

"My room is going to be blue and yellow. Me and Molly have already decided."

"You'd better talk to Anna before you two get too set. You know your sister hates yellow." Harriet laughed again. "My brood certainly has definite ideas about everything." She had the largest family in the new town. In addition to four girls, she had three sons and another child was on the way. To Elizabeth she said, "Since Molly and Dorothy are all but grown and Anna is only eight, she gets left out of some of their decisions."

"I just hope I learn everyone's name," Elizabeth said with a laugh. "You all still confuse me."

"Well, you don't need to learn as many names for my family," Ella said. "We just have Darcy."

Once again Elizabeth had the odd sensation of how familiar Ella, and in some ways Darcy, looked. It was like trying to recall a name that eluded every effort to remember it. For some reason, she never felt entirely comfortable with them.

She sat down and picked up her needle, as had several others.

Dorcas looked around the circle. "I believe we ought to have a prayer first."

The other women looked at her in surprise. Elizabeth said, "All right, Mrs. Sanders. Will you say it for us?"

Dorcas lowered her eyes and began to pray in firm tones.

Elizabeth had trouble following the prayer. Dorcas was as fervent as her husband. Elizabeth had never known a quilting to start with a prayer. She wondered if it would be difficult to live so close to religious fanatics.

At last the prayer ended and as Elizabeth picked up her needle to begin sewing, she said, "I have some lemonade in that pitcher on the side table, and there are tea cakes on the platter.''

Dorothy looked up with interest. She tended to be on the heavy side, like her mother.

The conversation flowed into predictable channels. When the houses would be finished, whether the seeds brought from Missouri would prosper in Oklahoma soil, how hard they could expect the winters to be. Elizabeth listened to all of them and shifted her attention from one conversation to another. She had missed the talk that always accompanied gatherings of women.

Ella Barker puzzled Elizabeth. She was friendly, but Elizabeth instinctively distrusted her. Abner, her husband, was much the same. Her gimlet eyes seemed to miss nothing, and if Mary Kate was around, her attention was riveted to the child, yet she usually ignored the McGivens children. Elizabeth didn't trust Ella or Abner, but she couldn't have explained why she didn't. Ella didn't even show much interest in Charley McGivens, even though he and Darcy seemed to be falling in love.

''My Charley may make a nuisance of himself,'' Harriet was saying. ''If he does, just chase him away and send him home.''

''Charley doesn't wear out his welcome,'' Ella said quickly. ''Why, I've never seen a lad with better manners.'' Darcy smiled silently and kept her head bent over the quilt.

Elizabeth watched the steady rise and fall of bright needles. All the women were proficient needlewomen, as was she, and the quilt was quickly taking shape. She had used an old, worn quilt for the batting and occasionally her needle hit a knot of fabric, but in general it passed through the cloth smoothly. ''The batting is a quilt one of my cousins gave my mother years ago,'' she told Maida. ''I've used it until it's threadbare.''

''I love quilts. They're so colorful,'' one of them replied.

Dorcas gave the woman a warning glance. ''Too much color smacks of frivolity,'' she said in dour tones. ''I sew my quilts of somber colors. Since I wear only black and the occasional dark brown, it's not difficult to achieve this. White scraps from Brother Amos's cast off shirts lend enough color for me.''

Elizabeth thought about that for a moment. Quilts of black, dark brown and white didn't sound particularly pretty.

Dorcas continued, ''So much color hurts my eyes. I'm always surprised by color.''

''Abner has the schoolhouse all planned,'' Ella said. ''He's building it by the creek beyond that little bend. It won't be on our property but will be beside it. That way he won't have so far to walk and neither will the children. It can be real cold during the winter, I imagine.''

''Last winter was hard here,'' Elizabeth admitted. ''In the hut—'' She bit back her words but wasn't fast enough.

''What hut?'' Maida asked.

''I lived in one before moving in here.'' She didn't intend to elaborate. ''More tea cakes?'' she asked quickly. ''I have plenty more in the kitchen. Molly and I have been baking all morning.''

Dorcas shook her head dismally. ''We don't hold with much sweets. It's bad for your soul.''

Harriet frowned. ''How on earth can a cookie matter to your soul one way or another?''

''It's the luxury,'' Dorcas said seriously. ''If you get

used to having sweets, you come to expect it. Brother Amos and I eat a Spartan fare, and I believe we're all the healthier for it."

"If I served Tavish a meal with no 'pudding' as he calls it, he would likely send me packing. He does love a bit of sweetness, even if it's nothing but honey on a piece of bread."

"Mama," Dorothy said, "maybe Mr. Sims could stock some yellow and blue cloth in the general store that could be used for the quilt I'm planning." She hadn't been following the older women's conversation at all, lost as she was in her daydreams of finally having a real room to sleep in.

"Maybe so. That's assuming Anna will let yellow come in the door. I'm telling you, you have to talk to her before you get too far into planning this."

"*New* cloth for a quilt?" Dorcas asked rather sharply. "Isn't that a bit extravagant?"

"Not if I make dresses for the girls out of the cloth and give them what's left." Harriet fixed her second daughter with a wink of her eye. "I know exactly which one is going to wear that yellow dress." Dorothy ducked her head and grinned.

"Maybe I ought to make me a quilt, too," Darcy said in a low voice.

"It wouldn't hurt to add one to your hope chest," Harriet said approvingly. "You'll soon be of an age to need a trousseau."

"You're all welcome to use this quilting frame until you have your own built," Elizabeth offered. "I would enjoy the company. You can't imagine how lonely it has been here at times."

"I think we are all fortunate to have found a preacher, a teacher and a storekeeper all willing to make up the train," Maida said. "We have everything we need for the town to thrive."

"Abner loves to teach," Ella told her. "He had hoped we would have more than one child. When we didn't, he turned his hand to teaching because he loves having youngsters around him."

"The only shortage I see," Harriet put in, "is in young people. I'm hoping more families come to the town before the rest of my young'ns reach marrying age. Of course Charley and Molly are already there, them being nineteen and eighteen."

"Maybe there are eligible young men in Glory," Elizabeth suggested. "It's a fair-sized town by frontier standards."

"It's also a day's ride," Harriet said. "A bundling board is the answer."

Dorcas's face had gone white. "A bundling board! That's the height of impropriety!"

"Not at all," Harriet said in her own defense. "My family used one when I was growing up. We lived so far away from anything that it was the only way. If it hadn't been for the bundling board, most of us wouldn't have gotten to know any boy well enough to marry him."

"I'm sure that's true," Dorcas sniped.

"They are perfectly respectable!" Harriet wasn't going to back down on this, having admitted using one herself. "Ours was a wide pine board that attached to the headboard and extended over the footboard. The girl stayed on her side and the boy on the other and they couldn't even see each other."

"You can't escape the fact that they were sleeping in the same bed!" Dorcas shot back. "That's a sin no matter which way you turn it!"

"Not if the boy and girl behave themselves!" Harriet snapped back. "In my parents' house there weren't any extra beds, and I didn't have any brothers. There was no other place for the boys to sleep!"

"I'm sure nothing inappropriate happened," Ella said. "I've known many country people that used them and I never heard of a single instance of wrongdoing."

"In your case," Dorcas said, "the young man can just as easily sleep with your sons. Or I'll find a place for him in the parsonage, for that matter. Brother Amos would be unrestrainable if he thought a bundling board was being used by a member of his congregation."

Harriet opened her mouth to carry the battle further but Elizabeth hastily said, "Would you mind helping me with the lemonade, Harriet? I'm sure some of the women must be parched in this heat." Even though she succeeded in stopping the argument, she could tell that Harriet and Dorcas were accustomed to arguing with each other and would likely resume at some future time. All the others seemed to be on familiar ground with the disagreement. At least, Elizabeth thought as she poured the lemonade, it would be lively with the settlement only a short distance from the ranch.

The next day Brice was to go to the back pastures to check on the progress of a sick cow. A cow lying down was an easy prey for wolves and pumas, and it was unusual for one to stay down for any length of time unless it was ailing badly. He watched Elizabeth as she put away the breakfast dishes and tidied the kitchen. "I should be home before dark or soon after."

"I'll stay up and watch for you."

"But if I have trouble finding the cow, I may have to sleep under the stars tonight. Don't wait up." He knew he was being curt with her, but he was having to struggle continuously not to touch her. Only his concern for the consequences gave him the strength to keep his distance.

"I have food for you in this bag." She handed it to him. "It's some of the ham from last night and the rest of the loaf of bread. Maybe I should fry up some beef if you're going to be out there for two meals."

"This will be enough." It was time to leave but he was reluctant to go. "I'm going to look for the cow where Puma Creek winds around that tall rock. Lucky said he last saw her there. If he's right and she's down with sour stomach, it won't take long to get her back on her feet."

"Is Lucky going with you?"

"No, if she's still down I won't need anyone to hold her while I doctor her and if she's up, she won't need me."

Elizabeth looked up at him. "You'll be careful, won't you?"

"I always am." He had an almost overwhelming desire to touch her, to stroke the soft curve of her cheek and to bury his hands in her hair until it cascaded from her bun into waves down her back. "I'd better go," he said abruptly.

Elizabeth watched him walk out the door. She had seen the need in his eyes. Living in such close proximity was as difficult for him as it was for her these days. She put all her effort into scrubbing the kitchen. She had found hard work didn't stop her from thinking about him, but it exhausted her to the point where she could at least sleep at night.

After scrubbing for an hour, she happened to see the bag of food on the table. He had forgotten to take it with him. She looked out back. Brice was long gone by now and the men were busy with their own chores. "Molly?" she called out.

The girl, carrying Mary Kate on her hip, came into the kitchen. "You called me, Miss Elizabeth?" Like the hired hands, Molly had adopted that form of addressing her.

"Brice forgot to take his food with him and he may be gone all night. I'm going to take it to him. Will you watch the baby while I'm gone?"

"I sure will. We were learning to stack blocks real high, weren't we, Mary Kate?" Like Elizabeth, Molly had fallen under the little girl's charm.

"I'll be back as soon as I can. Her bottle is in the springhouse and I mixed up some extra milk for her." Lately she had been diluting the milk less but it was a process she was careful to do herself. When it came to Mary Kate's health, Elizabeth took no chances.

She removed her apron and donned her sunbonnet automatically as she went out the back door. As she had thought, Brice had already gone to find the cow. Elizabeth saddled a horse and rode away from the barn.

Elizabeth was always uneasy when she rode alone out of sight of the house and barn, but her mission was more important than the discomfort of her apprehension. In the distance ahead, she saw the silver ribbon of Puma Creek and she headed for it, knowing that if she followed it far enough, it stood to reason she would find the rock outcrop and Brice.

After nearly an hour's ride, the rock formation she sought came into view not far ahead. Nearing the marker, her horse pricked up its ears as it sensed Brice's horse and whickered softly. Brice looked up from the cow, more than a little surprised to see her there.

"You forgot your food," she said in explanation. "I didn't want you to go hungry."

He looked away. Rather distantly, he said, "It wouldn't have hurt me. I didn't eat all that regularly before you came to the ranch." Then he looked back at her and smiled. "But I'm grateful."

Relieved that he wasn't angry with her for riding out alone, she dismounted and tied her horse to a bush. "How is she?"

"It's sour stomach all right." The cow lifted her head and lowed mournfully.

"She doesn't sound too happy."

"She's not yet. Since you're here, you can help me get the medicine down her." A grin split his face. "I'll bet you didn't expect to have this much fun today."

"You're right." Elizabeth approached the animal warily. All of Brice's cattle roamed the range and were wild. She had seldom touched a cow in her life and knew very little about them.

"She won't bite," he assured her. Then, as if to belie Brice's words, the cow lowed again and fixed Elizabeth with a wild eye. "The medicine is in my saddlebag."

She untied the saddlebag and brought it to him. "Did she eat some poisonous plant?" The animal was in obvious distress.

"No, she made a meal of the wild clover in that field back there where the rest of the herd is, then drank too much water. It flushed the clover through her system too fast and it didn't digest properly." He sat back on his heels and rested for a minute before opening the saddlebag. He took out several vials of medicine and shook up the one containing the whitish mixture.

"That looks like milk of magnesia."

"It is. Count out forty drops of the oil of peppermint

into that empty bottle.'' He positioned himself at the cow's head and lifted it until her neck was perpendicular to the ground. She protested but he forced her mouth open and poured the medicine down her throat. The cow tried to rise in protest but wasn't able.

''I've counted the drops,'' Elizabeth said, handing him the bottle and tightly recapping the vial.

Brice added two ounces of laudanum to the oil of peppermint, then shook it up. ''She's going to feel as if she's been on a drinking spree after this.'' He again opened the cow's mouth. ''The trick with this is not to drop the bottle. This one is small enough for her to swallow.'' He carefully poured the mixture into her throat. The cow bellowed loudly and walled her eyes in search of an escape.

Elizabeth put the empty containers back into the saddlebag and buckled the flap. Brice again started stroking the cow's belly to relieve her pain. A few other cows came nearer out of curiosity but were afraid to get too close.

''They're pretty,'' Elizabeth said.

''People in Glory thought I was crazy to stock whiteface instead of longhorns, and it's a fact that they are more trouble. A longhorn can eat anything that grows, drink dust and never have a problem. I'm doctoring these cows every time I turn around.''

''Then why not get rid of them and buy longhorns?''

''Because when I sell these, I'll make three times the money. A longhorn is all horns and bones. Look at the body on those cows over there. They're almost square and it's all beef.'' He looked up from his strenuous effort to keep the sick cow still. ''See that bull? That's the one we were doctoring in the barn not long ago. He looks good now, doesn't he?''

"He does for a fact. He also looks mean."

Brice chuckled. "He won't give us any trouble. He's afraid we may cage him up and doctor him again."

Elizabeth hoped he was right. She had a healthy respect for wild bulls.

Suddenly Brice rose and stepped back as the cow rolled onto her stomach, looked around and got to her feet. She stood there for several minutes as if she wasn't sure why the world was dipping and swaying under her, then she trotted unsteadily toward the herd.

"That was fast," Elizabeth said. "I thought you'd be working with her all day."

"She wasn't as sick as she might have been." He watched her join the others. "Sour stomach clears up pretty easy if you doctor it early enough. We were fortunate that Lucky noticed that she was down. That's the other drawback with this kind of cattle. They're worth a lot more than longhorns. I don't want to lose one if I can help it."

Although Elizabeth could no longer pick her out once she had mixed into the herd, Brice was still following her movements. She realized that to him the cows were all individuals and distinct from one another. His caring went beyond the expense of losing a cow.

She strolled to the side of the creek and looked down into the water. It was cool here in the shade and the breeze brought the scent of clover. "It's so beautiful out here," she said almost to herself. "That's the first thing that struck me when I came to the valley. It's so pretty."

"Yes, it is." He was standing closer to her than she had thought and she turned to look up at him. "I love this place. When I saw it for the first time, I was on pins and needles until I had the ownership papers in my hand. Anything will grow in this valley, and the creeks never run dry. It's all I could ever ask for. Almost.'' He looked at her with the aching need back in his eyes.

Elizabeth touched his arm. ''You could have it all, Brice. You have only to ask.''

He was silent for a minute, then drew her into his embrace. She could feel him tremble slightly and knew how difficult it was for him only to hold her. They stood there quietly, embracing each other, reluctant to go back to their normal routine.

''Damn, but I wish we had met before Celia and Robert came into our lives!'' The admission burst from him and he held her closer.

''I know. I feel the same. Sometimes I imagine you riding up to my father's house in Hannibal. I'd be sitting on the porch, maybe sipping lemonade. You'd be hot and I'd offer you a glass.''

''I would accept it,'' he said, playing into her fantasy. '''Morning, ma'am,' I'd say. And I'd come up onto the porch.''

''I would give you the glass and our hands would touch. Just a bit, but we'd both feel it. I'd say, 'Sit here in the shade for a bit and be comfortable.' You'd sit beside me in the swing. 'You'll have to ask my father if you're to court me properly,' I'd tell you. 'He's in the back parlor.'''

''I'd ask permission to court you. If he didn't give it, I'd court you anyway.''

''We could slip out to meet in the barn....'' Her pulse was racing at how easily he fell into her dreamworld.

He tipped her head up and kissed her, gently at first, then slowly parting his lips he pressed his mouth more firmly against hers as she responded in kind. His tongue touched hers, sending shock waves of stimulation throughout her body, then he pulled back, separating them by only a whisper. Looking down into her eyes, he said, "And then I would make love to you on the hay." His eyes were dark and aflame with passion. "You would drive me wild there as much as you do here."

"You seem to know my fantasy as well as I do."

"I should. I dream variations of it every night and torment myself with new innovations of it during the day." His voice was husky with emotion. "Elizabeth, what in the hell are we going to do?"

She closed her eyes and held him close. She had ached to embrace him like this. "I don't know, Brice. I purely don't know."

"If I didn't want you, it would be so easy." He touched her face as if he were memorizing every feature, every curve and plane. "It hasn't been easy since the first time I saw you." He bent and kissed her again, this time more passionately than before. "Elizabeth, let's go to Glory and be married. That will solve everything."

Elizabeth turned away. "We can't. There's something I haven't told you. I looked at Robert's things again and…" she found it difficult to finish.

"You still love him?"

"No!" She looked back at Brice. "I haven't loved Robert in a long time. Brice, the color of the hair is wrong."

"Wrong?"

"Robert had brown hair. The clippings in the envelope are reddish." She drew a deep breath. "I'm not sure Robert is dead. I may still be married to him."

Brice drew her to him and held her tightly. "He may never come back. You could wait forever."

"Or he could return and find me married to you."

Elizabeth held him as if she would never let go. "We can't be married until I'm certain."

"You're right, damn it." He sounded as unhappy as she felt.

"Brice, what are we going to do? It's tearing me apart—wanting you and not being able to come to you."

"It's doing the same to me." He gazed into her eyes. "You really want me? You enjoy it when I touch you?"

Her heart turned over at the note of caring in his voice. "Of course I enjoy it." She ran her hands over his back, enjoying the feel of his taut muscles. "You feel so good to me! At times it's all I can do to keep from touching you. I had to force myself to be mean to you, to push you away."

"I didn't know you felt that way. You're a hard woman to understand."

"There's a lot you don't understand about me," she said softly. "It could be wonderful learning about each other."

"Or we could be the topic of Brother Amos's sermons for years to come."

"I don't care, Brice. I couldn't care less what the Sanderses think of us. As far as they know, we're married. I'm not going to tell them any different, and neither are you. How would they know we aren't?"

"This is true. My men are loyal to me. They won't talk about us to anyone. I'm sure of that. They all like you and feel the same loyalty toward you as they do toward me."

"But we have to be certain this is what we want," she said as she laid her cheek against his chest. "If we do this, there'll be no way to go back to the way we live now. Everything will be different."

"Very different," he agreed as he ran his hands over her back. "God, but I want you. I need you."

Elizabeth knelt in the grass and pulled him down with her. "Beneath your gentleness there's a passion that almost frightens me."

"I'd never hurt you."

"I know that now." She touched his sun-warmed cheek, then leaned forward and kissed him.

Wonderingly he pulled the pins from her hair and put them in his shirt pocket as her hair tumbled down her back. He laid her down and spread her hair on the grass, and it caught the patches of sunlight that filtered through the tree's leaves. Slowly she began to unbutton his shirt. "Are you sure?" he asked, catching her hand. "Here? Now? In spite of Robert?"

"Yes. Here and now. I'm no longer married to Robert in my heart."

She stood and took off her clothing while he watched. It amazed her that she felt no self-consciousness with him. Clothing was an impediment to be discarded, nothing more. When she stood naked before him, he gazed at her for a long time, then drew her back down to lie on the cushion of her dress and petticoat.

He also undressed, and Elizabeth watched him eagerly. "You're so beautifully made," she whispered. "I can picture you on Mount Olympus or striding through the Coliseum."

"You constantly amaze me," he said as he lay back down beside her. "You seemed so proper when we first met. Hungry, but proper."

"This is what you get for feeding strays. Sometimes they never leave."

He kissed her long and deep. "I never want you to leave. If you did, I'd go after you."

His hands caressed her body and Elizabeth drew in her breath as he found each spot that ached for his touch. She lifted her head and ran her tongue along his shoulder. "You taste so good," she murmured. "And I love the way you smell."

He laughed and held her close. "You make me more alive than I've ever been. I watch you move and speak, and I memorize every little detail so I can torture myself later when you're not around."

"Those days are over." She ran her hands over him, enjoying the feel of his flesh against hers. "I'm going to move my things into your room before tonight. I wonder if Molly will be shocked."

"She's probably more shocked that we have separate rooms."

Elizabeth moved beneath him, and Brice matched her motions instinctively. She opened herself for him and drew him inside, gasping momentarily at the intensity of the sensation of becoming one with him. "I want you. I can't stand not being a part of you." Her smile disappeared as passion thundered through her. "Make love with me, Brice." Her voice tipped up on the end but it wasn't a question. Her need for him was too urgent.

Their eyes met as they moved together, drawing their passion from desire to mutual demand. Sweat slicked their skin and Elizabeth's breath came quick and sharp. He filled her universe and was all of life to her. She knew she was the same to him. It was as if their souls met and merged to form a new, more vibrant part of themselves.

When she could hold the ecstasy back no longer, she cried out and held to him. At the same moment, Brice arched toward her and together they soared up the summit of love.

For a long time afterward they lay still entwined. At last he said, "Why have we fought against this for so long?"

A smile curved her lips. She picked a strand of grass and used it to tickle his face. He pushed it aside and rolled her over.

"On your feet, woman."

"So soon?" she protested. She wanted to lie in the warm languor of their loving for a while before dressing.

Instead, he pulled her to her feet and led her into the creek.

"You want to go swimming?" she asked in surprise. "Now?"

"It's not deep enough to swim here. Come on."

She followed him. The water swirled cool about her ankles. They waded out to the middle where the water was waist deep on her. Brice cupped his hands and began pouring water over her, rubbing her body and washing away the bits of grass that clung to her. Her hair floated about her waist in the current like dark river weed. Elizabeth bathed him in kind.

His fingers trailed down her breasts and she caught her breath as her body leaped with remembered passion. "If you want to get any more work done today, you'd better not do that."

He laughed and stroked her again before resting his hands on her hips. "The afternoon will seem like forever, knowing you'll be waiting for me."

"I know," she whispered. "Are you in a rush to get back to the barn?"

They made love in the river as the cooling water eddied around them and time lost all meaning.

Chapter Ten

Now that the church building was almost completed, Brother Amos had turned to erecting his own house. That was how he thought of it—*his* house. Dorcas understood this and kept silent about it.

"You'd think folks would understand the Lord's house comes first," he said as he paused for a drink of cool water she had brought him from the creek. Sweat plastered his dark hair to his bony forehead below the brim of his dusty black hat. He took off the hat, wiped the sweat on the sleeve of his shirt and put the hat back on.

"I expect they're all tired of living in their wagons," Dorcas said, choosing her words carefully. She sometimes spoke when she should have kept quiet.

Brother Amos frowned at her and past her to the group of five other houses under construction. "The pews still aren't built. I'm having to carve the altar cross myself!"

"They raised the walls and put on the roof," Dorcas reminded him. As forthright as she might be in the company of women, she was almost fawning in the presence of her husband. It was how she had been raised. Her father, like Amos's, was a preacher. He and her mother had taught her that the Bible said the man was the representative of the Lord in the house and was to be treated with the same deference.

"Pah!" Amos said, and gave the working men another glare. He picked up his hammer and pointed at the board he wanted Dorcas to steady for him.

They lifted the board in place and she obediently held it while he nailed it onto the uprights that supported the roof. The other men had given Amos a hand with the part that was too tall for Dorcas to reach or too heavy for her to lift. She had been grateful, but Amos seemed to think such help—and more—was due him.

"I reckon we can sleep inside tonight," she said as he put the last board in position. She stood on tiptoe to reach it and hold it in place. "I'm looking forward to getting out of that wagon."

He didn't answer until the board was nailed. "I reckon."

She hadn't expected him to agree. "I'll start moving our belongings in."

"Your room is the one to the back," he said without looking at her.

Dorcas nodded. She had figured this out on her own. They hadn't slept in the same room for years. Not since she had proved to be barren. Amos firmly believed that intercourse was only intended to produce children and was sinful even in that context. She thought he probably had been glad to have a reason to move her to a separate room. Even in the wagon, they had slept at opposite ends, as far from each other as space allowed. Most nights he had slept beneath the wagon on the ground.

She went through the door thinking, even though it was sinful, that she was glad to have a house to call her own. It was small, the smallest of any in the settlement, but it was a castle to her. There were three rooms, or would be once the inner walls were completed. Two bedrooms and a room with a fireplace in which they could sit to read the Bible and eat. Her room was on the west side of the house so she had a view of Ella and Abner Barker's house and beyond that, Puma Creek. Amos's overlooked the church. That seemed fitting and appropriate to her.

The room was so small she would have only enough room for a narrow bed and her trunk of linens. Her other two dresses would have to hang on wall pegs along with her nightgowns and winter shawl. That was fine. She hadn't expected a large room. She was glad she had one at all. For a while Amos had considered having her sleep in the common room and using the lumber he would have saved by not making her a room to build the needed pews. The only reason he had thought better of the idea was because it would have put him at risk of walking into the common room while she was in her nightgown or worse, changing clothes. The room he had built for her would not have been quite so tiny had it not been an afterthought.

Dorcas didn't really mind. She would only be in it at night and she wouldn't have to share any of its precious space. She was a bit embarrassed at first that the other men now knew of their sleeping arrangements since they had helped put up the studs for the dividing walls, but by now she had almost convinced herself that even that was all right. She and Amos would be a standard of righteousness for all of them. Maybe some of the others would be encouraged to sleep apart once their families were complete. It certainly wouldn't hurt the Mc-Givenses to follow suit.

At once Dorcas was mortified at her inhospitable

thought. It was between Tavish McGivens and God to determine how many children he brought into the world. She dropped to her knees and prayed on the spot for forgiveness. When she felt a measure of heavenly approval, she got to her feet and went out to get the bedrolls.

"Sister Dorcas," Amos called to her, "it's about time you got supper started."

"Yes, Brother Amos," she said. It wasn't as if she didn't know that, she thought with some resentment. She had been cooking supper for him for eighteen years, nearly half her life. She knew when he would get hungry as well as he did. If she hadn't been helping him build the house, she already would have started cooking. That, too, was an uncharitable thought, but she didn't have time to pray now. Not when he had told her to start the meal.

She left the bedrolls where they were and went directly to the campfire she used for cooking. Beneath the cooking pot that was suspended over the fire pit, she saw glowing embers and knew she had again succeeded in keeping the base of the fire going throughout the day. By carefully banking the fire at night, as well, bringing it to full flame for cooking the next meal was easier than starting a new fire. It would be much easier, still, once she had a fireplace and hearth, but she managed.

She stacked dry wood beneath the pot, then stirred the embers carefully until flames broke through the ashes and began consuming the new wood. Next she started filling the pot with water she had brought up in pails from the creek. At least she had water fairly close by. Her mother had had to walk half a mile to a town well for the family's water. It had been most inconvenient but that was where the church fathers had built the parsonage and, since it had no well, there had been no other way to have water. Having helped her mother haul water for so many years gave Dorcas a real appreciation for the close proximity of Puma Creek.

By the time she had cooked a stew of venison and potato, it was growing dark. She was tired from having worked since dawn and she still had the wagon to empty and supper dishes to wash. Amos had taken his position for the meal, sitting erect on their one ladder-back chair. Dorcas sat opposite him on her low stool, made intentionally close to the ground for use in milking once they had a cow, and bowed her head for his prayer.

Amos loved to pray. He could make a prayer last almost as long as a sermon. Dorcas tried to keep her mind on what he was saying, but she was so tired that her thoughts tended to wander. That was a sin, and she wondered if she should confess it to Amos. But he would likely want to pray over that, too, and she didn't have the time.

By the time he was finished and she could eat, the sky was dark except for a faint greenish rim to the west. A half-moon was rising and promised to give some light once it was higher. She hoped that later she would be able to see well enough in that silvery light to unload the wagon. She was determined to sleep in the house that night.

Amos ate with the same dedication that he did everything else. "The Harrisons' house is almost finished. Maybe Brother Edmund will help you build the pews for the church," she said, not looking at him.

"Maybe." Amos glanced toward the Harrisons' campfire. "It's a shame Tavish McGivens doesn't have more sons old enough to help finish his house. He's having to build one the size of a barn to house his family, and two of the larger children are only girls.'' Amos shook his head as if that was the real shame.

"What about Brother Abner? He has almost finished their house.''

Amos thought for a while. "I'm not sure about the Barkers. Have you seen Charley McGivens making eyes at Darcy Barker? I believe they're getting sweet on each other.''

"Surely not. Perhaps they were only being friendly.'' Dorcas had seen the same thing but she didn't want to upset her husband.

"I hope not. As I'm the only preacher around here, they are all my flock. A good shepherd watches after his own. The moral fiber of this settlement rests on me, and I shall not shirk my duty.''

"No, no. Of course you won't, Amos.''

He shot her a piercing glance. " 'Brother' Amos,'' he corrected between bites of stew.

"I'm sorry. I meant to say Brother Amos.'' This was something he had started when they moved to separate bedrooms. He had also begun referring to her as "Sister Dorcas,'' as if by labeling each other as such they could overlook the years they had tried in vain to produce a child.

"We can't afford to be slack. The others watch us and count on us to lead them to salvation.''

She couldn't see how calling her husband by his first name when they were alone would harm anyone but she didn't argue. She never argued. There was no point in it since Amos would win eventually, and she had to give him the respect that was his right. After all, she wouldn't argue the point if she were talking to Jesus, and Amos was his representative.

"They are our children, Sister Dorcas,'' he continued.

"And I'm worried about Charley McGivens and Darcy Barker."

"I still wish we had children of our own," she said almost to herself. "I would love to have a daughter to help me about the house and a tall son that could follow in your footsteps." She looked toward the McGivenses' encampment. There was no lack of children over there.

"If God had wanted us to have children, he would have sent them to us. No, he has something else in mind for us. If we had children, we might be caught up in the sinfulness of the world. We might give them more of our attention and less to the Lord."

Dorcas wisely didn't voice her opinion on that.

"I'm done." Amos dropped his spoon into his bowl and put it on the ground. He got to his feet and said, "I'm going out to pray."

She silently finished her own bowl of stew and started washing the bowls in the cooking pot that she had re-filled with water before sitting down to eat. By now the water was hot enough to do the dishes. She washed them by the firelight and dried them with a cup towel before carrying them into the house.

Amos always went away from the wagons to pray alone at night. At first she had been awed by so much devotion. Now she sometimes wondered if he was only staying scarce so their neighbors wouldn't notice that he did none of the chores.

She went to the wagon and lit their only lamp. There had been another but it had fallen out of the wagon during the trip and been stepped on by the Barkers' oxen. She guarded the remaining one as if it were gold. Since lamp oil cost money and firewood gave light for free, she almost never used it.

After it was lit, she carried it inside and put in on the

floor so she could see to walk around in the house without running into the walls and uprights. The house was snug and dry and she almost felt like singing despite her exhaustion, just because she was inside a real house. Not many women appreciated a house as much as Dorcas.

She carried Amos's bedroll in first and spread it on the floor in his room, a room not much larger than her own. She had a feeling he would have made it even smaller if he had been physically able to live in a smaller room. That was one more good thing about Amos: he didn't expect her to be the only one who suffered in order to glorify the soul.

She smoothed her work-worn hands over the pad and blanket, pushing the wrinkles away. A rare, sweet smile touched her lips. She remembered how Amos had been when he was courting her, all knees and elbows, as her father had said. A tall, awkwardly thin boy who found life so serious and such a challenge. Dorcas, scarcely more than a girl herself, had fallen under the spell of his words more than anything else about him.

They were going to save the world, according to their youthful plans. Shoulder to shoulder they would labor for the Lord and bring wavering and fallen souls to paradise. Looking back, she wasn't sure when the dreams had died and when Amos had turned into the dour man he now was. Perhaps it had happened gradually when year after passing year proved her to be barren, a vine unable to bear fruit. A vine blasted, according to the Bible. Her barrenness was a great shame to her and a constant reprimand to him.

With a sigh, Dorcas got to her feet. Amos would be back soon and it wouldn't do for him to find her lazing about by his bed. She brought in her own bedroll and hung a quilt over the studs on the future wall to separate herself from him. It was how he would want it.

Elizabeth was waiting for Brice when he came home, her heart light and happy. She had spent the afternoon moving her things into his bedroom. She had told Molly that she was doing spring cleaning, because she didn't want their private business talked about in the settlement. Molly had accepted the excuse and had asked no questions.

She was as nervous as a bride. Her body still sang from having made love with him that morning, and she felt as if she could fly. Surely no woman had ever been happier. She loved Brice and nothing else mattered, not even the fact that Robert might still be alive. Though he hadn't said so, she thought he must love her, too.

When Brice came in, he grinned at her in a way that told her he was also remembering that morning. He kissed her forehead as he passed, sending a wave of comforting warmth all over her body. Mary Kate, too adventurous now to be content in her corner, crawled to him and he lifted her high in the air. This, Elizabeth thought, was what a family was supposed to be like.

She had cooked all his favorite dishes that night. Roast and sweet potatoes glazed with brown sugar, beans, the indispensable corn bread and an apple pie. During the meal they exchanged glances as love-filled as any verbal declaration. Although they were alone except for Mary Kate, they didn't voice their emotions. Elizabeth wasn't too sure there were words to describe the love she felt.

Brice's every move was magical to her. She loved the way his sun-browned hands cut the meat and how white his teeth were as the meat traveled to his awaiting mouth. As always he had bathed before coming into the house and his hair was still damp and clean. No matter how hard he worked, he took care to be presentable when she was near. Elizabeth appreciated this thoughtfulness.

Mary Kate seemed to know they wanted to be alone and she was determined not to miss anything, fighting sleep and bedtime until Elizabeth took her upstairs against her protests. After a few token cries, she settled down for the night and Elizabeth left the hallway and started downstairs. She found Brice on his way up.

"I've turned out the lights," he said.

"There's no reason for me to go down then."

He stopped beside her at the head of the stairs. "Are you sure you want to take this step, Elizabeth?"

"I've never been more certain in my life." She reached up and touched his face. He had even shaved at the barn. Tonight was as important to him as it was to her.

He put his arm around her and took her into his bedroom. With him beside her, the room no longer seemed so large and its masculine tones framed him beautifully. This room, more than any other in the house, suited Brice.

As if he were hearing her thoughts, he said, "You can put some feminine touches in here if you like. Maybe some lace somewhere or other."

"I like it just the way it is." She went to the wardrobe. "I put my things in this bottom drawer. It was almost empty. Your things are in this one." She indicated the upper drawer. "I hope I didn't move anything you didn't want me to touch."

He smiled. "You can touch anything of mine you please."

She felt a blush rising as she focused on a more personal interpretation of his words but it wasn't uncomfortable. With a smile she went to him and put her arms around him. "I might say the same to you." She laid her cheek against his chest. "I do have one question. I couldn't find your nightshirts, and come to think of it, I haven't washed one since I've been here."

"I don't own one. But I could learn to sleep in one if you'd like."

"No," she said with a happy sigh. "I don't see any reason for you to do that."

"We could get rid of your nightgowns, too," he suggested.

"I've never slept naked."

"You might like it."

Elizabeth laughed softly. "I might at that."

"Do you think we'll be able to get by on two or three hours of sleep for long?" he asked with a laugh. "Starting tonight, I don't plan to be getting much more sleep than that."

"I think we could learn to do without sleep altogether."

Brice tipped her face up to his and met her lips with a tender, loving kiss.

She wanted to say she loved him, but she settled for holding him tighter.

As he began unbuttoning her dress somewhat hurriedly, her fingers flew over the buttons on his shirt. She was eager to lie beside him on the large feather bed.

Elizabeth sang as she churned butter on the back porch. She had always sung as she churned, but today she had been singing through nearly every chore. She knew Molly must wonder what could be going on, but the girl hadn't asked, and Elizabeth certainly wasn't going to tell.

The night before had been perfect. Brice was a wonderful lover, sexy and attentive to her every desire. He seemed to know exactly how to touch her and when to talk to her in his low, modulated tones that were a part of his lovemaking. She had never had a man talk to her as he touched her, and the effect had been sensual in the extreme. He knew just what to say to bring her to greater passion, and he had made her body explode with ecstasy time after time.

She looked up as Maida came around the house. "Molly told me you'd be out here. Do you want company? I like to churn."

Elizabeth surrendered the chore and picked up a dress she was embroidering for Mary Kate. "It's almost made butter."

Maida fell into a rhythm of peaceful churning. "I can't wait to get a milk cow so we can have butter and milk. Edmund has started on a pen and a barn, so it won't be much longer. And chickens. I want some nice chickens." She looked out at the yard where several hens of various colors were pecking at the grass in their search for bugs. "I've always been fond of chickens."

"I'm looking for a cat," Elizabeth said. "I can't imagine anyone with a barn that is used to store feed and corn not having one. I guess Celia didn't like cats." She realized her mistake as soon as the words left her mouth.

"Who is Celia?"

Elizabeth wasn't sure how to answer. At last she said, "She was Brice's first wife. He built this house for her. She's buried over that hill in what has now become the family cemetery."

Maida almost stopped churning. "Brice was married before? You never told me that. I assumed that the two of you built this house."

Elizabeth knew she had encouraged Maida to believe that. She had all but told her as much. "I would appreciate it if you don't tell the others. He doesn't like to talk about her. She died in childbirth," she added.

"How sad! Then you and Mary Kate must be a double blessing for him." Maida looked at the house as if she were seeing it in a new light. "But he obviously loves you. I've seen the way he looks at you."

"Yes," Elizabeth said with a satisfied smile.

"Edmund said he saw Dorcas moving their things into the house last night. He said he came upon Brother Amos sitting out in the dark just looking around and not doing anything in particular. If he was my husband, preacher or no preacher, he would do more of the work around there. He had her helping him nail boards all day. Why do you suppose she puts up with him?"

"Maybe she loves him?" Elizabeth had wondered the same thing herself but wasn't one to gossip. It was none of their business if Brother Amos expected Dorcas to do a man's share of the work.

"A woman has to work hard enough as it is without having to build her own house as well." Maida frowned at the dasher as it agitated the cream in the churn.

"You helped Edmund, didn't you?"

"Yes, but he didn't tell me I had to do it. I helped so we could get out of that wagon faster."

"Maybe Dorcas felt the same. You know they were the last ones to get their house finished enough to move in."

"They could have slept in the church. Anything

would be better than that wagon. I hope I never sleep in one again for as long as I live."

"So do I." Elizabeth placed a tiny stitch of pale pink in the flower she was embroidering. "I wonder if Mary Kate will like to sew. I've always enjoyed it."

"Not me. I can do it, but I would rather do something else."

Elizabeth looked toward the barn and saw Brice walking toward them. A warmth radiating from her heart quickly filled her, and she found herself smiling for no explainable reason. He saw Maida sitting with her and his steps faltered, but he came to the porch.

"Good morning," Maida said cheerfully.

"Morning," he replied. "I see Elizabeth has you churning."

"It was her idea," Elizabeth said in her own defense. "I expected you to be working on that line cabin today." To Maida she explained, "Brice is building a little cabin on our back acres so men can more easily check on the herds during the winter. It's hard to ride all the way out there and back the same day, especially when snow is on the ground."

"Cal and Avery are out there. I thought I'd stay close to the barn today. That cow with the bad leg needed doctoring."

"How is she?" Elizabeth knew very well he had stayed close to the house because he didn't want to be far from her today.

"Fine." He grinned at her. He knew she had seen through his excuse. "How's Mary Kate today? Doing better with her teething?"

"She's fine. Babies have been teething for a long time with no ill effects." She found she couldn't suppress her smile. What would Maida think? They were grinning at each other like newlyweds. But in a sense, that was what they were.

"I guess I'll be getting back to the barn so I can rub some liniment on that cow's leg."

"I'll see you at suppertime." She continued her sewing, putting in one tiny stitch after another, yet all the time she wanted to run to him and kiss him and have him embrace her. But that wouldn't do in front of company and whatever men were working within sight of the house. She gave him a smile full of promise, however.

He interpreted it correctly because his grin broadened. He tipped his hat to Maida and went back to the barn.

Elizabeth watched him under the pretense of examining her handwork. He was as nice to see from behind as from the front.

"Why are you smiling like that? If I didn't know better, I'd say the two of you have a secret."

Elizabeth almost dropped the dress she was sewing. "A secret? Of course not. What secret could we possibly have?"

"Maybe Mary Kate is going to have a little brother or sister?"

"No, that's not it. I mean, we don't have any secret. I was just glad to see him, that's all."

Maida smiled and put her head dreamily to one side as she churned. "I hope Edmund and I are like you and Brice after we've been married for years. You two are so much in love."

"He's an easy man to love." Elizabeth's voice was gentler than she had intended. More briskly she said, "Let's have a look at your progress." She reached for the churn and lifted the lid. "I think we're there. It's starting to gather."

Elizabeth took the dasher and gently stirred in a sideways motion that clumped the butter together. She washed her hands at the pump, then lifted the lumps of butter out, let the buttermilk drain from them and put them in a bowl. She took the bowl to the pump and splashed cold water over it to firm it.

Maida handed her the salt and Elizabeth took out a portion and kneaded it into the butter. She didn't own a butter mold so she pressed half the butter into a smaller bowl until it took that shape. Then she overturned it on the butter dish and it fit the shape perfectly. Elizabeth made a design on the top of the butter with a fork and covered it to keep it fresh. She repeated the process with the rest of the butter and wrapped it in a clean cloth.

Maida walked with her toward the springhouse. "On the way out, we passed some wagons of people heading back east. It was really disheartening. They had gone farther north and west than this and had run into unfriendly Indians. One woman said the Indians raided her farm, and if she hadn't hidden in the springhouse until they were gone, she might have been killed—or worse."

"We don't have problems with Indians around here," Elizabeth reassured her. "I've only seen a few since I've lived here and they were perfectly peaceful."

"All the same, it's frightening." She shaded her eyes against the sun. "Is that Ella walking up the hill?"

Elizabeth turned to see. "Yes, I wonder what she wants. She never comes to visit unless the other women will be here as well."

Across the yard Ella saw them watching her, stopped, then turned and went back toward the settlement.

"That's odd," Maida observed. "When she saw us, she went away."

"Maybe it only seemed that way," Elizabeth said doubtfully. "Why would she do that?"

"I don't pretend to know Ella. She and Abner joined the wagon train at the last minute. She's never been very friendly."

"Oh? I didn't know that."

"There was another family with almost as many children as the McGivens. He was to be the schoolteacher. Everything was all set, but at the last minute Abner showed up and bought him out, wagon, team and all."

Elizabeth stared at Ella's back as the woman walked away. "I guess she changed her mind about coming for a visit." She shook her head. "Let's get this butter in the springhouse before it melts."

Elizabeth put the butter on the shelf above the running water where the air was coolest. "It's so difficult to keep food when it's so hot."

"I know, but I enjoy summer more than I do winter."

"It's nice finally to have someone to talk to around here," Elizabeth said with a smile. "Those first months were terribly lonely."

"Yes, but you had Brice," Maida reminded her. "And there must have been a few men in the bunkhouse to speak to in passing."

Elizabeth nodded. If she had known at the time that she wouldn't be leaving, she wouldn't have lied herself into a box with her new friends. Now there was no way to gracefully retract all she had said.

Chapter Eleven

On the first Sunday after the pews were finished, Brice handed Elizabeth into the buggy and drove her down the slope to the church. The church was smaller than any Elizabeth had ever been in, but it was too large for the tiny congregation. Even with Brice's ranch hands there, half the pews were empty. Brother Amos had counted on the settlement growing.

Molly sat with Mary Kate on the back row so she could take the baby outside if she grew restless and noisy. Knowing the length of Brother Amos's prayers, Elizabeth expected the sermon to be long in the extreme. She wasn't wrong.

Amos took the pulpit and surveyed his congregation. There were the usual number of people shuffling and coughing because they were unaccustomed to sitting indoors but they were attentive. He waited in silence until a hush came over the congregation, then shouted, "But for the grace of God, you are all going to hell!"

Elizabeth listened as patiently as possible to Brother Amos citing numerous examples of what a sinner had to look forward to in the afterlife. She glanced from side to side when she thought he wouldn't notice. The others were listening in what passed as rapt attention. Was she the only one who wasn't enthralled? Elizabeth had never liked to be shouted at in church or out of it, and was wondering if she might find some excuse to avoid attending Amos's sermons every week. In so small a congregation, every absence would be noticed.

She saw Brice cover a sigh and she had to repress her smile. He was as ready to leave the church as she was. Like Elizabeth, he believed in a gentle God who didn't harbor ill will.

Looking directly at Elizabeth, Amos shouted, "One of the sins we must guard against particularly is fornication!"

She caught her breath. Was he talking about her relationship with Brice? How could he know?

"Fornication is the devil's playground! A person who lusts, even in his own heart, is as guilty as the dirtiest sinner." He waved the worn Bible over his head. "It says so right here in black and white!" He glared from Elizabeth to Brice, then at several others in the congregation.

Her heart was still thrumming like a trip-hammer. Surely he had only looked her way by chance. She began to pay closer attention to what Amos was saying rather than to the way he was saying it. The truth was abundantly clear. No matter how much she and Brice might love each other, they weren't married. How had they been so shortsighted as to think it wouldn't matter if they lived together as man and wife?

She wanted to look at Brice to see if the sermon was stirring as much guilt in him as it was in her, but she was afraid to show discomfort by any overt movement. Not when Brother Amos's eyes were sweeping over the congregation as if he were searching for the culprits.

Elizabeth glanced at Dorcas, who was sitting on the front pew and a bit to one side. She was listening in rapt concentration, now and then nodding her head in agreement. Her thin face was pale and drawn as if she had known more hard work than laughter in her life, and it occurred to Elizabeth that she might be younger than she appeared. How had a man like Amos Sanders ever courted a girl and won her heart? It was a mystery to Elizabeth.

She heard a sigh from someone sitting behind her. Unfortunately so did Brother Amos. He whipped his head around and his dark eyes glared past Elizabeth at Charley McGivens, who was seated just behind her. Amos directed the next few accusations and threats in Charley's direction, and Elizabeth heard the boy shift repeatedly on the hard pew. In the second row, near the window, Darcy Barker was also showing signs of discomfort. Ella Barker gave her daughter a remonstrative glance and Darcy settled down.

Brice eased his leg over until it contacted Elizabeth's to subtly get her attention. She knew he was following her thoughts. Maybe he was feeling guilt of his own. She shifted so the contact was broken. Amos's eyes were too sharp to miss anything.

The sermon was over at last. The congregation stood to sing "Amazing Grace," the only hymn everyone was sure to know. Eventually there would be hymnals, but for now they would have to rely on memory, or have Amos call out the words before they were sung. Amos raised his arms in benediction as the last of the notes died away and gave the last prayer.

Elizabeth was never so glad in her life as to hear him finally say "Amen." She filed out of church with the others, not making eye contact with anyone. No one else was in the mood to stand about and chat either. There were hungry families to feed and the sermon had left everyone in a despondent mood.

"Miss Elizabeth? Can I take Mary Kate over to my house for a while?" Molly shifted the little girl to her other hip. "Mama is fixing plenty of food, and I'll see that she eats."

"All right." Elizabeth looked up at Brice. "Is it all right with you?" She was so accustomed to her household authority she sometimes forgot she wasn't really Mary Kate's mother.

"Sure." Brice reached out and tickled Mary Kate's tummy and she giggled and squirmed in Molly's arms. "Do you want me to send the buggy down so you can bring her home?"

"No, sir. I don't mind carrying her up to the house. I won't keep her too long." She hurried away with Mary Kate waving her chubby arm.

Elizabeth waved back and found she was smiling. She loved Mary Kate as much as she would a child of her own.

Amos and Dorcas stood on the small porch, shaking hands with everyone as they left church. Elizabeth didn't want to touch him but she saw no way of avoiding it. His bony hand gripped hers too tightly and she was startled. For a moment his glittering black eyes pierced into hers, then he turned to Brice and released her hand. Dorcas captured it in an almost lifeless clasp. Her fingers were rough from work but there seemed to be no strength in them. Elizabeth was glad to escape to the wagon.

As they drove up the slope, Brice said, "What did you think of the sermon?"

"It was fine," she evaded.

"No, it wasn't. I don't like having someone yell at me. Especially when I haven't done anything wrong."

"Not done something wrong?" she asked. "How can you say that? We're doing wrong by living together!" She glanced around to be sure the ranch hands weren't near enough to overhear her. "You know we aren't married! I may not even be a widow!"

"Amos doesn't know that."

"But *we* do!" She stared straight ahead between the horse's ears. "Brice, what are we going to do?"

"I, for one, am not going back to church," Brice replied. "We can't get rid of Amos, and, since there's not another church, I just won't go."

"You can't do that! Everyone will wonder. It was part of your stipulation that a church be built in the settlement. You have to attend it!"

"No, I don't."

"I'm worried about us." Elizabeth's brow puckered in her concern. "What if Brother Amos is right? What if the way we feel about each other is a deadly sin?"

"Elizabeth," he said with a short laugh, "what are you talking about? Nothing I've ever done in my life has seemed as right as what we have between us. We were meant to be together. Can't you feel that?"

"I don't know!" She gazed over the hills that sloped up from the valley. "Maybe we're wrong."

"No. We aren't wrong." A muscle tightened in his jaw. "I was afraid you would be upset when the sermon was over. I knew what you must have been thinking."

She glanced around to see that the others were still at a distance. "He looked straight at me! Brother Amos was talking to me!"

"More likely he was talking to young Charley. He was sitting right behind us and is of an age to be more interested in girls than in common sense. I noticed Darcy Barker was fidgeting uneasily, too.''

"They are children. No, Brother Amos was talking about us. I'm sure of it.'' She caught her lower lip with her teeth. "I have to move out of your room.''

"What!'' Brice turned on the buggy seat and stared at her in disbelief. "You want to do that?''

"It's not what I want.'' She felt close to tears. "I have to think of the future. If it ever becomes known we aren't married, it may be less embarrassing if I've been sleeping in my own room.''

"Elizabeth, this is ridiculous. Everybody assumes you're sleeping with me whether you are or not.'' It was a poor choice of words.

"Don't you think I know that?'' She glared at him. "I felt as if I had a scarlet A sewn on my dress! I was mortified!''

"No one but you and I know how things are between us. If you don't act guilty, no one will ever wonder.''

"How can you suggest such a thing? I can't spend the rest of my life living a lie. How could you even think that? Brice, I'm speechless.'' She crossed her arms and glared at the horse's rump.

"No, you're not, unfortunately.''

"What does that mean?''

"You're going to keep on worrying until you move back into the other room, and we'll be right back where we started.''

"I'm sorry if that will inconvenience you.'' Ice formed on her words.

"'Inconvenience' wasn't the word that sprang to mind. Hypocrisy, maybe.'' His anger was rising to match hers.

"'Hypocrisy'? You're calling me a hypocrite?'' Her

voice rose and she glanced again at the hired men. Lowering her voice she said. "You're a fine one to call me that! You're the one who tempted me!"

"What?" he burst out, not caring who might hear him. "What the hell is that supposed to mean?" They had reached the house and he reined the horse to a stop. "I tempted you? It seemed pretty mutual to me!"

Elizabeth gathered her skirts and climbed down from the buggy without waiting for him to help her. She stalked around the house.

"Where are you going?" he shouted after her.

"For a ride!" she snapped back.

She went to the feedlot, caught a horse and saddled him. Her anger was still building and she didn't dare go near Brice until it cooled. She was too likely to say things she would regret.

She mounted and kicked the horse into a gallop. The wind whipped her hair, trying to loosen it from its bun, but she didn't care. All that mattered was putting distance between Brice and herself so she could think.

Without noticing which way she was riding, she soon entered familiar territory. She reined up the hill and into the yard of the mud hut she had previously occupied. She dismounted and tied the horse to a bush before going inside.

Winter and the spring storms had taken a great toll on the place. A large part of the roof had fallen onto the place where their bed had been. A startled field mouse scuttled from the warped tabletop to a hiding place behind the battered cabinet.

Elizabeth lifted one of Robert's cotton shirts off its wall peg and the cloth frayed at her touch.

She pulled gently on the material and watched it part in a long tear, not unlike the way she felt inside. She loved Brice with all her heart, but Brother Amos's sermon had torn at her soul. Whether they wanted it to be true or not, what they were doing was wrong. Or at least it was in society's eyes, and that mattered now that the settlement was a reality. Why hadn't she considered that before she met him in the pasture not too long ago?

She went back outside and sat on the crude bench beside the house and gazed out at the familiar countryside. How often she had sat here, wishing Robert would ride into sight. How often this bench had been her resting place in a hut that was barely habitable.

Elizabeth buried her face in her hands. What must Brice think of her? Her anger had leaped out of bounds and she had said too much, too fiercely. Anger had always been her primary shortcoming. Her father had prophesied that it would lead her to grief someday. She lifted her head to look out over the land again. There was no way Brother Amos could possibly know what lay between Brice and herself. As far as he knew, they were married and the parents of Mary Kate. Even if he knew the truth, it wasn't any of his business.

Right and wrong were clearer here at the hut. Here, life was stripped to its bare essentials. This wasn't Hannibal and the settlement wasn't exactly society. For that matter, there was no proof that any of the other couples were married either. People came west for many reasons, occasionally to escape a bad marriage. Bigamy wasn't as rare out here as it was in Missouri.

Perhaps someday she would be certain Robert was dead and Brice would marry her. There would be nothing to prevent it if she were truly a widow. Not if he loved her.

She went back to the horse and mounted. For a moment she sat in the saddle, gazing at the mud hut. In a year, maybe two, it would have gone back to the earth. In time all traces of her life here would be wiped away. The bench and table would rot along with the remains of Robert's shirt, and her past would be erased.

Elizabeth turned the horse's head east and rode back to the ranch and Brice.

She found him in the library. He looked up when she came in but he didn't smile. She hadn't considered that he might still be angry with her. "Is Mary Kate still with Molly?"

"Yes. I ate the cold chicken for dinner." He stood but he didn't come toward her. "I left it out for you."

"I'm not hungry."

"Suit yourself."

"I'm sorry, Brice. I have a quick temper and I know it. I said things I shouldn't have."

"I also apologize." His tone of voice belied his words.

"I guess I'll go up and change." She searched his face for a sign that he might be softening.

He turned and sat back down at his desk and seemed to be instantly engrossed in the papers he was perusing.

Elizabeth went to the stairs and paused before going up. Something was terribly wrong. She could feel it.

As soon as she went into their bedroom and opened the wardrobe, she knew what was wrong. Brice had moved her things out. She found them in the adjoining room stacked neatly on her bed.

Angrily she went back downstairs and into the library. "You moved my things out!"

"It's what you said you wanted!" His eyes met hers, and she could see the anger in them. "Have you changed your mind again?"

"No!" She glared at him. "I haven't changed my mind!" She wheeled and stormed from the room and ran up the stairs.

Tears clouded her vision as she rushed into her room, with its clusters of roses and violets on the walls, and began putting her things into the armoire. He had moved her out of his room without even attempting to try and change her mind! She was hurt and embarrassed and wanted to run to him and make up, but she didn't allow herself to leave the room. He didn't really love her or he wouldn't have done such a thing.

She went out onto the veranda and let the warm breeze dry her tears. Below her lay the settlement, which reminded her of the sermon that had ruined her relationship with Brice. Anger at Brother Amos caused her to tremble. If she hadn't gone to his church today, she would still be happy and living in Brice's room.

But if Brice didn't love her any more than this, why did she care?

The question brought all her pain to the surface and killed her anger. How could he have made love to her with such heart-stopping tenderness and not love her? How could he have said the right words so convincingly that she altered her life for him? The answers were obvious. She loved him so much that she would have believed anything.

How brief her happiness had been! Only a few short nights and the end she had feared had come to pass. He hadn't even waited to tell her to move herself but had done it for her! Elizabeth wasn't used to a demonstration of anger like this. Her father had shouted and grabbed the razor strap when he was angry. Robert had done more or less the same. But Brice had removed her from his room. Brice hurt her more deeply than her father or Robert.

Down in the library, Brice was living in his own hell. It was as if time had turned back and he was reliving the pain of Celia's rejection all over again. He had seen the anger pale Elizabeth's face and heard her say words he had never expected to cross her lips. She wanted to move back into her solitary room. If she had ever loved him, it was over.

Brice was accustomed to rejection. He had lived with it for many years, first with his family, then with Celia. He knew the pattern. It had nearly torn him apart to take her things back into her room but he wanted to spare himself the pain of having to watch her do it. This way he at least had the appearance of bending to her wishes.

If she loved him, how could a mere sermon turn her against him? If it hadn't been for his agreement with the settlers, he would have sent Amos packing that very day. Brice knew it would cause talk, but he never intended to set foot inside the church again. Not as long as Amos was its pastor.

He could hear Elizabeth moving about upstairs. That meant she was in her bedroom putting her things away. He rubbed his eyes tiredly. It was starting again, the strained tension, the conversations that were only spoken when necessary, the coldness that killed a marriage as surely as frost could nip an early crop. He would never stop loving Elizabeth. He knew that without a shadow of a doubt. She was part of his heart and always would be. Brice didn't fall in love easily, even though it had seemed that way with Elizabeth, and he fell out of love with even more difficulty.

He dreaded it starting again. The sullen silences, the

bursts of unexpected anger and continuous complaints. Nothing could be colder than a meal with no conversation. He knew that all too well.

A lonely bed was much worse.

He stood and went out onto the porch to look down the hill at the settlement. How had his world fallen apart in such a short time? All they had done was go to church. It had to mean that Elizabeth hadn't loved him as much as he had wanted to believe. Nothing else made sense.

Two days later while Maida and Edmund Harrison were riding for pleasure and exploring the area, they discovered Elizabeth's mud hut. They hadn't expected to find evidence of anyone ever having lived there. Maida had seen it first. "Look over there. Is that a house?"

On inspection, they had found it to be deserted but knew someone had lived there in the recent past. Maida held up the shirt and said, "Who could have lived here? I wonder where they went." She held it out to judge the size. "He must be about your size. Look, there was a woman here, too." She went to the shelf and picked up a hair comb. "I've seen one like this before." The memory of where she'd seen it, however, eluded her.

Edmund looked at it with little interest. "It looks like the ones Elizabeth wears. Can you imagine anyone living in this place? It makes our wagon look good. Admit it, now."

"I have to admit that this is worse than any wagon. It *does* look like Elizabeth's comb. Why would it be here?"

"I don't know. Maybe they lived here while they were building the house."

"That wouldn't make any sense. It's too far away. Besides, I don't think we're still on the ranch. Elizabeth told me once that the settlement is on the edge of it." She turned the comb over and inspected it more closely. Elizabeth wore black combs because they were the same color as her hair and therefore less noticeable, just as Maida wore amber ones in her red hair. Of course a lot of women had black hair, but where had this woman gone? "I can't imagine Elizabeth and Brice living in a place like this."

"Neither can I, but I guess someone did, or it wouldn't be here. They were the only ones around."

"No, wait. Elizabeth has said that the house was built before she and Brice married. That he had a first wife who died."

"There you have it. She must have left that comb here."

Maida shook her head. "Brice wouldn't be any more likely to live in a mud hut with his first wife than with Elizabeth. Especially not one that isn't even on his own land. That makes no sense."

"It doesn't matter. Whoever lived here is gone now."

"I suppose." She looked at the fallen roof, the uneven dirt floor. Even in the summer heat it felt damp and smelled like a plowed field. "I would hate to live here."

"Me, too." Edmund put his arm across her shoulders. "When the times are rough, let's think about this place and remember that we have it better than these people."

Maida put the comb into her pocket. "Let's ride some more. We'll have to go back soon." She was glad to leave, but couldn't resist a glance back at the hut before it was out of sight. The comb in her pocket certainly looked like the ones Elizabeth wore almost every day.

* * *

"I put it straight to Charley McGivens and Darcy Barker last Sunday," Amos said to Dorcas as he prepared to write his next sermon. "I wish you could have seen their faces. They knew I was talking to them. I'm telling you, they are fornicating as sure as they're breathing."

"I'm not so sure," Dorcas said as she folded the shirt she had just ironed. "Ella Barker is real careful with that girl, and I know Abner is strict. They don't have much to do with any of us."

"That don't matter. I can smell a sinner a mile off." Amos looked intently out the window toward the Barker house that stood at an angle from his front porch. "My father could, too. I've heard him say it many a time."

"So have I." Dorcas unrolled her Sunday dress, sprinkled it again and started pressing it on the ironing board that once had been a side plank on their wagon. Dorcas had covered the board with the remains of an old quilt. She was good at making do.

"Sometimes I think of the huge chore I've been given and it's all I can do to not get bigheaded."

She glanced at him. He seldom let down his guard enough to admit to anything as base as pride. "What chore would that be, Brother Amos?"

"Why, the salvation of all these souls, of course. I'm the only spiritual guide these people have. It's entirely up to me to get them into heaven." His eyes were bright with eagerness, and for a minute he looked like the boy who had courted her.

"You can do it if anyone can. I've got great confidence in you." She smiled and nodded to add impact to her words. "You're the best man for the job."

"Now don't go helping my head to swell." But he didn't sound all that displeased.

"It's a place for us to get a new start as well," she

added hopefully. "That's something that keeps coming to me. It's a new start. I wonder if it's not a heaven-sent message."

She had gone too far. Amos was frowning. "If God is sending anybody messages, it makes more sense that he would talk to me. After all, woman caused man to lose out on the Garden of Eden."

"You're right, of course, Brother Amos. I was talking too idly."

He nodded, his brief excitement gone. "I led you astray, talking about my own pride. It's all my fault."

"No, no. You didn't cause me to err. I did it on my own." Sometimes it was hard to tell what she could say to him and what was best left in her own mind.

He grew quiet as he pondered. She knew it was in earnest that he talked about spiritual matters. Amos wasn't a man to be light about any subject, but when it came to religion, he didn't allow anyone, even himself, any latitude. He was convinced, as was his father before him, that it was no small thing to be the shepherd of a congregation of sinners.

"Brother Amos, did you ever consider what you would have been if you hadn't received a calling to preach?" she asked as she traded the cooling iron for a hotter one. The fire made the house almost unbearably hot but he didn't like for her to iron outside where everyone could see her pressing their clothes and turning them every which way.

He was quiet for so long that she thought she had made another major mistake. "I reckon I would have been a farmer. I used to enjoy planting seeds and watching them grow when I was a boy. I used to think I might own a small farm some day."

Dorcas smiled. "I'd have been a good farmer's wife."

"You're a good preacher's wife, too."

She looked up at him, startled. "Why, thank you, Amos."

"Brother Amos," he corrected automatically.

"I'm sorry. Brother Amos." But all the same, she felt a warm glow inside. His compliments were rare, and she would treasure this one for a long time to come. The house didn't seem quite so miserably hot now and she hummed a hymn as she pressed the wrinkles from her best dress.

Chapter Twelve

Brice hated the silence. He couldn't bear to be around Elizabeth and not be able to speak to her or hold her in his arms. If he hadn't loved her so much, he would have ignored her wishes to live apart, swept her off to the bedroom and made love to her until she forgave him. But he did love her, and she apparently didn't return that love.

"I'm going to ride into town today," he said to break the silence.

She glanced at him as she gave Mary Kate a piece of fried bacon. "All right," she said calmly, then looked away.

He finished eating breakfast, but only because he needed to fuel his body. He hadn't tasted any of it. Elizabeth wasn't even pretending to eat. She kept her full attention on the baby as if Brice were not even in the room.

He stood and left the table without a word. He was so determined not to show his heartache, he didn't notice the telltale tremble of Elizabeth's hand as she fed scrambled eggs to Mary Kate. Her expressionless face was all he noticed.

He cut several slabs of roast from what had been left from the night before and a wedge of crusty bread. After wrapping it all in a clean cloth and knotting the corners to make a bag, he went out to the barn. Within a few minutes he was riding past the settlement and on his way to Glory.

The trip was lonely. Now that the settlers were here, the route to town was marked by the wheels of their wagons and animals. Some day he thought it might be a real road. The frontier was changing, and in a way that was as sad as having Elizabeth stay in her own room all night. Brice wasn't fond of change for the most part. It was one reason he had settled so far from a town. If only, he thought bitterly, he hadn't been so foolish as to bring a settlement to his very doorstep! Then Elizabeth wouldn't have had people about to make her feel ashamed and Brother Amos wouldn't have been there to deliver that cursed sermon.

Elizabeth gave Maida a cup of black coffee and one of the sweet rolls she had just baked. Maida bit into the bread and sighed. "I have to stop eating so much or I'm going to be as big as the side of a barn." She cheerfully ate another bite. "You sure are a good cook."

"Thank you." Elizabeth sat opposite the woman on the porch and sipped her own coffee. It was too hot to be drinking coffee but she was so tired from tossing and turning all night that she needed it to stay awake.

"I almost forgot," Maida said. She put the coffee and roll on the nearby table and reached into her pocket. "I came up here to give you this." She held out a comb.

"It's my comb." Elizabeth automatically touched her hair but found her hair comb was still in place. "Did I drop one at your house?"

"No, I found it in the most unlikely place. It is yours then?"

"Yes. I have several like this. It's not likely someone else has any like them. I brought them out from Hannibal."

"That's what I thought. I knew it was yours the moment I saw it. Edmund said I was wrong, but what do men know about combs?"

"Where did you find it?" Elizabeth turned the comb over in her fingers. It looked as if it had been out in the weather.

"It was in a mud hut back in the hills." Maida was watching her closely. "What were you doing out there? I can't imagine either you or Brice living in that place."

"A mud hut?" Elizabeth's fingers went cold and she found herself stammering. "No, I've…I've never lived in a mud hut." Her throat constricted as if her body intended to prevent her from telling any more lies since her mind was apparently incapable of stopping her. "Brice had built this house before I came here. Remember?"

"Well, that's what I thought you had said. You know what I think? I'll bet it was that hired woman you mentioned once. Consuela, was that her name? I'll bet she took it and left it out there."

"No. I mean, why would she? As I understand it, she lived in the attic room here in the house. She would have no reason to do that."

"What do you mean, 'as you understand it'? You must know where she slept." Maida gave her a puzzled look. "I heard Lucky tell Edmund she has only been gone since February. You were here long before that."

Perspiration popped out on her brow. "Yes. That is, I do know Consuela lived in the upstairs room. It was

furnished especially for her. I'm sure she lived there."
Elizabeth hated lying, but for the first time wished she
was better at it.

"Is something bothering you?" Maida leaned forward
earnestly. "Did I upset you over suggesting your maid
stole your comb?"

"No, not at all. Would you like more coffee?"

"I haven't finished this yet." She took another swallow. "How old is Mary Kate now? She's growing so
fast."

Elizabeth looked over the lawn where Molly was
playing with the child under the shade of one of the
cottonwoods. "She will have her first birthday this coming winter. It doesn't seem possible that she's grown so
fast." This was true. It was hard to believe the months
had passed so quickly since she came here. On the other
hand, so much had happened, a year might as well have
gone by.

"I'm making her a doll." Maida smiled at the thought
of how pleased the child would be. "It's like one my
grandmother made for me when I was little. I've used a
corncob for the face and I'm sewing a dress out of one
of those really pretty feed sacks."

"She'll love it. She has a doll that she sleeps with
every night. She's old enough to care about things like
that." She watched Mary Kate crawl after the tasseled
grass Molly was dangling in front of her. "She will be
walking soon."

"I wish we had a baby. I'm scared at times it will
never happen. We've been married for months!"

"You're still newlyweds. The babies will come soon
enough."

"How long were you and Brice married before you
found out you were going to have Mary Kate?"

"Is that someone calling me?" Elizabeth stood and looked toward the barn. "I thought I heard Avery call my name."

"I didn't hear anything."

"He's little more than a boy, you know. I feel almost like his mother, especially since he had scarlet fever and almost died. You've never seen anyone so sick!" As she had hoped, Maida took up the new stream of conversation.

"I'm afraid of fevers. One of my brothers went to New Orleans several years ago and the whole city was down with yellow jack. He was plenty glad to get out of there, I can tell you. That's the thing about yellow fever. He said it's so bad that you catch it if someone just looks at you."

"My father believes the same thing. Thank goodness the two of us had both had scarlet fever already. She wasn't as sick as Avery, but we were worried to distraction."

"I guess so! And you the only woman around here at the time. At least now you have women nearby to help you in times of sickness."

"Brice helped me. He stayed at the house all day every day until she was out of danger."

"You're so lucky to have a man like him."

"Yes." Elizabeth dropped the comb in her pocket. "I know."

"I have to be getting back. It seems positively lazy for me to sit up here talking when I have so much work to do at home. And I know I'm keeping you from yours."

"This is ironing day. I don't mind being distracted." Elizabeth wrinkled her nose. "The kitchen is too hot as it is."

"I know. But we have to do it." Maida cheerfully skipped down the steps and detoured so she could speak to Molly and Mary Kate before heading around the house.

Elizabeth went down to the springhouse to get the clothes to be ironed. She had sprinkled the clean clothes the night before and left them in the springhouse to keep them cool overnight so they would be easier to iron. Her irons were already lined up on the hearth where she had left them when Maida came to the house. They were heated and ready to use.

A sound toward the front of the house drew Elizabeth's attention. It couldn't be Brice home from Glory so soon, and Molly was outside with the baby. Moving silently, Elizabeth went to investigate.

Ella Barker was on the stairway. When she saw Elizabeth she jumped and turned pale.

"What are you doing?" Elizabeth demanded. "Why are you in my house?"

"I...came for a visit. I knocked on the door, and I thought you called out for me to come in."

"Why were you going upstairs?" Elizabeth knew the woman was frightened and lying.

"It sounded like you were up there. I was going to save you a trip downstairs. I was just being neighborly."

Elizabeth stared at her and she tried to think of any reason Ella would want to slip into her house and go upstairs. Had she intended to steal something? Why would Ella think she could get away with it?

"I reckon I'll be going," Ella said as she edged down the stairs and to the front door.

"You found me, what did you come to tell me?" Elizabeth knew something was very wrong here.

"Nothing was on my mind. I saw Mr. Graham riding toward town and just thought you might be lonely."

"Brice is rarely at the house during the day. I have no particular reason to be lonely."

"You're right, of course. Well, I'll be going." Ella all but ran out the door and across the yard.

Elizabeth watched her leave. Ella was obviously lying. She went upstairs and looked around, but saw nothing missing or anything that would tempt a thief in broad daylight. She went back to the front door and closed it in spite of the heat. She felt more secure when the bolt slid into place. She was still puzzled but there was no explanation for Ella's odd behavior.

The next day was even hotter. By late afternoon, she was so hot and sticky that her skin itched. Since Molly was busy outside with the baby, leaving Elizabeth alone in the house, she decided to take a bath.

She hauled out the copper tub and put it in the center of the kitchen floor, then began the laborious task of filling it.

Once the tub was ready, she laid a clean dress and fresh underclothes on the nearby bench and stripped off the clothing she was wearing. Even the hot breeze passing through the kitchen felt cool without all the layers of clothing against her skin. Wasting not a moment, she stepped into the cool water and sat down.

Elizabeth closed her eyes and leaned back against the tub. Nothing felt better than a cool bath on a hot day. Already she could feel her muscles relaxing. Slipping lower in the tub, she wet her hair and rubbed soap into it. Elizabeth washed her hair frequently, despite her mother's warnings against it, and had suffered no ill effects. Clean hair was as important to her as a clean body. She was teaching Mary Kate to follow in her footsteps.

Maybe someday, she thought, Brice would make a bathing room out of one of the smaller rooms upstairs. Elizabeth had heard of them before she came west and, while she had never seen one, she was all for the idea.

She heard a sound from the front room and decided Molly must be bringing Mary Kate inside. She stood and poured a bucket of clean water over her head to rinse away the soap. So much for her bath, but at least she was cooler and cleaner. "I'm in the kitchen," she called out as she wrapped a linen towel around her. "Molly? Did you hear—" She turned and found Brice staring at her.

Instantly she was embarrassed. The fact that they had seen each other naked before no longer mattered, not since he had moved her out of his room. She clutched the concealing towel. "I didn't know it was you."

"I'm sorry." He turned away, but with obvious reluctance. "I wouldn't have walked in on you if I had known you were bathing."

"I should have waited until night, but it was so hot and I had no idea you'd be back so early." Her voice was stiff with her embarrassment.

"I got something for Mary Kate while I was in Glory." His voice sounded tight as if he were upset over discovering her naked in his kitchen. "It's a stuffed bear."

"She will love it." She hastily dried herself and reached for her chemise. Keeping her eye on Brice's back, she dropped the towel and pulled the light garment over her head. Then she stepped into white cotton drawers and tied the ribbon at the waist. She hadn't worn a corset since leaving Hannibal. Quickly she tied the pink ribbon that kept her chemise from falling off her shoulders.

Brice glanced back at her. Elizabeth's fingers faltered. Their eyes met and for a long time neither spoke.

"You're a beautiful woman, Elizabeth," he said softly. "I think you may well be the most beautiful woman I've ever seen."

"Thank you." It seemed strange, standing in the kitchen in her underwear and hearing Brice say she was beautiful.

"And you're certainly clean. No one could ever accuse you of not being that."

"No. No one ever has." What was he getting at? Was he trying to smooth matters between them?

"Your hair is dripping."

She automatically gathered it up, not noticing that the water had rendered her chemise almost transparent. Quickly she coiled her hair into a bun and shoved the pins into it, then pulled on her fresh dress. "I'll start your supper."

He turned away again as she buttoned her dress and tried to smooth the skirt into place. She hadn't dried completely and the fabric tended to stick to her. Also her wet hair was heavy. She could feel drips of water running down the back of her neck but at least she was properly clothed again.

Brice glanced back and saw she was dressed. Without asking if she wanted help, he picked up the heavy tub of water, carried it out the door and dumped it off the porch. Elizabeth heard her chickens squawk as they ran to examine the wet spot and scratch for food. He wiped the tub dry and hung it back on its peg. "I'm going down to the barn."

"All right." She wanted to bridge the painful rift between them, but wasn't sure how to go about doing it. Without another word, Brice left the kitchen.

She went out onto the porch and got the mop and wet it using the porch pump. Water splashed onto the yard and again the chickens made a dash to see what it was. Nothing was more curious than a chicken, she thought.

Back inside, she mopped the kitchen floor to clean up the puddles she had made with her bath. Then she paused and looked around her. She loved this house. She enjoyed keeping it clean and running smoothly, and she was skilled at it. Brice would have to look long and hard to find someone better than she was at the job. Maybe he would let her stay even if he had moved her out of his room.

There was no guarantee. She hadn't been all that sure he wouldn't hire a woman to replace her while he was in Glory and return to her with word that she had to leave. After all, she was back to the role of housekeeper and nanny.

What on earth would she do if he told her to leave?

Elizabeth sat on the bench and leaned the mop against the wall beside her. If he still cared for her, would he have turned his back while she was wrapped in nothing but a cloth? Wouldn't a man have reacted differently if he still wanted her? In her experience, a man would have done anything but look away whether he wanted her or not. And if he didn't care for her, why would he say she was beautiful? Why didn't Brice ever react the way she expected him to?

Brice was at the barn, stripped to the waist and pumping water over his head and torso. Seeing Elizabeth all but nude had almost been the death of his resolve to follow her wishes and stay away from her. If he had known she bathed at this time of day, he would never have invaded her privacy like that.

He couldn't wash away the image of her standing under that stream of water as she rinsed the soap from her body. He had stared at her for several seconds before she became aware he was there. Her skin was pearl-white and softer than any satin. When it was wet, her hair was pure black and slicked over her body like seal's fur. He might never forget the sight of the water, touched with sunlight streaming through the window, running down the slender curve of her waist and hanging in teasing drips from her nipples.

When she bent to put the bucket on the floor, her hips had gleamed in the sunlight, and as she raised her arms to smooth the water from her hair, she could have been mistaken for a nymph from some fairy tale. She was no less enchanting.

He had somehow managed to turn his back and give her the privacy any woman would desire, but it hadn't been easy. Nor did he feel particularly gentlemanly since he had had a clear reflection of her in the glass doors of the china cupboard. No gentleman would have watched her dress, but he couldn't help himself.

Brice had never wanted any woman as much as he wanted Elizabeth. He was having to sluice the cooling water over him to keep from going back to the house and trying to change her mind about not wanting him.

"Drowning yourself?"

He looked up to see Cal watching him. "I'm considering it."

"Cow pond's quicker."

Brice stopped pumping water and straightened. "Have you ever been married, Cal?"

"Nope." He seemed to find the idea amusing.

"Women can put you in a living hell."

"Some can."

"I purely don't understand them." Brice shook the water from his hair and ran his fingers through it. "You'd think they would follow some line of logic. That a man could eventually learn it, like you can learn a foreign language. But no. They keep changing the rules."

"Yep."

"Now you take Celia. I learned the best way to live with her was to pretend we were strangers. That was the only way to keep the peace, and even that didn't always work. But with Elizabeth, that's not possible." He glanced around to be sure they wouldn't be overheard. "I know I can talk to you because you never talk enough to tell anybody anything."

Cal nodded and leaned back against the stall.

"I'm in love with her. I've tried not to be and it just makes me love her more. I thought she was falling in love with me. But then we went to church last Sunday and Amos Sanders preached a sermon about hellfire and damnation and she got mad at me. Tore into me like a wet hen on the way home!"

Cal nodded again but kept his opinion on that subject to himself.

"The upshot is that I had to move her out of my room and back into the one Celia used!"

Cal got a perplexed look on his face. "Why would you do a thing like that?"

"It's what she wanted. She must have. She never said anything about not wanting to move back. Since then she hasn't said much of anything at all."

"Damn fool thing to do. Should've given her time to cool off, gone on with your living."

"That's why you're still single, Cal," Brice said as he shook his head. "You don't understand women any better than I do."

Cal shrugged and went back to work.

Chapter Thirteen

"**L**ook what I made for you, Mary Kate," Maida Harrison said as she handed the little girl the doll she had
made.

Mary Kate crawled over to her and pulled up on her
skirt. She grabbed the doll enthusiastically, then dropped
to the floor and started examining it minutely.

"Say thank-you," Elizabeth prompted.

"It won't be long before she can talk," Maida said
as she watched the child. "She's going to be a heart-
breaker when she gets older. I think she's the prettiest
child I've ever seen."

"I think she looks like Brice," Elizabeth commented
as she smiled at her foster daughter.

"I don't know," Maida said loyally. "I think I see a
bit of you in her eyes."

Elizabeth laughed. "My eyes are gray, not blue."

"Brice's are brown, aren't they? She certainly didn't
take them from him." Maida bent and touched Mary
Kate's blond curls. "She has hair like an angel. Where
did she come by such beautiful hair?"

"There are blondes in her family." Elizabeth smiled
at her friend. "She certainly likes that doll. It was kind

of you to make it for her. I've started piecing a quilt for her bed. It won't be long before she won't be able to sleep in the small one anymore, and she will need a new cover.''

''That reminds me. Is there anything I can do to help you get ready for the quilting bee tomorrow?''

''No, Harriet has already brought the quilt top up and I've strung it on the frame.''

Maida shook her head. ''I don't know how they all sleep in that one house. There seem to be children running everywhere. And there were originally two more. She told me they lost two boys in a drowning accident just before they decided to come west. Can you imagine anything so terrible? They were between Brian and Anna in age. That's why she has a gap in the family there.''

''That's so sad! I had no idea.''

''When she told me, she cried. I think that's why this coming baby is so precious to her. If it's a boy she's going to name it after the two they lost.''

''That's sad, too. I think I would want to find an entirely new name.''

''So would I.'' Maida looked thoughtful. ''I may have news to tell at the quilting. I can't decide if I should wait until I'm positive or not. Well, I'm almost positive.'' She laughed and said, ''Edmund and I are going to have a baby!''

''Are you! That's wonderful news.'' Elizabeth knew how much Maida wanted a family.

''Tell me, Elizabeth, when you were expecting Mary Kate, did you feel queasy every morning or did it sometimes happen in the evening? Because I feel sick when I'm making supper, not breakfast.''

Elizabeth thought back to her cousins' numerous pregnancies. "It can happen at any time of the day, but I think it always tends to happen at about the same hour."

"That's exactly what I thought! When the 'stranger' didn't pay me a visit last month, I started to wonder." She clapped her hands like an excited child. "I didn't get a visit this month either!"

Elizabeth laughed along with her. "I'm so happy for you!"

"The only thing that would make me happier, would be if you were expecting now, too. We could go through it together and our babies might be best friends. Or if one is a boy and the other a girl, they might eventually marry. Wouldn't that be something?"

"Maida, that baby isn't even here yet and you're marrying him off?" Elizabeth shook her head in amusement.

"Do you think it'll be a boy? Edmund wants a boy really bad. He would grow to be such a help around the place. Edmund has sent word around to ask who owns the land right across the creek from our cabin. If he can, he wants to buy several acres and grow crops to sell."

"It should be good land for it. This whole valley is as fertile as any land I've ever seen. I don't know who owns it, but Brice may. It could be that nobody has claimed it at all."

"That's what we're hoping. We don't have much money, you know." Maida touched her middle. "What does it feel like to have a baby inside you? What does it feel like when it kicks?"

"You'll see soon enough." Elizabeth stood. "Would you like some lemonade? Lucky went into Glory yesterday and brought me some fresh lemons."

"I'd love some. I do love lemonade. Maybe if I drink enough, this baby will have yellow curls like Mary Kate."

"Maybe so." Elizabeth wondered how she was going to be able to answer all the questions Maida would be sure to ask in the coming months. She had stayed with numerous cousins after their babies arrived, but almost none of them prior to the event. Elizabeth knew next to nothing about pregnancy. As an unmarried girl, it hadn't been proper for the married women to tell her about such things as what happened between a man and a woman, or about pregnancy and birthings.

"Maybe you could even be my midwife!" Maida exclaimed as the idea struck her. "I'd want you to be there anyway and I would certainly trust you."

"I don't know," Elizabeth evaded. "I think it would be better to ask Harriet. She has far more experience than I do. I'll hold your hand, but she would be better to serve as your midwife."

Maida looked slightly disappointed, but her mood was too buoyant to fall. "I'll think about that later. I have plenty of time."

"I'll start sewing baby clothes for you. A baby needs more things than you could ever imagine." She picked up Mary Kate off the floor and put her comfortably on her hip.

Together they went into the kitchen to make lemonade.

After supper Brice and Elizabeth took Mary Kate into the back parlor to play before bedtime.

"She's carried the doll and bear all day. She will wear them out at this rate." Elizabeth watched the child hug the bear and doll in one arm while she tried to stack her blocks with the other hand.

"She's growing too fast."

Elizabeth watched Mary Kate. "What are we going

to tell her when she gets old enough to ask questions? I had a hard time answering Maida today. She and Edmund are going to have a baby, and she had more questions than I had answers.''

"Maybe we made a mistake in not setting everyone straight at the beginning. At the time, it seemed like the thing to do.''

"It's too late to change that now. Everyone believes we're married and that she's our child.''

"We could tell her that she is. She would never know. You're all the mother she's ever had.'' Was he suggesting that he wanted her to stay indefinitely? She was afraid to ask.

"No. We can't do that. She deserves to know who she really is.'' If Brice had misstated his intention, this would give him the chance to correct it.

"She's Mary Kate Graham. That's all that's important. She has a mother and father to love her. There are a lot of children in the world who don't have that much. I don't see how her knowing Celia's name will help her any. It would just make her curious about her relatives in Texas. I want her to know as little about them as possible.''

"I don't think that that's possible. They came once, they could come again. Celia's family has a claim to Mary Kate, too. Have they written lately?''

"No, and that has me puzzled. I know the Lannigans far too well to believe they gave up on taking Mary Kate just because I said no. Lorna Lannigan never lets go once she has her teeth set into a matter.''

"You think they will be back?'' Elizabeth remembered all too well how uncomfortable the visit had been.

"At the time I was amazed they had come so far,

stayed one night and left again," Brice said. "I never heard of anyone coming so far and doing that."

"Neither have I."

"And they were in a buggy. No one would think of driving a buggy all the way from Texas."

"I assumed they rented it from someone in Glory."

"Apparently they did, but why? It makes no sense."

"I know." These questions had bothered Elizabeth, too, but she wasn't sure how far their ranch was from the Lannigans' home in Texas, or whether the Lannigans knew other settlers in the area. "I suppose we'll never know the answer to those questions."

Elizabeth watched the little girl at play. "I can't understand them not writing to ask if she's doing all right."

"They have a closed-rank sort of family. I was never allowed in even before I moved out here. Maybe if we had stayed in Texas and I had gone to work in the family store, I would have been accepted. But I would have died a little every day, working in a store and having my father-in-law for a boss."

"I can't imagine you in a store."

He smiled but it was touched with sadness. "I had a lot of grand hopes. Not all of them are working out."

She wondered if he was referring to Celia. Certainly his ranch was prosperous. "There's talk in the settlement of making you mayor someday."

He looked at her in surprise. "Mayor? Of a settlement?"

"Tavish told Harriet that he figures it may be a real town some day and he wants to name it Grahamville."

"That's more than a mouthful." All the same, he looked flattered.

"I think you would be a wonderful mayor."

"I think the settlement is just fine the way it is."

"Edmund wants to buy the land across the creek from their house. Maybe the town will expand in that direction."

"That's the only way for it to go. I gave a parcel of land to them, but I'm not giving up any more. They're close enough to the house as it is."

"Do you regret it?"

"I regret Brother Amos being among them." He looked at her. "He's caused more trouble with one sermon than an army of men with guns!"

"I guess the others are used to hearing him. I'm sure he was preaching at every opportunity in the wagon train."

"More than likely."

"Maida didn't seem to think there was anything out of the way in that sermon." She was on thin ice with this conversation. She knew she had done wrong to get angry at Brice when she was as guilty as he was, but he had been the one to move her out of his room and that still hurt every time she thought about it.

"Maida and Edmund are properly married. Of course she wouldn't have taken exception to it."

The clock on the mantel chimed the hour. "I guess I should take Mary Kate upstairs." She was reluctant even though it was past the child's bedtime. These days she and Brice rarely talked, and she hated to end it.

"Yes, it's long past when she should be in bed." He sounded tired as he said the words, as if he were reluctant, too. Or maybe he was only thinking that Mary Kate would be cross the next day if she missed too much sleep.

Elizabeth went to the girl and picked her up. "Give Papa a kiss," she said as she took her to Brice.

Mary Kate threw her pudgy arms around Brice's neck

in a bear hug. She babbled her own language into his ear and put a wet kiss on his cheek. When Elizabeth took her back, Mary Kate gave her a kiss, too, and giggled happily. She was an unusually happy child and Elizabeth couldn't help laughing along with her. "Come on, buttercup, it's past your bedtime."

She took Mary Kate to the nursery and got her ready for bed. Mary Kate was agreeable and yawned several times, but she firmly clasped the doll, the bear and one block, and refused to put them down. Elizabeth tucked them all in bed with her and blew out the lamp. "Good night, Mary Kate." She watched for a few moments as the child played quietly with the toys, arranging them so they, too, were covered and in a row beside her.

Elizabeth left the door ajar and went to her room. There was no point in going back downstairs. By now Brice would be in the library and deep in paperwork over a proposed sale of one of the herds. He wouldn't want to resume their conversation.

Instead she went out onto the veranda. The air was cooler now that the sun was down but her dress's long sleeves and close-fitting bodice were still too warm for comfort. In the concealing darkness, she opened the buttons down to the lace of her chemise and let the sweetly scented night air touch her skin.

During the time she had lived in the Territory she had known more highs and lows of emotion than she would have thought possible. Never had she been so happy or so sad, never had she known she could love so deeply, or be so heartbroken when it wasn't returned.

She leaned on the railing and looked out at the stars. She remembered the night Brice had talked about the stars and all the other unanswerable questions of the universe and of life. Until that night, Elizabeth hadn't known men had such thoughts. No man she had known prior to Brice had, or if he had, he certainly hadn't expressed them to her.

That was one of the things that made her love him. He questioned everything and had as much curiosity as she did. Brice felt finer emotions and wasn't afraid to admit it. Once when he was playing with Mary Kate, Elizabeth had been certain she saw tears of tenderness well up in his eyes. Yet she had no doubt that Brice would fight to the death to protect what was his. Along with the tenderness, there was an untamed edge that fascinated her equally as much.

His lovemaking was gentle but it was equally passionate, too. When he held her, she could feel primitive emotions crying to be unleashed. His sheer physical strength made his gentleness more poignant.

It wasn't safe to think about their lovemaking. She was too tempted to go to him.

Elizabeth went back into her room and pulled the double doors closed. If she was lucky, sleep would block out her yearnings for Brice. All too often, however, her dreams were such that she woke aching for his embrace.

Brice wasn't in the library. He had come upstairs soon after she had. Because the moonlight was bright, he hadn't bothered to light his bedroom lamp. When she had stepped out onto the veranda, he had seen her but she couldn't see him.

He had watched as she loosened the buttons that held her dress close to her neck. The night air was still warm as the earth was slow to release the heat it had stored up during the day, and she looked as if she was searching for relief. He had wanted to go to her but held himself in check. There were so few chances for him to look at her. He drank in the sight of her standing slender against the night sky. She was illuminated from behind by the lamplight from her room so he could see her clearly.

Her hair, as dark as the night itself, was still in its neat bun, but in his imagination it was free and flowing down to her hips. He could still remember the smell of it when he had held her, soft and sweet, as if she washed it in flower petals. Her skin had the same delicate scent. He wished he could bury his face in her hair again and feel the magic of her naked flesh pressed against his.

After several minutes, she went back inside and he heard her close the veranda door. A few moments later, he went out to stand where she had stood. Even though the sky was brilliant with moonlight, he could still see the stars beyond. The night was like velvet. The breeze carried the scent of prairie grass as well as that of the four-o'clock flowers Elizabeth had planted around the porch.

He smiled when he thought of the flowers. He had brought her the seeds almost on a whim. There weren't many flower seeds in Glory's limited stock. Most of the seeds were for plants that would feed man or beast. She had cherished the flower seeds as if they were diamonds. After planting them, she had hauled water out to nurture them into life, and when the first shoots came up, she had been jubilant. He took so naturally to prairie life that he sometimes forgot that a woman liked pretty things like flowers. Now the flowers bloomed every evening from about four o'clock until dawn in vivid clusters of bright pink, white and yellow, and their scent was a joy.

He was pretty sure the four-o'clocks were the basis for the scented soap and hand lotion Elizabeth made. Nothing else around the ranch smelled that sweet.

He wondered if roses would bloom here and how he

could get some cuttings for her. He figured all women loved roses. His own mother had kept several rose beds and had used the petals to scent everything from pot-pourri to sugar to lotions. As much as Elizabeth liked the lowly four-o'clocks, she would certainly love a rose-bush or two. And roses wouldn't hide their petals until evening the way the four-o'clocks did.

He turned and saw her moving about in her room. Through the lace curtains on her door and illuminated by the soft lamplight, she appeared to be floating around the pink and white room in a golden nimbus. She lifted her arms and when she removed the pins from her bun, her hair billowed in dark waves down her back to well below her waist. Brice felt his pulse quicken.

As she unbuttoned her dress and started to step out of it, he hastily turned and went back to his room. Sitting amid the darkness of his room, he could see in his mind's eye everything that was going on in the adjacent room. The few nights they had been together he had watched her carefully and memorized every movement she made. He knew just how her hair wrapped around her shoulders as she brushed it and how her chemise sometimes slipped, exposing the soft skin of her shoulders and the rounded curves of her breasts.

Brice closed his eyes and rocked forward, cupping his face in his hands. How much longer could he stand to live in such torment, knowing the woman he loved was separated from him by only a thin partition? That a door led conveniently from his room to hers. When he had installed the door, he had thought only of creating a path for cooling breezes. The door had come to symbolize the barrier that separated him from everything he wanted and couldn't have.

He undressed in the dark, and although it impeded air

flow through his room to do so, he left the hall door closed. If Elizabeth had reason to get up during the night, he didn't want his nakedness to dismay her if she should pass by and glance in. He opened the doors that led to the veranda and got into bed.

He could hear her moving about in the next room. What was she doing in there? Surely she wasn't cleaning at this time of night. Did she read or sew when he wasn't with her? The yellow light from her doors and windows splashed onto the veranda, taunting him and daring him to follow his instincts.

What would she do if he went to her? Would she give herself to him in order to appease him or would she be more likely to turn on him in anger? Neither was acceptable to Brice. If he made love with her, it would be exactly that. He didn't want to merely use her body for his own gratification. He wasn't that sort of man.

At times he wondered if he would ever be able to make love with her again.

The women Elizabeth had invited to the quilting arrived promptly at nine o'clock in the morning. Elizabeth had put the finishing touches on her house and she, along with Molly, had baked a supply of cookies and squeezed enough lemons for plenty of lemonade.

Harriet's quilt wasn't as expertly done as Ella Barker's had been the week before, but what it lacked in design was made up for by the bright flashes of color she'd chosen. Dorcas blinked when she was confronted with it and murmured, "My, my!"

Harriet was as pleased as if Dorcas's praise had been lavishly bestowed. "I got this pattern from Tavish's mother. She calls it a string quilt, and it's one of the easiest I've ever worked on."

"I can see how that would be," Dorcas said.

The quilt was made from blocks of strips of fabric sewn together, one stripe design going one way and the next going the opposite. Even a beginning quilter could have accomplished it.

Harriet confirmed this when she said, "My youngest girl, Anna, did most of it. She's only eight and is quite pleased with herself."

"Pride goeth before a fall," Dorcas replied automatically.

"It's very pretty," Elizabeth said quickly in Harriet's defense. She liked Harriet and thought the woman might not be as thick-skinned as some of the others believed her to be.

"There's cloth in it from dresses my mother wore as well as some of my sisters'. Anna sewed on it all the way out here."

"I think it's good to teach girls to use a needle early," Ella commented. "I had Darcy sewing by the time she was five."

"Well, I would imagine so." Dorcas sounded as if she couldn't fathom what else girls would be doing at that advanced age. "I've been sewing ever since I was old enough to hold a needle. A girl needs to be broke to the yoke early in life if she's to pull her weight. It's the same as it is with a horse. You can't wait until either are grown and settled in their ways before you try to train them."

Harriet frowned at her. "There's nothing wrong with a child having some enjoyment, either."

"I've always found my joy in service to others." Dorcas looked as if she didn't care any more for Harriet than the older woman did for her.

Harriet muttered something Elizabeth was glad neither she nor anyone else overheard clearly.

"I've put the chairs around and there are refreshments on the table there. You ladies just help yourselves." Since their quilting bees had become a weekly activity, the other women had begun bringing sweet breads and cookies to lighten Elizabeth's load and the table was covered with an assortment of food.

"I hope my Molly is still working out well for you," Harriet said as she lowered herself onto a chair and took her needle from the bodice of her dress. "She's become so attached to your Mary Kate that it would break her heart not to see her every day."

"I think the world of Molly. I'm glad she's happy here." It was true. Elizabeth had never known a more congenial girl. She wasn't one to keep a spotless house, but Elizabeth didn't mind. Molly could be trusted completely with Mary Kate. That left Elizabeth time to clean whatever Molly missed.

"Where is Mary Kate?" Ella asked. "I haven't seen her lately."

"Brice hung a swing for her in the backyard and she plays there most of the time." Since Elizabeth had found Ella in her house, she hadn't tried to further a friendship.

"I could keep her from time to time," Ella surprised her by saying. "My Darcy likes little ones as much as Molly does."

"Thank you, but that won't be necessary." Elizabeth had no intention of entrusting Mary Kate to a woman she disliked.

Ella shrugged and threaded her needle.

Maida couldn't keep her good news secret any longer. "Edmund and I are going to have a baby!" she burst out. Her cheeks grew pink at the thought of her accomplishment.

"That's real good news!" Harriet said. "I said to my Tavish only a few days ago that you looked right perky. It's a sure sign that a baby is on the way. It puts a spring in anybody's step."

"That's an odd way to put it," Dorcas said, ignoring Harriet. "You'll find out soon enough that it's you and not your husband that's having it. Men don't have anything to do with it after they get things started."

Harriet opened her mouth to point out that Dorcas wasn't in any position to know about that, but Elizabeth intercepted her skillfully. "I've told Maida that I'll start sewing baby things for her."

Harriet nodded. "It's a pure wonder how many things a baby needs. They go through clothes like corn through a goose. If they aren't wet on one end, they're wet on the other." Ella nodded in agreement.

"The next time anyone goes into town, I want them to pick up some cup towel material for diapers," Maida said.

"I'll show you how to cut them and fold them," Harriet offered. "I'm the expert on that." She laughed good-heartedly. "Are you hoping for a girl or a boy? You fold the diapers differently, you know."

"Surely there's time for that later," Dorcas said coolly. "As for which kind of baby she wants, she doesn't have any choice about it. The good Lord will send her what he sees fit to send. I think it's bad luck to want one more than another. Besides, it's almost blasphemous to show such a lack of faith in the good Lord's judgment."

Ella shook her head. "I've never heard that. I know it's unlucky to pick out names beforehand."

"Especially long ones." Harriet poked her needle into the quilt and drew it out again on the other side. "You shouldn't name it anything too long. Short and simple. That's the ticket."

"We like Amanda Althea Elizabeth if it's a girl," Maida said with a smile at Elizabeth. "If it's a boy it will be Edmund Aloysius Barclay after Edmund and both our fathers."

"Now see? You've already broken both rules," Ella said. "You've picked out a name and it's a mouthful. You'd do well to throw those names out of your head and start over later. There's time enough to name a baby once it's here."

"But I want to decide now," Maida objected.

"I reckon it would be all right if you don't go around telling everyone what names you picked out," Harriet said. "That's the way Tavish and I do it, and we've had good luck with ours." A cloud passed over her face and Elizabeth wondered if she was thinking of the two little boys who were no longer with them. "At least we've had good luck with our babies. All of them were born alive and healthy."

"I asked Elizabeth to be my midwife," Maida said.

"And I told her to ask you, Harriet." Elizabeth was determined to stick to her guns on this issue. She didn't know anything about childbirth.

"I'd be glad to," Harriet said. "By then my newest will be old enough to be no trouble."

"I'll help out, too," Ella said. "It's been a long time since mine was born, but I know how it's done."

"I think you're all risking fate in planning all this," Dorcas said as she added another tiny stitch to the others she had done. "There's plenty of time when the event is nearer."

"Elizabeth, will you be my baby's godmother?" Maida asked.

"I'd be honored."

"Our church doesn't believe in godparents," Dorcas said firmly. "I'm positive Brother Amos won't allow it."

"I'll be its godmother unofficially then," Elizabeth said to keep peace.

Maida smiled. "I guess that's good enough. I'll teach him or her to call you Aunt Elizabeth."

Dorcas snorted her disapproval. "You're putting the cart before the horse."

As the other women argued dispassionately, Elizabeth sewed in silence. She was growing used to the minor disputes that seemed part of the women's lives. Every quilting day was spiced with terse comments from Dorcas and arguments from everyone else. It created a sort of verbal tapestry of its own over the quilt they were sewing.

Back at the church, Brother Amos was polishing the pews and altar in preparation for the Sunday service. He considered the building and its contents his personal responsibility, and never asked Dorcas to clean it. He was sure that would be acceptable according to scriptures. Every passage he knew spoke of women as being suspect, if not downright unclean and of the devil. It seemed unlikely, therefore, that one should ready the church for its services.

He didn't mind. Amos had a set idea on how to do everything. He had learned it from his father, who had always cleaned his own church back in Missouri. It was Amos's father who had pointed out the Bible verses to Amos and encouraged him to handle his church in this manner. Amos wasn't sure what Dorcas did all day but it seemed to take her all day to do it so she didn't have time to clean the other building anyway—at least not as Amos wanted it. Anything less than spotless was sacrilegious in his opinion.

He cleaned in silence. Occasionally a hymn tried to surface but he sternly suppressed it. He had shaped many sermons while he cleaned his church or his father's before it. To write down the ideas as they occurred, he kept some paper close at hand.

Therefore, he was clearly able to hear the conversation that started taking place just behind the back wall.

At first he thought he was imagining it. No one had any reason to be back there. Eventually that would be part of the cemetery but now it was only untouched land. When a higher, more feminine voice added to the deeper one, he stopped cleaning and went closer to the wall.

Although he put his ear to the wood, he couldn't make out what was being said, but he could hear enough to know it was a man sweet-talking a woman. Amos frowned. There were no single adults in his congregation.

He went out the front door and circled around the building. He heard the couple before he saw them and recognized the voices at once.

"I love you, Darcy. I don't see why you won't let me," Charley McGivens said.

"It's not that I won't," Darcy Barker replied. "It's just that it's broad daylight and anybody could happen upon us."

"Not if we go down the creek to that stand of scrub oak. No one will see us there."

"I just don't know. If we were married..."

"We will be. You know I want to marry you." His voice was earnest and beseeching.

Amos had heard enough. He burst around the corner like an avenging angel swooping down on Adam and Eve sharing the apple. "Sinners!" he shouted. "Fornicating sinners!"

Darcy screamed and shrank against Charley. He was backing away so fast she almost fell. He stared at the preacher. "We weren't doing anything! Honest we weren't!"

"You're a disgrace to this community!" Amos shouted. "Not doing anything? That's the devil talking through your mouth, boy!" He was so angry he was shaking. "You deserve a sound thrashing, both of you!"

"Don't you lay a hand on Darcy!" Charley shouted back, stepping between his love and the preacher. "Don't you threaten her!"

"Are you threatening me?" Amos was shorter than the boy by several inches but he shoved his face fiercely close to Charley's. "Are you planning to hit me, boy?"

Charley unclenched his fist. "No, sir, I'm not aiming to hit you. But don't you go scaring Darcy!"

Darcy was sobbing and trying to hide behind him. "We didn't mean any harm, Brother Amos. We didn't!"

"No harm!" he bellowed. "You were planning a fornication and you didn't mean harm?" His voice was drawing attention all over the settlement. The women were all up at Elizabeth's but the men were gathering.

"What's going on here?" Tavish McGivens demanded as he stepped close to his son.

Abner Barker was coming on a run and when he reached them, Darcy threw herself into her father's protective embrace. "Papa, we weren't doing anything wrong! I swear we weren't!"

Amos pointed his long, bony finger at the boy and girl. "I heard them plain. They were planning to go down to the oak patch and fornicate. He was talking her into it and she wasn't putting up much of an argument." He was so filled with righteous anger that his hand trembled and he felt shaken to the core. It was almost like a religious ecstasy, this power that filled him. "I denounce them both as sinners of the worst sort!"

"We love each other," Charley protested. "We want to get married!"

Abner and Tavish exchanged glances. Amos felt certain that they had at least suspected this of their children. "I won't have behavior like this in my congregation! It's up to me to get all your souls into heaven, and God frowns on sinners. Do you know what that means, Darcy Barker?" He honed in on her because she was crying and less belligerent than Charley. "It means you'll burn forever in hell!"

Darcy cried harder and buried her face in her father's shoulder.

"We didn't mean nothing!" Charley protested. "I just wanted to kiss her!" He didn't meet his father's eyes.

Tavish drew in a deep breath and gave Charley a warning look. "I believe my son. His word is good with me."

"So do I," Abner said. He wasn't eager to have his daughter looked upon as a harlot in the making. "My Darcy has never lied to me in her life!"

"We were only talking about kissing, Papa!" Darcy said quickly. She burst into fresh sobs.

Amos drew himself up to his full height. "I know what I heard. These two are tainting their souls further by lying about it. They're bringing shame on your heads by what they planned to do and by lying when they were found out. I just hope to God I have stopped them before irreparable harm was done. Otherwise, no prayers will save them.'' He knew by the worried look on Charley's face and Darcy's louder sobs that it had already gone beyond the talking stage. ''I place these two under the ban of being shunned.''

''What?'' Tavish exclaimed.

''No one will talk to them or have anything to do with them until they make reparation to the Lord. You parents can feed them and tell them to do chores, but you're not to speak to them unless necessary, and no one else is to talk to them at all. If any of you break the ban, I'll have you shunned as well.'' He looked at the shocked faces of his congregation. ''I've been called by the Lord to polish your souls until you're not displeasing in his sight. And I'm going to do just that!''

Amos gave them all another long look, then turned and stalked back into the church. He was still shaking all over. At times like this he delivered his best sermons. He thought something like this must be what caused the Quakers and the Shakers to have earned the names they had been labeled with. To shake with righteous anger was a fine thing indeed.

Amos didn't take up his cleaning rag again, but went to his sheet of paper. Within minutes he had filled it with his sermon for the next service. He was positive he had a true calling and that times like this were proof that he was sent to scour souls clean for God. Shunning was a serious measure, but if he could impress everyone in the congregation early on, he would be better able to control their sinning in the future. Amos had no doubts as he went back to cleaning his church.

Chapter Fourteen

"Sin must be plucked out like weeds!" Brother Amos shouted from the pulpit at his congregation. "If we don't stand for the Lord, we surely stand for Satan!"

Elizabeth glanced around while he was looking away. Brice hadn't come with her. He was standing fast in his refusal to attend a service and be yelled at. She wished she had been able to stay at home with him, but Amos's sermons had become a point of honor with her and she was a stubborn woman.

The rest of the congregation seemed as ill at ease as she did. Word had spread fast and everyone knew about the romance between Charley and Darcy, as well as the tryst Amos had foiled. Both youngsters were staring miserably at the floor. Their parents were trying to appear stoic but Elizabeth saw the flush of angry embarrassment spreading in Ella's cheeks.

Like Brice, Elizabeth thought Amos should have minded his own business. Darcy Barker was as good as any girl Elizabeth had ever seen, and young Charley McGivens, while he had a streak of wild oats to sow, was a fine young man. Left to their own devices, they might have done more kissing and touching than they should have, but Elizabeth doubted they would ever really jump over the traces. After all, Darcy had been finding excuses not to go to the oak woods with Charley, and by all accounts except Amos's, Charley hadn't been that insistent.

"It's up to me," Amos said. Beads of sweat had gathered on his pale brow and his eyes seemed darker and shinier than ever. "I've been placed as shepherd over you all. If one sheep strays from the fold, the good shepherd goes after it and hunts until he finds it and brings it home. We've got two strays. I'm calling on all of you to help me bring them back to the fold."

Elizabeth wasn't too sure this was a good analogy since Amos had just labeled them as sheep and now he was asking them to behave as shepherds. Charley's head dropped lower on his chest and his mother gave him a sharp look. He straightened somewhat but his mouth still held a rebellious line. Elizabeth looked back at Amos before he could catch her attention wandering from him.

He paced the width of the pulpit area in silence as if he were pondering his next words and checking them out with God. "What I'm asking you to do isn't easy. The men already know what I'm going to say."

So did Elizabeth, as did all the other women. She felt as if they were all collectively holding their breaths.

"I've denounced Charley McGivens and Darcy Barker. That means they are to be shunned until they publicly apologize to this congregation for planting sin among us. There are younger children paying heed to these older ones and we must set an example now. We cannot allow Charley and Darcy to lead the others to a life of degradation and sin!"

Elizabeth shifted uneasily. She heard others doing the

same. Amos had gone too far in denouncing the young couple.

There was a sudden scraping of feet, and to her amazement, Tavish McGivens stood up and Harriet hurriedly got to her feet as well. Their children quickly followed suit. Without a word, they filed out of the church.

Elizabeth wanted to follow them out but was afraid to call attention to herself. Her own life wouldn't bear close scrutiny, even though she and Brice were now sleeping in separate rooms. She kept her face expressionless and staring straight ahead.

Amos's face grew red with a surge of anger and he seemed shocked speechless over them walking out before he dismissed them. For the next hour he shouted and declared against the wages of sin and described the hellfire awaiting those who strayed from the path of righteousness. Elizabeth barely heard him.

As soon as the service was over, she hurried outside and to her buggy. None of the others stayed around to talk either. Everyone was eager to get away from Brother Amos's domain.

When she reached home Brice had a cold dinner on the table. Their best meal was always saved for supper. "I was wondering if you decided to attend church in Glory today. Amos must have been in rare form."

She removed her hat and stroked Mary Kate's blond curls. "He was. He formally declared that Darcy and Charley are to be shunned. The McGivenses stood up and walked out on him."

"Good for them. Tavish isn't going to be bullied by him."

She sat at her place and helped herself to a slice of boiled ham. "I was glad you weren't there. You probably would have left with them."

"You know I would have." He handed her the corn bread left over from the evening before.

"Can't you see we have to be careful?" she asked. "What if he starts looking too closely into our relationship?"

"Let him. I haven't done anything to be ashamed of. Have you?" He frowned at her over the table.

"Of course not." She avoided his eyes. "But we would be shunned, too, if he knew about us."

"If he does, I'll run him out of the valley. It's that simple."

She put down her fork. "You can't do that! You can't invite people to move all the way out here and chase them away at the first disagreement. Amos and Dorcas left their home, families and friends to come here. You promised the settlers a preacher to induce them to settle here. Where would you find another who could uproot his family and come all the way out here? Surely you knew there would be conflicts from time to time."

"If I had foreseen Brother Amos I wouldn't have made the offer in the first place. I'm not all that fond of civilization."

She frowned. She already knew he had made the offer of the settlement to please Celia. Over the months Elizabeth had revised her feelings toward her. She stabbed the slice of ham and cut it with angry strokes of her knife.

"Am I that ham?" he asked.

"What a question," she snapped.

"Have you noticed we have our worst arguments when you've been to Amos's church?"

"Certainly I have. I can't help but notice that." She ate the ham and tore her slice of corn bread in half. "If there were another church around here, I'd go to that one, but there isn't so I'll just have to make do.''

Brice sighed and gave Mary Kate more peas. "There's another choice. You could stay home.''

"And have him talk about us the way he is the McGivenses and Barkers? I don't think so.''

"You worry too much what people think. I figure if something is making your life unhappy, you ought to change it.''

"I wish my world was as simple as yours,'' she shot at him. "I really do. I could do as I pleased and not give a flip what everyone else thought.''

"What would you change if you could?''

His question surprised her. "I don't know,'' she evaded.

"I know what I would change.''

"Oh?'' In spite of herself, she asked, "What would that be?''

"I'd change the way we're living. And I'd send Amos back to wherever he came from.'' He got up from the table and left the room.

Elizabeth and Mary Kate stared after him. "Eat your peas,'' she said to the child. Mary Kate willingly obeyed since she was particularly fond of peas with pepin on them. Elizabeth wondered if Brice meant he wanted her to leave the valley or if he wanted her to move back into his room. She was worn out with trying to figure out what he meant and she was too afraid to ask him. She chewed her ham with a vengeance.

Early the next morning there was a commotion in the settlement. Elizabeth went down to meet Maida on the green between the general store and the school. Most of the other settlers were also milling about there. Charley McGivens and Darcy Barker were conspicuously absent.

"Have you heard? Charley and Darcy are gone." Maida looked as if she had no idea what to expect next. "They left sometime during the night."

"Where have they gone?"

"Most of us think they eloped," Maida replied. "Harriet is beside herself."

"Maybe they just went for a ride."

"Before daylight? I'm positive they eloped. I can't blame them after all Brother Amos said."

"He was awfully hard on them. Maybe they only went as far as Glory and we can convince them to come back."

"I know I wouldn't come back to be shunned."

"Neither would I," Elizabeth admitted. "They can't have gone back east. It's too far, and they wouldn't know the way without a trail master. They must be in Glory."

"By now they are probably married."

"But they are so young! Darcy just turned seventeen!"

"That's old enough. I was only a year older when I married Edmund. I've heard of younger ones getting married."

"So have I," Elizabeth admitted. "It's just that seventeen seems so much younger to me now than it did when I was that age. What will Harriet and Tavish do? Or Ella and Abner?"

"Tavish and Abner have already left for Glory. They want to find them and bring them back. Abner is furious, and so is Ella. I don't know why, since it's been obvious to everyone that Charley and Darcy were falling in love. They could both do a lot worse."

"Do you think I should go talk to Brother Amos? Maybe if he lifts the ban against Charley and Darcy, we can get back to the way we were."

"Talking to Amos won't change a thing," Maida said. "Believe me. I know, because I got to know him on the trip out here."

"I have to tell Brice. He needs to know what happened." Elizabeth dreaded the conversation. She could already hear what Brice would say. "What do you think would happen if he told Brother Amos to leave?"

"I don't know. The settlement wouldn't have a preacher. Edmund and I wouldn't leave, but I can't speak for the others. Harriet and Tavish are bound and determined to go to church. Or they were until yesterday. I'm not so sure now. This has upset everyone."

Elizabeth nodded. "I know. Well, Brice has to be told."

"If I learn anything else, I'll come up and tell you."

Elizabeth set out in search of Brice.

Dorcas sat quietly at her sewing. Across the room Amos was reading silently from his worn Bible. She had learned the quickest way to find out what he was thinking was to wait him out.

She knew what had happened. Everybody in the settlement was talking about it.

She knotted her thread in the cloth, snipped it, and carefully threaded her needle again. She sewed as she did most things, slowly and precisely. Although she never wasted time, she didn't speed through it, either. She was sewing a tiny gown for Harriet McGivens's expected baby. Because Dorcas didn't like Harriet, she was sewing it for the betterment of her own soul. As the preacher's wife, Dorcas always made a garment for the new babies in her husband's flock. It helped her quell the disappointment of never having needed baby garments for a child of her own.

"Maybe I was too hard on them."

She looked up in surprise. Of all the things she would have guessed Amos was thinking, this wasn't one of them. She wasn't sure how to answer him so she said nothing.

He closed the Bible and put it back on the shelf. Going back to the window, he gazed out at the empty valley that sloped up to the plain where Glory lay. "I never expected them to elope."

"Neither did I," Dorcas said truthfully. She would have been far too frightened of her father to dare such a thing.

He continued gazing out the window. "I had to do what I did. Can you imagine what it would be like here if everybody did as they pleased? There would be no civilization before we knew what was happening. I couldn't allow Charley and Darcy to go sinning once I knew what was on their minds."

She put her sewing aside and went to him. She stopped a step or two away and folded her hands together. "I know you did what you thought was best. You always do." It was true. She might not always agree with him, but Amos was a man to follow his conscience above all else.

"I did for a fact." He sighed and looked years younger in his uncertainty. "I did what I had to do. I did what Papa would have done."

"Yes, you did. My father would have done the same."

"So why do I feel so bad? I ought to rejoice that they won't be around to lead the others into sin by example.

When you find a rotten apple, you don't pack it in a barrel with the good ones.''

She thought for a minute. ''Maybe you feel bad because you don't know where they've gone, and you wonder if Charley and Darcy will be able to take care of themselves?''

He looked at her. ''You always take me so literally. I can figure out why I'm sorry they left.''

She gripped her hands together. ''I'm sorry, Brother Amos. I thought you were waiting for an answer.''

''Maybe I shouldn't have preached over them in church.'' Amos rested his hand on the windowsill. ''Everybody already knew Charley and Darcy were to be shunned. I didn't have to harp on it.''

As he stood there, alone, he looked so much like he had when he came calling on her in their youth, that Dorcas forgot herself and went to him. She put her arm around his waist and hugged him. ''Don't beat yourself over this, Amos. I don't think you made a mistake, and maybe the others won't either once they get word that Charley and Darcy are all right.'' This wasn't likely, but she wanted him to feel better. ''You did your duty. No one can do more.''

He put his arms around her and they stood in an embrace for several seconds. Then he released her and stepped away. ''I didn't mean to do that. I forgot myself for a minute.''

She smiled and instantly looked younger. ''That's all right. A wife is supposed to be there for her husband to lean on from time to time.''

He seemed to be thinking that over.

Dutifully, she went back to her sewing and placed more tiny stitches in the fabric. In that moment, when they embraced, she had seen more tenderness in her hus-

band than she had seen from him in years. If he embraced her once, he might eventually do it again. Not
that she had carnal lusts, she reminded herself quickly.
All that had died years before. Even brothers and sisters
hugged from time to time, she assumed. She just felt too
lonely when no one touched her for weeks on end.

A tiny rebellious thought formed in her mind. If Amos
had come this far today, she might someday rediscover
the young man she had fallen in love with and married.
It wasn't impossible, perhaps. Now that Amos was many
miles away from his domineering father, he might
soften. Dorcas had harbored many treacherous thoughts
about her father-in-law. She didn't like him, though she
had never admitted that to a living soul. Because of him,
Amos had buried the vulnerable young man he had been
and had done everything in his power to be exactly like
his fire-breathing father.

They might even fall in love again.

No, she told herself firmly. They were past the foolishness of youth. Both of them were nearer forty than
they were to thirty. Any love between them would have
to be a platonic sort.

All the same, she had noticed how Tavish still looked
at Harriet, and she wasn't that much younger than Dorcas.

"What do you mean they left?" Brice asked.

"They were gone when everyone got up this morning.
Their fathers have gone to Glory to look for them."

"I should never have advertised for an unknown
preacher. For that matter, we don't know if Abner can
teach. I should have left well enough alone."

"It's not your fault," she said. "No one is blaming
you."

"Why in the hell couldn't Amos have been the one to decide to move away?" Brice kicked dirt around the fence post he had just dropped into the hole and stamped the dirt firmly into place. He wiped his sweaty brow on his shirtsleeve and surveyed how far he had to go before finishing for the day.

Lucky and Avery were some distance behind him, stringing wire between the posts he had already put in place. Fencing the pasture hadn't been an easy decision for Brice. He favored open grazing. But if he was going to raise purebred Herefords, he had to keep maverick bulls away from his cows. "I sure don't have time to think about this now."

"I wasn't trying to give you more to worry about. I just thought you needed to know."

"I did." He looked at her as if his thoughts were taking a different course but his countenance remained unchanged. "You're looking pretty today."

As always his compliment came completely unexpected. Elizabeth was caught off guard. "Th-thank you," she stammered.

"I'd like to stand and talk to you, but I've got to get these posts set so the men can string the wire." He seemed reluctant to go back to work. "I'll see you in a few hours."

She nodded. "Yes. I didn't mean to interrupt you."

"I'm glad you did." He smiled at her.

Elizabeth felt her heart do a flip-flop. She went back to her horse and Brice held the bridle while she mounted. She opened her mouth to speak but closed it again. How was she to know what to say to a man like him? She had expected him to be upset or worried about the young couple, or too busy to talk, but had never expected the compliment. She tried not to read too much into it, but she couldn't help but be touched.

She nudged her horse into a canter and headed back toward the ranch. His compliment might have meant nothing at all. That smile that stirred fires deep within her might also mean nothing. But for the intervening hours, she could hope and dream.

Now that she had known what it was like to live with him as opposed to merely dwelling under the same roof, she wasn't so sure her determination to stay away from him had ever made sense. It had been his idea to move her out of his room. What would he do if she simply brought her things back in again? Elizabeth decided she wasn't quite brave enough or confident enough to try that as yet, but she was determined not to put those thoughts aside forever.

Two days later Tavish and Abner returned to the settlement. The runaways had been found in Glory and were married by the time their fathers had arrived. In spite of their fathers' arguments and threats, Charley and Darcy refused to have their marriage annulled or to return to the settlement. Tavish, being the more softhearted of the two, gave Charley money to take Darcy to the McGivens clan back east.

Harriet grieved over not knowing if she would ever see her eldest child again. Ella became more withdrawn and bitter, and her behavior even more odd.

Chapter Fifteen

By October the summer heat was past and the cottonwood trees had become patches of gold across the valley. Elizabeth was relieved that the heat had finally given way to cooler weather, though she dreaded the onset of winter. Her memories of the mud hut were still too fresh. Although the summer had been hot and there had been little rain, Puma Creek hadn't run dry and everyone agreed that this was a good sign. No one could afford to live in a place that might run out of water in a bad summer. Household wells had been dug to tap the water deep in the valley, freeing the creek's supply for the livestock and putting a source of water closer to each home.

The most exciting news was that a railroad spur had been completed to Glory as had been rumored. They also heard another settlement was being founded between the ranch and Glory and that it was populated by an entire wagon train. Soon supplies would be available within a few hours' travel instead of requiring a two-day trip. One of the families among the new arrivals had a handsome son by the name of Henry Wells. When Henry accidentally met Molly McGivens while out riding, a new romance began to flower.

"I hope Amos keeps his nose out of this one," Brice said as he watched Molly daydreaming while she was supposed to be sweeping. "I would hate to see her heartbroken or eloping like her brother."

"I think Molly is more stubborn than to let Amos drive her away. She told me Henry is thinking of building a feed store beside that land Edmund bought across the creek." Elizabeth smiled. "That sounds as if he plans to marry her."

"I guess that means there will soon be reason to put up another house. You may lose a good housekeeper once she has a family of her own."

"Her sister Dorothy has already asked if I'll hire her someday. Mary Kate is almost as fond of Dorothy as she is of Molly." She stirred the stew she was cooking for supper.

"It would be nice to see you alone in the house sometime," he said almost as if he were thinking aloud.

She glanced at him in surprise. "We see each other alone after Mary Kate goes to bed every night."

"I was thinking of the daytime. I've almost never been alone with you during the day." He came to her and helped her swing the heavy pot over the hotter part of the fire. "Are you happy, Elizabeth?"

"Happy? Of course I am." She kept her face turned away from him so he wouldn't see the concern she was feeling. "Why wouldn't I be happy?"

Brice crossed to the kitchen door and pulled it shut so Molly couldn't inadvertently overhear their conversation. "I've been giving it a lot of thought these past few weeks. I'm not."

Her heart dropped and she pretended to be too busy

with the meal preparation to look at him. "I'm sorry. Is there something I'm doing that you'd rather I didn't? I know stew isn't your favorite dish, but Mary Kate loves it and—"

"I'm not talking about food, Elizabeth."

She put the ladle on the hook and turned to face him as she straightened. "Maybe you should explain it to me."

He came to her and put his hands on her shoulders. "Damn it, I'm lonely. I miss you."

"I don't see how that can be. I'm right here every day."

"I miss us being together. Really together, the way we were before that first sermon of Amos's. Don't you ever miss me?"

She met his eyes. "Of course I do. Haven't I made that clear? At times I've felt as if I'm throwing myself at you. You're the one who wants us to keep our distance."

His brow furrowed in confusion. "No, it was your idea."

"Brice, you moved me into the other room! You're the one who didn't want me, not the other way around."

"Not want you? How can you say that? I've loved you since the first time I saw you. Where did you get the idea that I didn't?"

She stared at him. "You love me?"

"Of course I do. You already know that," he said with a frown.

"If you love me, why did you move me back into a separate bedroom?"

"It's what you wanted! You said so when we left church!"

"No, I didn't! I went for a ride and by the time I

came home, I was living in the other room again!'' She made an effort to keep her voice down despite the closed door between them and Molly.

"You didn't move your things back," he said in defense. "You haven't complained about it a single time."

"It's not my place to complain! You own the house. I can't figure out exactly what my position is here, if you must know the truth. Sometimes I'm just the housekeeper and Mary Kate's nursemaid. Other times I've been more. What exactly do you want out of me, Brice?" Exasperation was causing her temper to rise. Was he telling her they had wasted three months on a misunderstanding? That couldn't be! "You never said you loved me. I would certainly have remembered that."

"I must have!"

"Why would I stay in the other room if I thought you loved me? Give me credit for having better sense than that!"

"I assumed you were angry with me."

"For this long?" she demanded. She made an effort to calm down. "Maybe you should tell me exactly what you're trying to say."

"You confuse me. I never know where I stand with you. I don't fall in and out of love that easily, but you seem to. I never fell in love at first sight before you came along. It caught me off guard. I know women don't like to hear declarations of love every five minutes and—"

"Hold it right there!" She advanced on him, her eyes flashing a warning. "I'm not Celia! I'm tired of living in her shadow! She hurt you and gave you some of the worst information about women that I've ever heard!"

Brice refused to back up. "You're the one who has always professed to somehow have been her friend. You only saw her once! I assumed if you found so much in common during one short visit, you must share the same views.''

''I was wrong about that. I know more about her now. It may be wrong to speak ill of the dead, but she was a cruel and selfish woman!''

''I already know that!'' He frowned back at her.

''Then why in the world do you believe all her misinformation?'' Elizabeth put her hands on her hips and glared up at him. ''Not want to hear you love me? I live for those words! There is nothing I want more than to know you love me and want me and that you would welcome love from me! You never asked me!''

''I also didn't stop you from bringing it up on your own,'' he pointed out. ''If you loved me, what made you keep your distance from me?''

She stared at him a long moment, then turned and left the room.

He opened his mouth to call her back but stopped. Molly was in the house and he didn't want the settlement to have gossip to pass about. He hurried after her and saw her going upstairs. If she saw that he was following her, she gave no sign.

Elizabeth marched straight into her room and propped open the door between the bedrooms. Then she opened her wardrobe and gathered up an armload of her clothes. Seeing Elizabeth in his room, Brice stopped in his doorway and stared. She yanked open the drawer of his wardrobe, shoved his things over, and deposited her own. In the next trip she brought everything else. She kicked the drawer shut and crossed her arms as she scowled at him. ''We've lost too much precious time, Brice. We're not going to have this anymore.''

He shut the bedroom door for privacy and went to

her. "All this time we've been misunderstanding each other?" He still couldn't believe what he was hearing.

"I want you to tell me you love me every time you think about it," she told him. "I intend to do the same. I don't want you to assume that I will react the same way Celia would have to anything ever again. Do you understand me?"

"Perfectly. The same goes for Robert. I'm not going to desert you and I'm not going to throw you out. Every time we have an argument, you seem to think I will." He knew he was right by the way her glance wavered. "You have to promise me this."

"All right."

He studied her. "I wish it were dark already so we would really have each other alone."

She came to him and put her arms around his waist. Brice held her. "I remember one day we made love in the daylight. As I recall there was a whole herd of cattle looking on."

"I've spent a lot of time remembering that day. I rode by there with Avery the other day and all I could think about was how you looked lying on your dress with the shade making dapples of sunlight on your body."

"I think about every time we've made love," she admitted in a softer voice. "I treasure them all, and when I'm busy doing my work around the house, I bring them into my mind and look at all of them again and again."

He pulled her close and buried his face in her fragrant hair. "God, Elizabeth, have we really lost so much time because of a misunderstanding?"

She nodded, holding him as close as possible. "I was brokenhearted when I came back that Sunday and found my things in there."

"If you had said a single word, I would have brought them back."

"If you ever move me out again, I'm going to say more than a word to you."

"I'm not fool enough to do it twice. I love you," he said.

"I love you, too." Her voice broke with emotion. He wasn't far from tears himself.

"When I think I could have driven you away and not known I was doing it, I..." He stopped. "I guess I'm speechless. If only you had let me know how you felt."

"How could I make it any plainer? I wasn't sure if you wanted to hear that I love you."

"We have to do away with the past. If any two people have been haunted by it, it's us. We have to put all of it behind us."

She gazed up at him. "I'll never leave you, Brice. Nothing and no one is going to tear us apart. Not ever." She resolutely put aside the idea that Robert might still be alive. She belonged with Brice and no one could take her away.

"I love you," he murmured as he bent to kiss her.

Elizabeth thought the evening would never end. Mary Kate was in a playful mood and had stalled her bedtime until Elizabeth had no choice but to take her upstairs over much protest. For a long time afterward, Elizabeth could hear her babbling to the toys in her bed in an effort to keep from falling asleep. Eventually Mary Kate stopped struggling, and as soon as she became quiet, she fell asleep.

"Finally!" Elizabeth said as she met Brice in the hall. "I thought she was going to stay awake forever!"

"So did I." He took her hand and led her into their

bedroom. As he closed the door, he said, "I've wanted to do this for so long. To shut this door with you on this side of it."

She came to him and they kissed. "I love the way you taste," she said. "And the way you smell and the way you feel and the sound of your voice."

"That pretty well covers it," he said with a laugh.

"No, I also like the way you look. You're a handsome man, Brice Graham. That was the first thing I noticed about you."

"What was the second?"

She laughed. "That you were the most exciting man I've ever seen, bar none." She reached up and caressed his face. "I've dreamed about you for so long. About being with you like this."

"So have I. I'm surprised that I managed to keep that door shut." He motioned his head toward the door that separated their rooms.

"It never will be closed again, even if I have to take it off the hinges and hide it."

He put his arms around her waist and lifted her from the floor in a twirl. When he deposited her, she was on the footstool beside the bed. "That's better," he said. "Now we're closer to the same height. You're a tiny thing, you know that?"

She stood with her eyes almost on a level with his. "Maybe it's just that you're so tall."

"I'm going to put a footstool in every room," he teased. More seriously, he said, "I do love you to distraction, Elizabeth."

She smiled and kissed him with growing passion. "I love you with all my heart."

He began unfastening her dress. It was all Elizabeth could do to stand still. She wanted to rip it off and tear his clothes from his body. But she forced herself to submit to the sensuous torture of waiting. Brice clearly wasn't going to be rushed.

He kissed each inch of her skin as he revealed it. When the buttons were open, he eased her dress off her shoulders. Elizabeth put her arms behind her and drew the cuffs over her hands. The dress pooled about her feet on the stool.

With a gentle tug, Brice released the ribbon that gathered her chemise above her breasts, and on its own, the chemise slipped off one shoulder. He untied her petticoat and guided it over the curves of her hips and let it fall onto the dress, then ran his hands over her hips again, this time taking her underdrawers away. His eyes roamed over her naked body and Elizabeth tingled all over from the knowledge that he was looking at her and loving all he saw.

She sat on the bed and he knelt before her and removed her shoes and white cotton stockings. Elizabeth lifted her arms and removed the pins from her hair, then lay back on the coverlet, her hair spreading about her.

"You're the most beautiful woman I've ever seen," he said almost with reverence. "I can hardly believe that you could be here, loving me, looking at me the way you are." He leaned on the bed over her, his hands planted to either side of her.

Elizabeth drew him down and kissed him. Her nipples brushed against his shirt and she drew in her breath.

He smiled and traced his fingers down her shoulder and over her breast. "You enjoy being touched, don't you?" He cupped her breast in his hand and lowered his mouth to take her nipple between his lips.

She moaned with desire. Her body was crying out for his and she had to will herself to slow down. She wanted this to last for as long as possible. The anticipation was almost as good as what she knew was still to come.

Brice got off the bed and removed his clothing, never taking his eyes from her. Elizabeth curled to one side so she could watch. It was erotic the way he opened his shirt, removed it and tossed it aside. His body was well muscled and as lean as a panther's. As he began unfastening his pants, she moistened her lips.

When he was naked, he came to her and drew her to her feet. Still standing on the stool, she put her arms around him. Her body fit perfectly with his, as if each had been designed to the pattern of the other. He reached behind her and pulled the bedcovers down. Their eyes never wavered. It was as if she could see the love burning in the depths of his brown eyes. The intensity of his gaze excited her in the extreme.

Brice put his arm on her waist and pulled her closer to him in a possessive gesture. Elizabeth pressed her hips against him in invitation. He lifted her in his arms, still gazing into her eyes, and laid her on the bed. She ran her hands over the warm muscles of his arms and drew him down beside her.

He knotted his hand in the dark silk of her hair and lifted her face to his. His lips claimed hers, and his kiss was eager and demanding. Elizabeth met it with an equal passion. She parted her lips and ran her tongue over the cushion of his lips and into his mouth. His tongue met hers, and her pulse quickened.

She rolled on top of him and braced her hands on his shoulders to look into his face. He had left the lamp burning and she was glad. She wanted to feast her eyes on every inch of his magnificent body. With her hair making a curtain about them, she traced her finger over the line of his lips and down the column of his neck, over the hard wall of his chest and lower to where their bodies met. She smiled when he moved impatiently. He wanted her as badly as she wanted him.

Elizabeth rocked back and he encircled her waist with his hands and guided her onto him. Her breath caught in her throat as they became one. "I wanted it to last longer," she murmured. "Yes. Don't stop." Her head rolled back in ecstasy.

Brice smiled, his eyes intent with desire. "What makes you think it won't last a long time?"

She laughed softly, delighted to be making love with him and knowing his question was his promise that it wouldn't be over until they both were well satisfied. "I may never get enough of loving you," she whispered.

"You were made for loving," he said as he smiled at her expression of obvious satisfaction. "I love watching you." He encircled both her breasts with his hands and teased her to greater desire. "You so thoroughly enjoy it."

"Yes," she murmured, "I love for you to touch me and to look at me." Her eyes closed as she concentrated on the magic his body was making with hers. Again she looked into his eyes. "Am I wanton?"

"Yes, and I'm glad," he replied. With a smooth movement, he rolled them both over, their bodies still linked in loving. "I'm going to satisfy you in ways you never imagined," he promised as his hands caressed her. "I'm going to make my dreams a reality."

"Yes," she whispered. "I've had dreams of my own." She lifted her head and ran her tongue over his chest, flicking it across his hard nipples as he had done hers. "I want to touch you all over and get to know every part of you again and again."

"You're almost too good to be true." His hand glided

across her belly then lower to the moist nest of curls between her thighs. With the tip of one finger, he sensuously stroked the most sensitive spot as his tumescence continued to move inside her.

Elizabeth gasped and opened her legs wider to give herself over to him. He was sending waves of fiery delight throughout her. Within seconds her body was racing toward a culmination and when it arrived, it almost overwhelmed her. She held to him in desperate passion, willing it never to stop even as she was unsure if her body could take any more pleasure. She thought he was through with her, and she felt a pang of regret as the waves of love faded. Instead, he begin to move again.

Soon she had lost count of the times they had made love. Her ecstasy was increased by knowing he was deriving great joy from satisfying her over and over.

As her body tired, Elizabeth locked her legs around his and together they moved in the deep, sensuous rhythms that brought him the most pleasure. Brice moaned as she gave him as much satisfaction as he had given her. In doing so, her body responded yet again.

When they at last lay quietly in the tangled covers, she felt as if they had invented lovemaking. Surely no one had ever experienced so much love. Her head lay cradled on his shoulder and when she looked up at him, believing him to be asleep, she found him watching her, a gentle smile on his face.

"I love you," he said softly.

"I love you, too," she murmured with a smile of her own.

"Can you think of any reason Ella would be sewing dresses for a little girl?" Maida asked as they sat on

Maida's front porch.

"Maybe she's making something for one of the McGivens children."

"It was too small for little Anna and too large for a baby. I saw it when I went over to repay the sugar I borrowed from her last week. When she saw me looking at it, she grabbed it and put it out of sight."

"That's odd, even for Ella." Elizabeth watched Mary Kate playing in the soft sand beside the porch. "Ella makes me uneasy. I have the feeling she's watching me all the time. Do you sense that?"

"I often see her walking to or from your house. I thought you must have hired her to help Molly during harvest."

"Molly and I have our hands full with canning and preserving, but I haven't hired Ella. I don't like her."

"How strange," Maida mused as she set her chair to rocking. "Why would she go there? Surely she has enough around her house to keep her busy. I certainly do!"

"Will you help me keep my eye on her? I haven't trusted her since I found her in my house one day."

"Inside your house? Without your permission?" Maida was shocked.

"She said she knocked and thought she heard me say to come in, but I found her going upstairs."

"Upstairs? She has no business going upstairs in your house!"

"I know. And she had the most peculiar expression on her face. I hate to accuse her of anything, but she looked guilty."

"Well, I should certainly think she should. I never heard of such a thing!" She rocked for a minute in silence. "I'll keep an eye on her from this end. If I see her going up to the house, I'll follow her."

"Thank you. I feel more relieved knowing that." Elizabeth glanced at the Barker house. No one was in the yard or on the porch, but Ella could be watching her from inside. She felt a shiver run up her back.

Two days later Anna McGivens came running up the hill with the news that her mother was ready to have the baby.

Elizabeth called out to Molly and hurried down to the McGivenses' house. Anna gathered up her younger brother, Andrew, and her next older brother, Brian, and took them out to play games in the barn. Elizabeth found Maida and Ella already at Harriet's bedside. Harriet smiled when Elizabeth came in, but another labor pain seized her before she could speak.

Maida looked at Elizabeth in concern. "She seems to be having them awfully close together."

Ella said, "It will be over all the faster for it." She lifted the sheet and checked Harriet's progress. "I don't see the baby's crown yet."

Harriet groaned. "I hope this one isn't as hard as Andrew was. He was late and was a big one. I think this one is close to being early. Maybe it won't be so large?" Her voice tilted up questioningly.

"Can't tell," Ella said with a shake of her head. "Try not to push yet. It's way too early."

"Why shouldn't she push?" Maida whispered to Elizabeth. "Wouldn't that bring it faster?"

Elizabeth had been wondering that herself. "Is there water on to boil?" She knew this was part of the process, and she knew how to boil water.

"Tavish put on a pot before I chased him out of

here.'' Ella patted Harriet's arm. ''Just relax as much as you can and don't worry. That baby is the size it is, whatever that may be, and worrying won't help at all. Could be a tiny little girl and she just hasn't dropped far enough yet.''

Harriet seemed to be hanging hope on Ella's words. Elizabeth had seldom seen Ella show a willingness to help another. She wondered if there might not be a kernel of empathy in the woman after all.

After six hours passed, Ella drew Elizabeth out onto the porch, ostensibly for a breath of air. ''What do you make of it?''

''I don't know,'' Elizabeth said truthfully. ''Shouldn't the baby be visible by now?''

''It sure should. Harriet told me she started having pains last night right after supper. That puts her in labor nearly twenty-four hours. That baby should be here by now, and I don't see a thing. Do you have any ideas?''

''Not a one.'' Elizabeth was growing afraid. She knew now why Ella had sent Anna to fetch her. Neither Dorcas nor Maida ever had a child, and Elizabeth was presumably the only other woman in the settlement who had undergone a successful delivery. As the presumed mother of Mary Kate, Elizabeth should have knowledge to add to Ella's.

''Was Mary Kate a difficult birth? Mine was an easy delivery. I don't know what to do.''

''No. She wasn't difficult.'' Elizabeth had to tell the lie or explain her ignorance. ''I don't have any idea what to do.''

''Who helped you? Maybe we could find her.''

Elizabeth shook her head. ''Consuela helped Mary Kate be born, and she left here nearly a year ago.'' She knew this was true. She also couldn't forget that Celia had died having her baby. It happened to women all too often.

When they went back inside, Harriet said, "Send Tavish over to the new settlement. Molly has said Henry's mother is a midwife."

"That would take several hours," Maida objected.

"I reckon we don't have much choice," Harriet said as she bit back a pain. "She may be the only chance I have."

Elizabeth touched her arm reassuringly. "I'll go find Tavish."

Four hours later Leona Wells was there with them in the tiny room. Harriet had tired a great deal and was obviously sinking fast. She was no longer talking between contractions and her hair was matted to her head with sweat. Elizabeth wasn't positive she was aware Leona was in the room.

Leona lifted the sheet and tilted her head to one side as if she were thinking. "My guess is this little fellow is coming hind part before."

Ella's eyes met Elizabeth's. Although Elizabeth didn't know what that meant, she knew it wasn't good news. "What can we do?"

"I'm going to try and turn it." Leona pushed up her sleeves and placed both hands on Harriet's rounded abdomen. "I'm going to have to hurt you a bit," she warned. "But it's the only way I know to do this." When she shoved, Harriet screamed. It was the first outcry she had made in more than an hour.

Leona reached in and pushed against the baby as she applied pressure outside at the same time. "Don't push! Hold off!"

Harriet seemed to be trying to comply.

Elizabeth noticed Maida was getting so pale that her freckles were becoming quite visible. "Maybe you'd better go outside."

Maida shook her head silently. She went to Harriet's side and held her hand as the woman strained in agony. "Breathe deep," she said, "Try to breathe."

Leona straightened and reached for a linen towel. "I think it turned. It felt like it did." The worry on her face was still present.

This time when Harriet was seized with a spasm, she cried out and the baby fell into place the way it should have hours before.

"You did it!" Ella exclaimed. "I can see its head, Harriet! It's coming now!"

Harriet was gripped in another contraction. Her pain was evident.

Leona yanked the sheet all the way off the bed. Carefully she guided the baby into the world. "It's a little boy, Harriet! You've got another son! And he's a beauty!"

Harriet gasped for air. She was crying and trying weakly to raise herself enough to see her baby.

"He's not crying," Maida said in a low voice to Elizabeth. "Shouldn't he be crying?"

Leona had noticed the same thing. She held the baby up by his ankles and swatted his bottom. Nothing happened. Harriet gave a keening wail. Elizabeth stepped nearer to comfort her.

Leona called to Maida, "Dump the water into the washbasin!" By the time Maida had done it, Leona had cut and tied the cord and was there with the baby. She plunged him into the cold water as her finger explored his small mouth for obstructions.

Suddenly the infant let out a cry. Then another. He gasped air into his tiny lungs and screamed a protest.

"He's fine," Leona said with relief. "See, Mrs. McGivens? He's breathing just fine." She wrapped the baby in a clean towel and carried him to the bed. "You hold him while we finish up here." She put the baby in the curve of Harriet's arms.

Harriet was laughing and crying at the same time despite her exhaustion. "Look at him. Isn't he the very image of Tavish?"

Elizabeth found she was crying and laughing, too. The baby really did look like his father with his wrinkled red face and sparse hair. "He's a beautiful baby, Harriet. A fine son."

Later as they walked toward their homes, Maida said, "I thought she was going to die."

"So did I. Thank goodness Tavish found Leona and she knew what to do."

"I hope I don't have that much trouble. I've heard the first ones are really difficult sometimes." Maida put her hands over her middle as if to protect her unborn child. "What if something goes wrong with me?"

"Nothing will," Elizabeth reassured her hastily. "You're young and healthy. Nothing will go wrong."

"If anything happens to me," Maida said in a low voice, "will you promise to raise this baby for me?"

"Hush! Don't even talk like that." Their mutual fear for Harriet's safety was still too recent.

"But I can't rest unless I know." Maida caught Elizabeth's arm and made her face her. "Promise me? You're my best friend and the closest thing I have to family. Just to be on the safe side, we changed the names we had picked out and we aren't telling the new ones."

Elizabeth nodded, "Nothing will happen to you. I

won't let it. But if it makes you feel better, I promise.''
She hoped her words held more assurance than she felt.
She had seen how easily a woman could slip away in
childbirth and it had frightened her as much as it had
Maida.

Chapter Sixteen

Little Nial Anthony McGivens was the darling of the
settlement. He bore a startling resemblance to Tavish,
even to the red hair that lay close to his head, and Harriet
was positive his eyes would eventually turn Irish green.

"He's a beautiful child," Elizabeth told Maida a few
days later as they left the McGivenses' house after a
visit. "And little Andrew dotes on him."

"I think Andrew was tired of being the baby of the
family. You know how Brian teases him at times."

Elizabeth laughed. "Andrew can take care of himself.
He may be only five, but I've seen him tear into Brian
as if they were the same age."

"I just hope I don't have as much trouble with my
baby as Harriet did in giving birth to him." Maida
frowned. "I'm afraid."

"You should never have been in the house. It's done
nothing but worry you. Leona told you there's nothing
for you to worry about. She said babies almost always
turn properly before the labor pains start. As young and
strong as you are, she doesn't think you'll have a hard
labor at all."

"I just wish you were going to have one, too. We

could give each other moral support. You've had Mary Kate and I would feel safer somehow.''

''You're a funny one, Maida. How would my being in the family way help you at all?'' Elizabeth's smile held a secret. She had good reason to believe Maida might get her wish.

''I don't know.'' They reached Maida's house and went inside. ''Things are changing so fast these days. There will be a wedding soon. Henry Wells placed the cornerstones for his house yesterday. Tavish and Edmund and the other men have agreed to help him build it as well as his feed store. By the time the wedding is here, Molly and Henry will have a lovely house all their own.'' She wrinkled her nose. ''I'm not sure I would want Brother Amos to marry me but I guess Molly has no other choice.''

''Neither would I, but I guess it would be all right if he only performed the ceremony.''

Maida laughed. ''You know that's what I meant. You do beat all, Elizabeth. Marry Brother Amos indeed!'' She poured them each a cup of coffee and they sat by the fire. Cold weather had settled in and the warmth of a fire was welcome.

''Dorothy has been coming to work with Molly the past couple of weeks so she will be ready to step in after the wedding. It's just as well. Molly is so much in love she's addled. I found her putting the milk pitcher in the warming oven yesterday.'' Elizabeth smiled. ''It's beautiful to watch a young couple in love. They think they invented the emotion.''

''I've seen you and Brice look at each other the same way. I hope when Edmund and I have been married as long as you have, we are still that much in love.''

''It hasn't been so long.'' Elizabeth blushed at the

realization that their love was visible to their friends. How had they ever expected to hide it from anyone? "And it hasn't always run smoothly."

"It wouldn't be very exciting if it did, now would it? I know I kept Edmund on pins and needles before I accepted his proposal. Even after that I saw to it that I wasn't taken for granted. I think he breathed a sigh of relief when I said 'I do' in front of the preacher.'' Maida laughed. "And we were childhood sweethearts and never really stepped out with anyone else. How did you and Brice meet?"

"It's a long story and I have to be getting home. It looks as if it may rain and I don't want to be caught in it."

"You never tell me anything about how you met or when you married," Maida complained good-naturedly. "I force stories on you about Edmund and me all the time."

"I enjoy hearing them. I will tell you this. I knew from the first moment I saw Brice that he was a man I could love forever."

"Love at first sight!" Maida sighed. "I should have known it. Did he come to Missouri to meet you or did you come west?"

"Like I said, it's a long story." Elizabeth took her cup to the sink and dipped water into it to rinse it, then tossed the cupful of water out the back door. "It's already starting to mist. I have to go or I'll be soaked."

Maida took the cup. "I'll see you tomorrow at Harriet's house, won't I?" The quilting had begun to circulate to other houses now that other husbands had time to construct frames for their wives.

"Unless it's pouring down rain. I'll stay inside if the weather is very bad."

"That's one convenience of living in the settlement. None of our houses are far apart. I'll go to Harriet's rain or shine."

Elizabeth wrapped her woolen shawl about her. "I'll try to make it."

Maida opened the door and saw her off the porch before she shut it. Elizabeth started up the slope toward her house. She had considered riding down, but had hated to leave a horse tied outside in such weather. Maida's barn was only large enough to hold their horses and the wagon.

Halfway up the slope the mist turned to drizzle and by the time she was in her yard, it had become a steady rain.

Elizabeth hurried into the house. Molly, Dorothy and the baby were in the back parlor, and she spoke to them before going upstairs to change into dry clothes.

There was no fire in the bedroom since no one was likely to be in that room at this time of day, and Elizabeth shivered as she peeled the wet clothes from her body. Although wood was plentiful in the valley, cutting and splitting it was hard work and it wasn't to be wasted. All the same, she wished for a fire.

As quickly as she could, she pulled on dry undergarments, then her heaviest wool dress. She was thoroughly chilled and was still shivering. She took the wet clothing downstairs to the kitchen and draped it over chair backs to dry in front of the hearth. After standing as close as possible to the coals, she finally began to get warm.

Thinking about Brice being out in the weather, she went to the back door and looked out at the slanting rain. It wasn't freezing, but she knew it was almost cold enough. She felt sorry for Brice and the cowhands for having to work in such miserable conditions. They were stringing more of the new barbed wire in the back pasture. Brice wanted to get his land under fence before they acquired neighbors with herds of their own.

In the distance thunder rumbled. A gust of cold air whistled around the door and sent a draft into the warm room. With her foot, Elizabeth nudged the rolled towel closer against the door to stop the draft. The rain increased steadily and before long it was blowing in sheets across the yard. The cottonwoods, devoid of leaves now, bowed and scraped at the wind's passing. She hoped Brice wouldn't be out too much longer.

"Miss Elizabeth?" Molly said from the doorway.

Elizabeth turned. "Yes?"

"Would it be all right if Dorothy and me leave early today? It looks like it could get worse before it gets better."

"I was about to come to the parlor and suggest that to you. Did you both wear slickers?"

"No, ma'am, but we can run fast. We won't get too wet."

"You'll be drenched before you get out of the yard." Elizabeth had them wait while she got her oiled cloth cape and Brice's oiled poncho and gave them to the girls. "You can bring these back next time you're here. I don't want you to get sick."

Dorothy pulled the poncho over her head. It dwarfed her. "I'm much obliged."

Elizabeth saw them out and closed the door behind them. It was already colder than it had been when she had walked up the hill.

She went into the parlor and sat on the floor to play with Mary Kate. The toddler was stacking blocks as high as she could before they fell. Behind her a fire burned in the grate and the room was warm and comfortable.

Elizabeth felt tears of happiness rise in her eyes. She had wanted to live like this all her life, and she still could scarcely believe it was happening.

She brushed Mary Kate's hair back from her face. "Your papa will be home soon, I hope. We'll have to make him a nice hot supper, won't we?"

Mary Kate looked up and said, "Papa."

Elizabeth's mouth dropped open. "You said Papa! Say it again. Can you say it again?"

"Papa," the child said, then clapped her hands gleefully.

Elizabeth picked her up and hugged her. "What a wonderful child you are! I love you so much!"

Mary Kate hugged her enthusiastically in return.

Suddenly it occurred to Elizabeth that Mary Kate would have to be taught a word to call her as well. Some of her joy died. The only possible name would be "Mama" and that would be teaching her a lie.

She put the little girl down, and Mary Kate immediately resumed stacking blocks.

It was one thing to pass herself off as Brice's wife to the settlers and another entirely to do the same with Mary Kate. Whether Elizabeth and Brice liked it or not, she had a right to know about her real mother and the other family she had living in Texas. What would it do to Mary Kate if she later learned the people she considered to be her parents weren't even married? As long as Brice's and Celia's families existed, there was the chance someone might visit and tell Mary Kate the truth. The Lannigans had been here once; they could come back again.

The families would never know for certain that she and Brice weren't married, but wouldn't it seem odd to Brice's family that he had never informed them that he remarried? They had no wedding certificate on file in any courthouse, and someone might eventually learn this.

Elizabeth's joy became bittersweet. She was happier with Brice and Mary Kate than she had ever been in her life, yet the happiness could be swept away at a moment's notice.

She heard the back door open and went to see who had come in. Brice was standing in front of the fire, wet and shivering. "I'm glad you came in early," she said. "You look half frozen."

"I feel as if I am." He tossed another log on the fire. "I'm soaked. Could you bring me some dry clothes?"

She looked in the parlor to be sure the fire screen was safely in place to keep Mary Kate away from the hearth, then went up to get him some dry clothing.

He stripped off in the kitchen and dressed in the dry clothes as she put his wet things near hers to dry. "We got most of it done before the rain started. Damn, but it's cold out there. The wind felt like it was blowing straight from the North Pole."

"I wouldn't be surprised if it didn't freeze overnight."

"I think it's cold enough to freeze now." He buttoned his shirt and stuffed the long shirttail into his pants. "Where is Mary Kate?"

"In the back parlor. I let Molly and Dorothy leave early." She smiled at him. "Guess what! She said her first word today."

"She did?" He looked as pleased as if he had just heard that his daughter had recited Shakespeare. "What did she say?"

"She said Papa."

"That's my girl!" He went into the parlor and picked

Mary Kate up to hug her. "What's this about you talking, young lady? Can you say 'Papa' for me?"

"Papa," Mary Kate said obligingly, then burst into giggles.

"You're precious. Do you know that?" Brice kissed her cheek. Mary Kate examined the raindrops that still clung to his hair.

"She certainly does know it," Elizabeth said with a laugh. "We'll have our hands full with her someday. She's going to be the belle of the valley." She paused and her smile faded. "What will she call me?"

"Mama, of course. What else would she call you?" He tickled Mary Kate's neck and she giggled harder and squirmed around to tickle him back.

"I knew the time would come when she would start to talk and that this decision would have to be made, but somehow it slipped up on me. Time has passed so quickly."

"You've been here a year." He looked at her over Mary Kate's head and his eyes shone with the love he felt for them both. "At times I forget we haven't been together years, then at others, it seems like minutes."

"Now that she's starting to talk, we'll have to be more careful what we say in front of her." Elizabeth touched Mary Kate lovingly. "We can't afford to make any mistakes that we would have to explain. And that brings up the really big decision. What do we tell her?"

"We'll say we're her parents. It's the truth."

"When she gets old enough to ride a pony in the field and happens to see the cemetery with Celia's grave in it, what do we tell her? You see, Brice? It's not going to be simple."

"Celia was my first wife. You're my second," he said firmly.

Elizabeth stood quietly, letting him think about what he said.

"All right. So it won't be easy. But you're my wife, Elizabeth. Whether we had a formal ceremony and registered it somewhere or not, you're my wife. I'm married to you in every way that counts. If you ask me, Robert is dead and gone forever."

She touched his arm. "I wish I knew for sure. I feel married to you in my heart, too."

"Then that will be good enough." Brice met her eyes. "We love each other and that's what's important."

"I know." But she was thinking about Robert and Brother Amos and how a slip of the tongue could bring their world tumbling down like a house of cards.

The cold rain continued into the night. Elizabeth put Mary Kate to bed and met Brice in their bedroom. He was looking out into the night. Frequent lightning made the landscape a garish study in silver and black, then was gone again.

"This is quite a storm," he said as he put his arm around her and held her by his side. "I think it's the worst I've seen since coming here."

"Thank goodness I'm not in that mud hut." She looped her arm around his waist. She loved to feel him beside her. His body was so lean with muscle and so protective.

"In a rain like this, you wouldn't have been in it for long."

"I love it here, Brice. Not a day goes by that I don't give thanks for finding you and coming here to live."

He smiled down at her. "You've made this place a home." He bent and kissed her. "I love you, Elizabeth."

"I love you." The words were so simple, yet they gave meaning to her life.

He held her close as thunder roared just outside the house. "Someday I want to make love outside in a storm. Think how exhilarating that would be."

"Especially if we were struck by lightning," she teased.

"Maybe it would be better to settle for making love in here and just listen to the storm."

She smiled and started unbuttoning his shirt. "You've never settled for anything in your life. You're not likely to start now. I have a feeling I'll hear about this again when summer rolls around and it's warm outside."

"You might. We could go to that place downriver. We already know it's private."

"We'll see." Personally she also thought making love in a storm would be exciting. "Maybe a year from this summer we could give it a try."

He kissed her. "Why wait? We'll have a perfectly good summer this year."

"I may be busy."

He laughed as he pulled the pins from her hair. "I wasn't aware you had such a hectic social calendar. What will you be busy doing?"

"I might be giving birth to our baby."

His jaw slackened and he stared at her for several seconds before speaking. "Our baby? We're going to have a baby? You and I?"

She nodded. "Don't look so amazed. We haven't missed any opportunities to create one."

He put his hand on her flat stomach. "You're certain?"

"As sure as I can be."

"You'll have to take it easy. Have Molly and Dorothy

do everything. Or I'll do the heavy chores when I come in from the fields." He grinned and repeated. "We're going to have a baby!"

"I don't need to take it that easy. Not for a while yet."

His smile disappeared slowly. "I'll move your things back into the other bedroom tomorrow. Do you want me to do it tonight?"

"You do that, and I'll move yours to the bunkhouse," she threatened. "I'm staying right where I am."

"You'll need uninterrupted rest."

"I'm not made of spun glass, Brice. I'll rest just fine in here. Better, in fact."

"I'm not sure I can keep my hands off you if you're in my bed. That's the real truth, Elizabeth. You know how I feel about you."

"Don't you dare even think about not touching me. I can tell already that I shouldn't have told you this early. Maybe that's why women often don't tell their husbands until the man figures it out for himself. There's no reason to take a vow of chastity just because I'm going to have a baby."

He stared at her.

"Brice," she said softly. "Don't worry so much. I love you and I want you in every possible way, just as I always have. All that will change is my shape. No one is moving into a separate room or abstaining from anything. At least not for a long time yet. I'm healthy and I'm strong. Nothing is going to go wrong. Trust me."

He gingerly put his arms back around her. "I just don't want to endanger you or the baby."

"You won't. And that's another thing. I'm not going to die in childbirth. I'm not even worried about it. Leona Wells is a fine midwife, and she's not all that far away.

When the time comes, she will take care of me. Having a baby is perfectly natural.'' She kissed him. ''Stop worrying. I can see it in your eyes.''

''I'm not worrying,'' he lied.

''Brice, it's a good thing you aren't fond of playing poker. We wouldn't have a cent left.'' She kissed him again. ''Now where were we? I think you were in the middle of a seduction.''

He held her close to him, his face buried in her hair. ''I love you, Elizabeth. Don't leave me.''

She was serious when she said, ''I never will.'' She led him to the bed and turned back the covers as he undressed.

She removed her clothing as he watched. A teasing smile was on her lips. ''Don't look so speculative.'' She turned for his perusal. ''I don't look any different than I did last night or the night before and I was just as pregnant then.''

''But I didn't know it then.''

She slipped into bed and snuggled close to his warmth. ''If you're going to be odd about this, I won't tell you next time.''

''Can't you see why I would be uneasy? Celia died in childbirth. I can't put that out of my mind. It was my fault. She never wanted children.''

''But I do. She wasn't healthy and if she didn't want the baby, that had to make it more difficult. I want to give you lots of children. I want to put the McGivenses to shame and be the gossip of the entire valley.''

''Let's just have this one and then see.''

''I think it's going to be a boy. A healthy strapping son to fight all the boys who want to make eyes at Mary Kate.''

''Or it might be a girl with hair like the night and

eyes the color of storm clouds," he said softly. "I hope it looks like you, whichever it is."

"I love you, Brice." She kissed him long and lovingly and soon felt his body responding.

They made love slowly and passionately as the storm rattled around them. Lightning flashes threw lemony light into the room and the thunder crashed as darkness returned. Elizabeth gave herself to him eagerly and Brice gave her pleasure again and again.

When at last they lay in each other's arms, listening to the storm move down the valley, there was a tenderness between them that was deeper than ever.

Brice touched her stomach and said, "It could be a son," he said. "If it's another daughter, that would be wonderful, too. I'll love it as much as I do Mary Kate, whichever it is."

Elizabeth smiled in the darkness and rubbed her cheek against his bare shoulder. "We will be such good parents. We have so much love to give."

"We already are good parents," he reminded her. "All you have to do is look at Mary Kate and you can see it. You're a good mother."

"Lots of children," she said as she closed her eyes happily. "I want a big family."

"I'd say we're off to a good start." He held her more securely.

Elizabeth knew him well enough to know he would try to carry her on a pillow for the next few months. He didn't take automatically to reassurances. But she was positive from deep in her soul that she had nothing to worry about. She and the baby would be fine.

Chapter Seventeen

More contented than ever before in her life, Elizabeth rocked back and forth at a gentle pace, feeling the cooling breeze of evening wafting across the front porch. Brice was sitting beside her. Mary Kate was playing in the yard, running in a futile attempt to catch the butterflies hovering over the April flowers. She pointed at a small yellow one and called out, "Pretty!"

Elizabeth smiled and nodded. To Brice she said, "Once she started talking she hasn't stopped. I often hear Dorothy and her talking nonstop as Dorothy cleans the house. Of course, most of Mary Kate's words are still of her own invention, but that doesn't seem to slow them down."

Brice watched his daughter with amused indulgence. "She's like a butterfly herself, isn't she? With all those blond curls?"

"She's beautiful." Elizabeth touched her rounded stomach. "I wonder what the new one will look like."

"It will be beautiful, too. How could it be anything else with you as its mother?"

"And you as its father," she replied with a smile. "You are a handsome man, Brice Graham."

He reached out and took her hand. "I should spend more time at the house. I like sitting on the porch with you."

"I like it, too. We ought to be picking out a name for the new baby."

"I know. But none of them seem just right." He frowned in concentration. "I don't want a family name or one that's so long it will be shortened into something silly. I'm not that fond of Biblical names either. Everyone uses those and I would like something different."

"I know. I think about names off and on during the day but I haven't thought of one that seems just right. You don't think it's bad luck to choose a name ahead of time, do you?"

"No. As much trouble as we're having, we might not name the baby until it starts to school."

She laughed. "I think we'll come up with something before that. Maida fancies names from books for her baby. She won't tell me what she has in mind, though."

"It won't be long before hers comes. Edmund is as nervous as a long-tailed cat in a room full of rocking chairs. I hope for his sake that the baby comes while he's working in the field and that it's all over before he knows what's going on."

"I do, too. Maida says he's driving her to distraction." Her baby kicked and she shifted and rubbed her stomach. "Ours is a strong one. Feel right here."

Brice put his hand on her stomach and laughed when he felt the kick from a tiny foot. He was enjoying the pregnancy as much as if he had never been through one before. Celia had kept him at such a distance that, in a way, he really hadn't. "I can feel it!"

"You're a good husband," she said softly. "And a wonderful father."

"You almost never refer to me as a husband. I'm glad that's changing."

She nodded. "It's time. I love you and I'm never leaving."

"Damn right. Even if you tried, I'd come after you and haul you back."

She laughed as she said, "I don't think I'll be able to outrun you for a while yet." Her face became more serious as she said, "If Robert was alive he would be back by now."

They held hands as they watched Mary Kate run about in the grass. "When you're ready to go to Glory and be married, just let me know."

"Soon," she said. "We'll go after the spring rains stop."

Word of Maida's labor came soon after Brice had ridden out to start the branding. Brian McGivens had run all the way up the slope to tell her the baby was arriving early. Elizabeth left Dorothy playing with Mary Kate and went down to lend her help and support to Maida.

On Maida's porch she paused to wipe her feet free of mud from the rain the night before. Across Puma Creek she could see two houses now. Not long after Henry married Molly, his parents had moved to the settlement. Their house sat behind the one belonging to Molly and Henry. As Elizabeth watched, Leona came across the bridge. She didn't seem to be in a particular hurry. Everyone now considered her to be the official midwife and this gave her a bit of prestige. She waved when she saw Elizabeth and Elizabeth waved back.

Rather than wait for Leona, Elizabeth went into the house that was almost as familiar as her own. Maida was walking about in her nightgown, with Harriet holding her securely. She smiled when she saw Elizabeth but her face was pale with fear.

Elizabeth took Maida's other arm and matched her steps to hers. Harriet's baby was playing on a pallet by the door. "Where's Ella?" Elizabeth asked.

"She said she couldn't come," Harriet answered. "I was counting on her being here to help watch my baby."

The women paused when another labor pain gripped Maida. When it passed, she said, "So far they aren't bad. Leona told me to walk for as long as I felt I could. She says that brings the baby faster."

"What reason did Ella give for not coming?" Elizabeth asked as they resumed walking again.

"She said she was busy." Harriet's tone of voice told what she thought about that.

"Where's Edmund?" Elizabeth asked.

"He had to go into town yesterday. I don't look for him to come back until midafternoon, if that early." Maida clutched Elizabeth's hand until the next pain passed. "I wish there was some way to tell him to hurry home. I shouldn't be having it this early!"

"You're better off with him out of the way," Harriet said. "Men aren't any help at a time like this. As for it being early, you may have been further along than you thought. That happened to me with my second one."

"I always feel safer when Edmund is around."

Elizabeth looked at the door as Leona came in.

"You're walking like I told you. Good." She put her bag of knitting on the table. She had come prepared in case the birthing took a while. Leona never sat idle if she could help it. "It's the Indian way, and they don't seem to have as much trouble birthing babies as we do."

"Where did you ever learn Indian ways?" Harriet asked.

"My cousin, Amelia, was captured by the Indians when she was a girl. We only got her back a couple of years ago. She told me things that would curl your hair. She has a tattoo on her cheek! And her a good Christian woman!"

"A tattoo? Imagine!" Harriet marveled.

"She tried to tell us it was some kind of tribal honor and that she had actually married one of the braves. It's like they tried to turn her into one, too, and almost succeeded." Leona scowled to show her disgust. "For the first few months, we had to watch her to keep her from running away and going back to them."

Elizabeth was fascinated by the story. It sounded to her as if this Amelia had been happier among the Indians than back in civilization. "Maybe she fell in love with the Indian she married."

"My cousin? In love with a red Indian? Not a bit of it. They just twisted her brain into thinking she was. No, she's a Christian, born and bred. She'll get that nonsense out of her head eventually."

All the same, Elizabeth felt sorry for her. She would hate for anyone to "rescue" her from the man she loved, and she didn't share the fear and hatred of Indians that many of the families moving west did. Because her opinions were in the minority, she never talked about this to anyone but Brice, who shared her feelings.

Suddenly, Maida stopped walking and doubled over with pain. She would have fallen if Elizabeth and Harriet hadn't been there to support her. "That one was really bad," she said when she could speak.

"Good. That means the baby doesn't want to hold back." As another contraction began, Leona put her hand on Maida's stomach and stared up at the ceiling as if she were in deep concentration. When the contraction ended, she said, "I think it's time for you to go to bed. They're close together now and I don't want you to fall."

Maida eased herself down onto the oiled cloth that Harriet had spread over the bed. When she was in place, she gripped Elizabeth's hand. "I'm scared," she whispered. "Remember the promise you made me."

"I do, but nothing is going to happen to you."

Leona lifted the end of the sheet Harriet had put over Maida and nodded. "There's nothing to this, Maida. Don't start carrying on and scare yourself. The baby's already crowning."

"Already?" Maida clenched her teeth as another contraction came. Harriet brought her a clean cup towel to bite on so she wouldn't break her teeth.

There was a hesitant knock on the door and Dorcas came into the house. "Can I be of any help? I wondered if she was having it when I saw all of you congregating."

"We didn't know you would want to be here. This one is coming quickly," Leona said. "First babies don't as a rule. I think we're going to be through here before you know it."

Dorcas came to the bed. "Don't you worry none about your supper. I'll make enough to bring some to you and Edmund. And I'll pray for you and the baby."

"Thank you," Maida said. Then, she squeezed Elizabeth's hand as her body struggled to give birth. This time the contraction only subsided a bit, then slammed into her again. Maida cried out.

"Push!" Leona shouted from the foot of the bed. "I've almost got it!"

Maida groaned and pushed with all her strength.

Elizabeth watched intently as Leona leaned down with

her arms outstretched and a moment later rose holding the squalling baby by its feet.

"You've got a fine girl! She's a real beauty," Leona announced over the baby's shrill complaints. "Listen to those lungs!" All the women laughed because the tiny baby was crying lustily. "You won't sleep through that at night! I bet we even hear her over at our house!"

"Get on with you! She's not all that loud," Harriet said in the baby's defense. "She's a lady if I ever saw one."

Leona handed the baby to Elizabeth to wash and finished up the birthing process. She had never held anything so tiny. The baby's hands were dainty and already turning pink. Her face was screwed up in protesting screams but she was indeed pretty. When Elizabeth finished washing her up, she said, "Maida, wait until you see this baby's red hair! She took after you."

"Let me see." Maida tried to raise herself in the bed.

Leona pushed her firmly back down. "You just stay where you are, missy. You're not getting out of bed for at least a day or two. More if I have my way."

Elizabeth wrapped the baby in a soft blanket and carried her to her mother's waiting arms. Maida curled the baby in the crook of her arm and pulled the blanket aside so she could see her daughter close up. "She really does have red hair, doesn't she! And look at her tiny little fingers!"

"They're all there," Leona said. "I counted them."

Dorcas leaned closer and gazed wistfully down at the infant. For a moment her face softened and she looked young again. Elizabeth wondered if her childless state was a source of unhappiness. It was difficult to imagine Dorcas softening enough to give a mother's love to a child.

Maida was crying with happiness as she stared at the baby. "To think I was afraid of something that would give me a treasure like this!"

Elizabeth smiled in relief to see Maida was already discounting the pain. Maybe having a baby wasn't as bad as it seemed. She wished again that she could confide in someone and ask exactly what it would be like. "What are you going to name her?"

"We've picked Mahalia Elizabeth Harrison." She smiled at Elizabeth. "And remember, you're her godmother, whether Brother Amos makes it official or not."

"I remember." She touched the baby's soft red hair. "I never had a baby named after me before." She felt near tears herself.

"We're going to call her Mahalia to keep from confusing the two of you. Maybe you'll have another girl and they can be best friends."

"Or if it's a boy," Harriet put in, "he and my Nial can fight over who gets to walk out with her when the time comes." The women laughed. Although the babies in question were years from caring about such things, it made the settlement seem more deeply rooted to think about the coming generations.

Ella Barker knew Maida was having her baby and that Elizabeth was certain to be in attendance. They were such close friends there was no question of Elizabeth leaving Maida's side.

"Have you got everything?" Abner asked.

"It's all in the wagon. Pull the tarp over it so it's not so obvious and hitch the team. Do it in the barn so nobody sees you."

"I know what to do," he snapped. "I'm not the fool

you take me for.'' He looked around the house. ''I have friends here. I hate to leave.''

''I told you not to take up with these people. We knew we wouldn't be here that long.''

''We've been here for months. I thought you had changed your mind and that we might be here from now on.''

''You're proving yourself to be a fool. I promised Cousin Lorna to do this for her and I won't break my word. I feel bad that it's taken so long but they watch that baby every hour of the day.''

''Dorothy will be with her now. She won't give her to you.''

''I know that,'' Ella snapped. ''But neither Brice nor Elizabeth will be there. All I have to do is tell Dorothy that Elizabeth sent me to fetch Mary Kate and she will give her to me. There's no reason for her not to believe me. You just see to it that you're ready to go as soon as I get back here.''

Abner frowned but he nodded. Ella knew he would do it. Her cousin, Lorna Lannigan, had paid them handsomely to steal Mary Kate and deliver her to Saxon, Texas.

Ella wrapped her largest shawl about her and left the house. The shawl was voluminous enough to conceal Mary Kate when she returned to the settlement. Not that anyone would be about to notice. All the men were working and the women were attending Maida. It had been a long time in coming, but the opportunity was perfect.

Elizabeth took the cup of coffee Harriet poured for her and sipped it carefully. Harriet was known for making the strongest, hottest coffee anyone had ever tasted. This cup supported the legend.

"Would you look at that red hair? My lands, she has a head full of hair! Won't she and my Nial make a pair?"

Elizabeth laughed and nodded. "We're going to have a valley full of redheaded children, the way we're going."

Leona shook her head. "I'm not looking for yours to have red hair. Your hair is nearly black and Brice's is brown."

"Yes, but look at their Mary Kate," Harriet said. "She's got hair as yellow as a buttercup. You can't always tell."

Elizabeth smiled. "I'm looking forward to having this baby. I already get tired so easily."

"It's a boy," Leona predicted. "Look how low you're carrying."

"I don't know. I carried my girls lower than my boys," Harriet said.

For several minutes the women argued pleasantly over how to determine if a baby would be a girl or a boy, then Elizabeth went to Maida's bedside. "She's a beautiful baby."

"I think so, too. Won't Edmund be surprised when he comes home?"

"Was he determined to have the first one be a boy?"

Maida shook her head. "I don't think he cared which it was. We plan to have a large family."

"You can say that even having just given birth?"

"You know, I wouldn't have guessed I'd be talking about it so soon, either, but I still want more babies." Maida looked up at her. "You told me not to worry, I know, but I just couldn't help it."

"Then it wasn't all that bad?"

"It was at the time, but she was more than worth it." Maida couldn't take her eyes from the infant. "Look at her little fingernails! How can anything be so tiny?"

Elizabeth leaned near Maida and marveled over the miracle of little Mahalia.

When she started for home, the afternoon sun was still high in the sky but arching toward the horizon. She smiled as she walked, looking at the drifts of pink and yellow wildflowers. It seemed to be the perfect time of the year for a baby to be born. Everything was fresh and new from the winter and the whole world was lovely.

She was almost in her yard before she saw Dorothy step out onto the front porch. Mary Kate wasn't with her.

"Where's Mary Kate?" Dorothy asked.

"What do you mean? She's here with you." Instant fear leaped in Elizabeth's middle. "What do you mean, 'where is she?'"

"Mrs. Barker came after her. She said you sent for her because Mrs. Harrison's labor was lasting so long." The girl wrung her hands and bit her lip. "I didn't want to let her take her, but she said you sent her up here to fetch her."

Elizabeth stared at her. "I haven't seen Ella all day. Maida had an easy delivery. A little girl."

"Why would Mrs. Barker tell me such a thing? What did she want with Mary Kate?"

Elizabeth whirled and stared back at the settlement. She could see a wagon leaving town in the direction of Glory and the team of horses looked like the Barker animals. As she looked, a thin thread of smoke began spiraling up from the church. "Get Brice and the men!

Hurry!'' She gathered up her skirts and ran down the slope.

Henry Wells was unloading his wagon at the feed store when the fire bell began to ring. At the same time, Elizabeth ran to him. Her face was flushed from exertion and she was gasping for breath. ''Mrs. Graham!'' he exclaimed. ''You shouldn't be running in your condition! What's on fire! It's not your house, is it?''

By this time Elizabeth had climbed into the wagon. Without giving him any explanation she released the brake and slapped the reins hard on the team's rump. They bolted forward and sent Henry toppling off the wagon.

Elizabeth barely noticed. She had finally realized who Ella Barker looked like. She resembled Celia and was the image of what Lorna Lannigan would have looked like if she were younger and thinner. And she was stealing Mary Kate.

Dim shouts could be heard behind her as all the men ran to save the church. Elizabeth pushed the team to a speed that was unsafe over the rain-rutted ground. She had to stop the Barkers and get Mary Kate back.

The Barker wagon was fully loaded, and even though Abner was pressing his team to go as fast as possible, Elizabeth caught up with them and stopped them by driving her team in front of theirs. She grabbed at the Barker horses' bridles and held them firmly. ''Give me my daughter,'' she demanded.

''You stand aside,'' Abner threatened. ''Let us pass!''

''Give her to me!''

''Run her down, Abner,'' Ella shouted.

''I can't do that!'' he snapped at her. ''You can see she's in a wagon and besides that, she's a woman carrying a child.''

"Mary Kate isn't your daughter," Ella shouted. Mary Kate was terrified by now, and her screams rent the air. "Celia was her mother and I'm taking her to Cousin Lorna where she belongs."

"You will not take my daughter," Elizabeth told her with grim determination.

"Shoot her, Abner! We have to get out of here!"

"I can't shoot a woman!" he gasped as he stared at his wife. "No one was supposed to get hurt! I never agreed to that."

"Give her to me, Ella," Elizabeth demanded.

Ella held the squirming child above her head. "If you try to take her, I'll kill her! Lorna told me she wasn't to stay with you no matter what!"

"Lorna never meant to kill the child!" Abner exclaimed. "Have you gone plumb crazy, Ella?"

Elizabeth saw Brice riding hard toward them but she tried not to let her face give this away. Mary Kate's screams drowned out the approaching hoofbeats. "Don't hurt her, Ella," Elizabeth said. "Don't hurt her!"

"It's Brice's fault that Celia is dead!" Ella was sobbing now. "We were close as girls. Like sisters! Even after I married Abner and moved away, we wrote. Brice treated her awful! He's not a man—he's a monster! He killed Celia by forcing her to live out here, a delicate woman like her! It's his fault she's dead!"

Brice didn't slacken his speed. He galloped by the wagon and plucked Mary Kate from Ella's grasp. Elizabeth's heart skipped when she thought the baby might fall, but Brice had her firmly in his arms.

Elizabeth released the Barkers' reins. "You can leave now. If I were you, I'd do it before the others find out you were stealing Mary Kate."

"I'll see you pay for this," Ella shrieked. "I'll get her again! You'll see!"

Abner gave her a disgusted look. "Shut up, Ella!" He slapped the reins on his team's back and rode past Elizabeth's wagon.

By this time Brice had reined in and ridden back. He handed Mary Kate to Elizabeth. "I'm going after them!" he said grimly.

"No, don't." She hugged Mary Kate and kissed her to quiet her screams. "Mary Kate isn't hurt, and Abner will see to it that Ella goes far from here."

"You're positive Mary Kate isn't hurt?"

"She's only frightened." Now that it was over, Elizabeth was also trembling. "Let them go. I never want to see them again."

"But I should take them to the jail in Glory," he protested.

"Yes, and that would leave them in the area. Abner won't stop until he's back east where they came from. He knows you'll shoot him on sight."

"I'd like to shoot both of them!"

"I'd rather you take us home and get Henry's wagon back to him." She set her jaw firmly. "And I can tell you this—we aren't putting our lives on the shelf any longer. It's time to do what's right. Robert is dead and I no longer doubt it."

"Why did you suddenly reach that conclusion?" Brice asked.

"I could wait forever and not know. I'm positive the gun belt and coin purse were his. Maybe I just don't remember his hair having a reddish cast, or maybe the sun and weather bleached it before his body was found. It has to have been him."

"I agree. I've thought so all along."

Elizabeth hugged Mary Kate tighter. "We came so close to losing everything. Let's not wait any longer."

"You took the words right out of my mouth," Brice said with a smile.

By the time they returned to the settlement, the fire at the church was extinguished and everyone was puzzling over how it started in the first place. Elizabeth knew either Ella or Abner had started the fire to cover their leaving. Everyone would be too busy saving the church to notice Mary Kate in the wagon and to ask questions.

Elizabeth held Mary Kate tightly as she drove up the hill to their home.

Chapter Eighteen

By the following day everyone in the settlement had pieced together what had happened. As Dorcas left Maida's to pray in thanksgiving that the baby and mother were safe, she had seen Abner hurrying from the church. Tavish had happened to step out on the porch of his store and glimpsed Mary Kate's blond curls beneath the shawl Ella had wrapped around her. Everyone in town, with the exception of Maida, came to find out why the Barkers had gone to such lengths to steal Mary Kate.

Brice was all for giving them no explanation but Elizabeth could no longer live with lies and half-truths. Putting her hand in his, she stood beside him on the porch and met the gaze of the settlers.

"My name is Elizabeth Parkins," she began. "I'm a widow. Brice was married to Celia Lannigan, who was Ella's cousin. When Celia died in childbirth, I came here to look after Mary Kate and keep house for Brice. We fell in love." She glanced up at him for reassurance.

"How come you didn't tell us all this from the beginning?" Tavish asked.

She drew in a deep breath and plunged on. "Because we aren't married."

A murmur ran through the crowd and Brice's hand tightened protectively on hers. He took up the story. "By the time we wanted to be married, you were all here. You had assumed we were husband and wife and we were afraid to tell you differently."

"You can't continue living in sin!" Amos looked as stunned as if he had been poleaxed.

Dorcas stepped closer to him. "You could marry them, Amos. That would fix everything."

"No, it wouldn't!" he blustered. "They're worse sinners than Charley McGivens and Darcy Barker! They are living together openly! She's with child by him!"

"You can't drive them out," Tavish growled warningly. "They gave us our land and the lumber for our houses. This place belongs to them." The others muttered in assent.

"Marry them, Amos," Dorcas repeated. "Our religion is based on forgiveness."

Amos looked as if he wanted to argue the point but saw the foolishness of doing so. "I reckon I could marry them."

Elizabeth looked up at Brice. "How do you feel about this?" She knew how much he disliked Amos.

He smiled at her. "How can you ask such a question? Wait here." He went back into the house.

Elizabeth was embarrassed to stand alone on the porch under the gaze of everyone who knew the secret she and Brice had shared, but she saw no censure on anyone's face but Amos's.

"I think it's a good time for new beginnings," Dorcas said quietly to her husband. "I saw the birth of a baby yesterday. The first one I ever saw! Now Elizabeth and

Brice are going to be married. I think it's time for us to start our lives all over, too. I want us to have a new beginning, too.''

"What on earth are you talking about, Sister Dorcas?" he demanded in an exasperated tone.

"You think on it a bit, Amos. I'm sure you'll understand once you put your mind to it." She smiled and was almost pretty.

Amos stared at her.

Just then Brice returned. "We're ready if you are, Amos." He put his arm around Elizabeth and they made room for Amos to stand in front of them. Elizabeth pulled off the narrow wedding band she had worn for years. After thinking a minute she threw it as far into the yard as she could hurl it. Brice chuckled.

"Dearly beloved," Amos began.

She heard little of the ceremony. She and Brice made their vows as a mockingbird sang in one of the cottonwood trees. When Amos declared them husband and wife, Brice reached into his pocket and slipped a ring on her finger.

She looked at it in surprise. It was beautifully made. Garnets were mounted in the band and connected by filigree of gold. She looked up at him questioningly.

"It was my mother's wedding ring." His eyes searched hers to see if she was pleased. "I can get you one of your own next time I go to Glory."

"No," she said with a smile. "I'd rather have this one." She tiptoed up and kissed him.

The townsfolk grinned and nodded their approval.

Epilogue

Autumn came early that year. Elizabeth was glad for the break in the summer's unrelenting heat. "I never thought I'd look forward to winter," she told Maida as they sat on her back steps and watched the children playing.

"Neither did I. Look at those two! Aren't they a pair?"

Elizabeth smiled as little Mahalia reached out to pat Court, who was contemplating his toes beside her on the quilt. "He looks more like Brice every day, doesn't he? And Mary Kate still isn't tired of being a big sister."

"They look as different as day and night. Court has all that dark hair and brown eyes, while Mary Kate is as golden as an angel."

"That's assuming angels have gold hair and blue eyes," Elizabeth replied with a smile. "Personally, I think some of them have dark hair and brown eyes."

"Or red hair," Maida said loyally. "Mahalia certainly has plenty of it."

Court rolled over, his newest accomplishment, and reached for Mahalia's red curls. She evaded him, having learned from past experience, but he reached for her again, bent on having a handful of her colorful hair.

"He's going to drive her to distraction," Elizabeth said of her son. "Once he gets his mind set on something, he doesn't turn aside easily."

"I don't understand why you named him Valancourt. Is that a family name?"

"No." Elizabeth smiled as Court caught Mahalia's pudgy hand and held on. Mary Kate ran to Mahalia's aid. "It's a name from a book Brice and I both love. It was one of the first things we discovered we had in common."

"I've never been one for reading much myself. It's a good name, Valancourt. It has substance, like Mahalia."

"So it does." Elizabeth looked up as Brice drove up in the buggy. As always when he appeared unexpectedly, her heart beat faster. Since Court was born, they had fallen more in love than ever.

"You two are like a courting couple," Maida teased her in an undertone as Brice got out of the buggy and came to them.

"I feel as if we are."

"Afternoon, Maida," he said as he drew near. He ruffled Mary Kate's curls and bent to scoop up his son. Court crowed happily and patted his father's face. "How's Edmund today?"

"He's worn out from harvesting, but that's a good way to be tired. We had a better crop than we expected."

"This valley's so rich it will grow anything," Brice said with pride. "It's good land."

"You didn't have to drive down after us," Elizabeth said as she stood and took the baby from Brice. "I was just about to start home."

"I thought we might take a drive. The trees over in

the back pasture are really pretty now. I want to show them to you.''

Elizabeth told Maida goodbye and let Brice hand her and the baby into the buggy, then boost Mary Kate into the back. As they drove away, she said, ''What's the real reason? You showed me those trees two days ago.''

''Do I have to have a reason to take my family for a drive?''

''No. I enjoy being with you.''

''I just had to see you. I still can't get over the miracle of having you, and the children.''

She laughed and tucked her arm into the bend of his elbow. ''You're hopelessly romantic, you know.''

''I am? You're the one who named our baby after the hero in *The Mysteries of Udolpho*.''

''You didn't object, as I recall.'' She always enjoyed feeling the hardness of his muscles beneath her hand as he skillfully drove the horse. ''Maybe we'll have a little Emily next.''

''There's no hurry,'' he said quickly. ''I'm not sure I want to go through that again so quickly.''

''Why, how you talk. I had a very easy delivery with Court. Leona almost didn't make it up the slope in time.''

''I know. I nearly got to deliver him myself. That took ten years off my life.''

''I doubt it,'' she said with a laugh. ''I recall you looking as proud as any peacock.''

He grinned. ''He's a fine boy, isn't he?''

Elizabeth hugged the baby closer. ''Yes, he is.''

''I'm fine, too,'' Mary Kate spoke up from the back seat of the buggy.

''Yes, you are,'' Brice agreed. ''This whole family is fine.'' He looked at Elizabeth and winked.

She settled closer to him and gazed out over the rolling hills that defined their valley. "I've never been so happy in my life," she said softly.

"Neither have I. And we have a lot of years ahead to be even happier."

Elizabeth kissed him on the cheek. "I'll always love you."

"I know." He put his free arm around her and held her close.

* * * * *

Harlequin® Historical

After the first two sensational books in award-winning author Theresa Michaels's new series

July 1997

THE MERRY WIDOWS—MARY #372

"...a heartbreaking tale of strength, courage, and tender romance...."
—*Rendezvous*

and

February 1998

THE MERRY WIDOWS—CATHERINE #400

"Smart, sassy and sexy...one of those rare, laugh-out-loud romances that is as delicious as a chocolate confection. 4☆s."
—*Romantic Times*

Comes the final book in the trilogy

July 1999

THE MERRY WIDOWS—SARAH #469

"Extraordinarily powerful!"
—*Romantic Times*

The story of a half-breed single father and a beautiful loner who come together in a breathtaking melding of human hearts....

You won't be able to put it down!

Available wherever Harlequin books are sold.

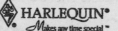

HARLEQUIN®
Makes any time special ™

Look us up on-line at: http://www.romance.net

HHWEST1

From bestselling author

Ruth Langan

comes a new Medieval miniseries

The O'Neil Saga

RORY
March 1999

CONOR
June 1999

BRIANA
October 1999

Siblings and warriors all, who must defend the family legacy—even if it means loving the enemy....

Available at your favorite retail outlet.

HARLEQUIN®
Makes any time special ™

COMING NEXT MONTH FROM

HARLEQUIN HISTORICALS